SOLDIER

SOLDIER

PARA-MILITARY RECRUITER™ BOOK 06

RENÉE JAGGÉR

MICHAEL ANDERLE

Copyright © 2023 by LMBPN Publishing
Cover by Mihaela Voicu http://www.mihaelavoicu.com/
Cover copyright © LMBPN Publishing
A Michael Anderle Production

LMBPN Publishing
PMB 196, 2540 South Maryland Pkwy
Las Vegas, NV 89109

Version 1.01, March 2025
ebook ISBN: 979-8-88878-266-8
Print ISBN: 979-8-88878-267-5

THE SOLDIER TEAM

Thanks to the JIT Readers

Zacc Pelter
Dave Hicks
Dorothy Lloyd
Jackey Hankard-Brodie
Diane L. Smith
Rachel Beckford
Wendy L Bonell
Christopher Gilliard
John Ashmore
Jeff Goode
Paul Westman
Kelly O'Donnell
Jan Hunnicutt

Editor
The SkyFyre Editing Team

CHAPTER ONE

Julie Meadows kept her pistol close to her chest as she jogged down the mineshaft. Her boots were nearly silent on the rocky floor, and her ears were filled with her heavy breathing. She could feel, more than hear, the rest of the Griffin unit behind her.

Her knee brushed something furry and solid, and she glanced down at Chester. He was barely visible in her night-vision goggles: a massive barrel-chested blond wolf, his shoulders almost as tall as her hip.

We're getting closer. The faintly British voice whispering in Julie's mind belonged to the helmet she wore. The other soldiers wore similar ones, except theirs were just helmets, not smartass shapeshifting magical artifacts.

Chester raised his head, sniffing. *Yep. I smell Alicanto and a ton of dwarves.* His words echoed in Julie's mind via the telepathic connection Hat had established among the whole unit.

Be specific, Chess, Julie reminded him.

He can't. There are too many of them.

When Julie looked back, Raven's red eyes glowed in the dark. The vampire flexed her fingernails and extended them into claws. *We're in for a big fight,* Raven added.

Many of them will be innocent workers. Remember, we're not here to create collateral damage, Jae cautioned. The Shajara Elf brought up the rear of the group. She had her medical pack strapped to her back.

Bummer. I love damage. One of the three faeries flitting over Julie's head performed a silly back-flip, clutching her tiny rifle to her chest.

The mineshaft split ahead of them, forking left and right. Julie halted, as did the rest of the unit, silent and seamless around her. Korin stepped up between her and Chester, glancing around. The dwarf had both hammers drawn. *Which way?* she asked.

Chester raised his nose, sniffing. *To the right. I smell metal and gunpowder.*

Julie nodded. *Then our intelligence was right.*

Seems that way. Raven sniffed, too. *We could be dealing with a small contingent of dwarf infantry armed with axes and hammers, plus two or three cannons.*

The Alicanto is definitely in there. Its magic feels nulled. Probably by iron, Hat told them. *And it's three cannons.*

What is this, the Civil War? Julie scoffed.

Everyone in the unit stared at her.

What Civil War? Isaiah asked.

Never mind. It's a human world thing. Julie waved a hand. *Overwatch, you get all that?*

Affirmative, Griffin Seven. The new, deep voice crackled faintly when it entered Julie's mind, telepathic interference marring his words thanks to the distance between them. *You are go. Diplomatic resolution has failed. Engage without hesitation.*

Jae sighed. *It seems the Silver Dwarves are jealous enough of Copper wealth that they won't let the Alicanto go without a fight.*

Then we'll give them a fight. Julie drew her second pistol and held one in each hand. *It's not fair to keep the Alicanto captive just because it senses silver ore.*

Julie glanced at the rest of the team. The faeries checked their rifles. Raven flexed her claws, fangs protruding from beneath her upper lip. Korin's hammers crackled with copper-colored dwarf magic.

Let's do this. Chester dropped into a crouch, hackles rising on his back.

No collateral damage. Okay? Julie glared at the nearest faerie.

The faerie sighed. *Whatever.*

Move out! Overwatch ordered.

Side by side with Korin and Chester, Julie jogged down the mineshaft to the right, carefully avoiding the minecart tracks that crackled with Silver Dwarf magic.

You're approaching a quarry, Overwatch told them. *Three guards straight ahead.*

Julie slowed and set her pistols to stun. After she rounded a bend in the tunnel, her night-vision goggles illuminated two figures straight ahead. Silver Dwarves. She caught the blurred impression of a weapon being raised and fired her pistol into the chest of the nearest figure. It fell to the ground, and the other spun. Chester was upon it and hurled it to the ground.

Good job, Ches— Julie began.

Nine o' clock! Hat shrieked.

Julie whipped around, blinding light searing her eyes as a hammer swung in her direction. She tried to block with one arm, but it was like blocking a landslide. The hammer thundered into her breastplate, sending her flying back into the tunnel wall. Her armor thudded into the rock, and she scrambled to her feet as quickly as she had flown back. By the time her boots hit the ground, the other five werewolves had overwhelmed her attacker.

Shit, Julie proclaimed. *Those hammers hit like a truck.*

Griffin Seven, report! Overwatch cried. *What's with Meadows' vitals?*

Just a scare, Overwatch, Julie assured him.

Overwatch sighed. *Proceed.*

Stepping over the unconscious bodies of the Silver Dwarves, Julie led her unit around the bend in the tunnel. Silver light etched the rough entrance to an open space. Its walls towered, cliff-like, littered with boulders where landslides had scarred their surface. Julie caught a glimpse of hulking machinery and stout, toiling figures. The rattle of machinery filled the air.

Your Alicanto is in the center of the quarry, Hat informed them.

Copy that, Hat. Julie checked her pistols. *Let's go.*

Is that moonlight? Jae asked. *Should we remove our night-vision goggles?*

I think so. Julie grinned as she touched the button on one side of Hat that caused her goggles to slide up inside her helmet. *It's a full moon.*

Sure is, Hat told her smugly.

The quarry swarmed with dwarves. Hundreds toiled on the walls, swinging pickaxes to fill barrows with ore, then loading the ore into one of the machines. Armored dwarves stood over them, hammers and axes hanging from their belts.

There! Jae gasped. *Eleven o'clock.*

Julie looked ahead. In the center of the quarry was a squat iron cage, ugly and medieval. She could make out a huddled lump of feathers behind the bars.

Its wings are dimmed because of the iron. Jae's voice trembled with anger. Stepping up beside Julie, the elf reached into a utility pocket in her belt, pulled out a handful of tiny seeds, and scattered them on the ground.

Noah, Blake, Austin, circle to the left. Chester, Isaiah, Teddy, you go right, Julie ordered. *Faeries, take the cannon dead ahead. Raven, cannon on the right. I'll take the one on the left. Korin, Jae, go for the Alicanto. Got it?* Julie hefted her pistols.

Oh, yeah. The faeries raised their rifles. *Got it.*

Go! Julie yelled.

They raced into the moonlight as one, and when the silver light fell on Julie's armored body, a jolt of power rushed through her veins. Three galloping wolves plunged past on either side of her, dwarves rushing to meet them.

Some broke past and headed for Korin and Jae on point. Jae let out a roar of anger, and roses exploded from the earth where she'd dropped the seeds, their roots shattering rock, sending dust into the air as they coursed through the dirt on either side of Jae and wrapped their sinuous thorny stems around the attacking dwarves.

Remind me not to piss Jae off. Julie raised both pistols and fired at two dwarves.

I quite agree, Hat told her.

There was an explosion, and the air filled with flickering silver light.

Cover! Take cover! Overwatch yelled.

The unit scattered. Julie threw herself behind a wheelbarrow of ore as a ball of crackling silver magic hurtled across the quarry. It slammed into the dirt a few feet from Julie, raking a black scar across the floor. One of Jae's roses withered and died, and the dwarf it held cut himself free and swung his ax toward Korin. She blocked with one hammer and hit him in the jaw with the other, sending him flying.

Faeries, go, go, go! Julie yelled. *We've got to take out that cannon!*

The three faeries didn't need to be told twice. Wings whirring, they plunged across the quarry to where the cannon waited, its black hulk shining against the cliff's face. The three dwarves manning it drew their weapons and swung. One faerie hung back, firing her rifle, and golden fairy dust exploded into the air, glowing. When it landed on the nearest dwarf's face, it melted her skin into a greenish ooze. She shrieked, clawing at her skin, and dropped, screaming. The other two faeries swarmed a second dwarf, their tiny fangs ripping into her flesh. They spat her blood everywhere.

That *is repulsive,* Hat opined.

Effective, though. Julie looked up and to her left. The second cannon hurled a ball of Silver magic at the unit. Korin and Jae both had to retreat several feet before it raked across the ground just in front of them. On either side of Julie, the Weres were fighting dwarf units, holding them back. Screams came from the cannon on the right.

Time for action. Julie looked at the cliffside, spotted the narrow trail leading to the cannon, and rushed forward. Her boots crunched on the rock and her breath rushed in her lungs as she bounded up the trail in giant leaps.

Look up! Hat yelled.

An armored dwarf on the trail above Julie seized one of the worker dwarves, shoved him roughly aside, and gave a wheelbarrow of silver ore a mighty push in Julie's direction. It thundered down the trail toward her, teetering wildly. She sped up, heading straight for it. Hat screeched panicked expletives in her head, but she ignored him. When she was feet from it, she jumped. Her leap propelled her high enough that her stomach lurched. Turning in mid-jump, she fired both pistols in unison, and the armored dwarf collapsed.

Julie's boots hit the dirt with a bone-rattling thud. She curled up and fell, rolling, pistols close to her chest. Coming up guns-first, she fired at another dwarf, who tumbled to the ground in front of her. She hurdled him at a dead run and bolted toward the cannon, which was a hundred feet away.

I haaaaaate thisssss, Hat squealed, sounding rattled as he bounced on her head.

Julie chuckled. *Moonlight is my favorite thing in the world.*

The cannon team swung toward her as she neared them. The first of the three fell to the ground, stunned by a bolt of magic to the chest from Julie's pistol. The second took cover behind the cannon, and the third charged her, swinging both hammers.

Julie threw up her arms to block. This time, when the hammers met her crossed forearms, they rebounded as if the dwarf had tried to strike a brick wall. His eyes widened in shock, and Julie drew back one arm and slammed her elbow into his chin. He reeled back, and she followed it up with a pistol butt to his temple. He collapsed to the ground, his helmet rolling away, groaning.

"Piss off!" she yelled at the dwarf cowering behind the cannon.

He didn't need to be told twice. Turning tail, he sprinted across the cliffside, screaming.

Julie stood over the cannon, looking down into the quarry. Faeries swarmed one of the cannons; Raven stood over the other, blood dripping from her fangs and claws. The Weres had formed a tight pack around Korin and Jae. They were heading for the Alicanto's cage, but the fight was thick. Blood dripped from a gash in Teddy's side, and Blake held up one paw as he fought.

Faeries! Raven! Get down there and help the Weres! Julie ran toward the wolves, worker dwarves scattering in panic as she bolted down the trail.

When she reached the bottom, Raven was on the dwarves, fangs slashing. Faerie dust burst from the faeries' rifles, sending screaming dwarves to their knees. Korin's hammers flashed brilliant copper as she slammed them into enemy chests and helmets. Roses writhed around Jae, jagged with thorns, striking like snakes. The werewolves were a mass of hairy forms and chomping teeth.

A dwarf swung his ax toward Raven. Julie raised a pistol and fired, and he crumpled, stunned. *It's beautiful, actually,* she commented.

Ah, yes. The kind of diversity I've always dreamed of, Hat agreed. *Even if it is rather on the violent side.*

Korin and Jae were a few feet from the cage when the dwarves realized their defense was pointless. With a last glance at the Alicanto, their leader shouted, "Retreat! Retreat!"

Dwarves scattered toward the mineshafts.

Faeries, Weres, Raven, pursue them! Overwatch ordered.

The wolves and faeries went after their prey, and a battered silence fell over the quarry. Julie shook sweat out of her eyes as she approached the cage. Jae was on her knees beside it, tearing at her med pack.

Up close, the Alicanto had smooth, slender lines and was the size of a peacock. It crouched miserably in the cage, trembling, its feathers dull browns and black. Its long tail draped behind it, smoking where the feathers touched the iron bars.

"Iron burns it," Jae called. "We need to get it out of there."

"Got it." Korin picked up her hammer and swung it at the lock on the cage's door. It shattered in one blow, and the door popped open.

The Alicanto raised its weary head. A crest of black feathers draped limply from the top of its head, and a tear escaped its dull eyes. The tear glittered; it was molten silver.

"You poor thing," Jae murmured. She reached toward the Alicanto, holding two silver pills in her hand. "You'll be okay. Just eat these."

The bird stared at her for a few moments, then stumbled forward. It missed the step coming out of the cage and fell to the ground with a thud that was heavier than its body should produce.

It's got a bellyful of silver ore, Hat told Julie. *That was why it led the dwarves to the silver. That's what it subsists on.*

The Alicanto raised a weary head and pecked the tablets in Jae's hand. It swallowed, then collapsed to the ground, motionless.

"Oh, no," Julie whispered.

"It's okay." Jae sat back. "It just needs a moment."

As if on cue, the Alicanto sucked in a breath. It sat up, then scrambled to its feet. It shook out its tail feathers. Then it reared back, spread its wings, and flapped them twice. Brilliant light filled the night, and a silver glow suffused the Alicanto's feathers, almost too bright to look at, and spread down the shafts into each feather. The long tail became a trail of silver light. The crest rose on its head, a perfect plume of silver.

The Alicanto threw back its head and let out a soft, belling cry. Then it sprinted toward the edge of the quarry.

Korin gasped. "Look at it go!"

"Come on!" Julie yelled.

They ran after it, weapons holstered, and followed it up the trail to the edge of the cliff. At the top, the Atacama Desert spread beyond them, shimmering silver in the moonlight, its distant mountains etched black against the stars. The Alicanto was a speck of brilliant silver, rapidly disappearing into the night.

Julie threw up her arms. "Whoo-hoo!"

"Yeah!" Korin punched the air.

Jae held up her hand for a high-five. Julie slapped it with enthusiasm.

Are you done? Overwatch enquired. *Can we get back to arresting those dwarves, please? We need to get them to Holding.*

Sure. Julie grinned at her comrades. They headed back into the quarry to mop up the last of the mess.

"Sorry." Julie hurried through the gilded double doors at the entrance of the main building at the Official Para-Military Agency Headquarters in New York City. "I'm late, I know."

The sumptuously carpeted entrance hall was empty except for a lithe, willowy Aether Elf leaning against the wall, scrolling through his phone. Taylor Woodskin looked up when Julie ran in. His soft brown hair fell in ringlets around his elegantly pointed ears, and when he saw her, his eyes widened.

"Julie!" Taylor shoved his phone into his pocket and strode toward her, holding out his arms. "You're finally here."

Julie walked into his embrace and wrapped her arms around his powerful torso, then buried her face in his chest. Taylor still wore his green uniform, but when she took a deep breath, the smell of the earth after rain filled her senses.

Taylor held her close for a few seconds after her arms loosened. He stepped back, his hands on her shoulders, and gave her a searching look. "Are you okay? I was so worried about you!"

"I'm fine, T." Julie smiled at him. "The mission was a huge success. It just took us a while to hunt down all those dwarves in the mine."

"I was scared for you." Taylor rubbed the back of his neck.

"I've been a full-fledged Special Forces soldier for six months, babe. I think it's time you got used to it." Julie laughed and took his hand. "And I'm also starving."

"Hmm." Taylor raised an elegant eyebrow. "Too starving for a drive across town?"

Julie snorted. "Never too starving to see Genevieve."

Taylor sighed. "I should have known you missed me less than you missed your car."

"She's not just any car," Julie chided.

She wasn't. A few minutes later, Julie and Taylor were driving across Staten Island, the roar of the 429 V8 Cobrajet engine filling the air. Taylor clutched the handle over the window in terror as Julie threw the 1971 Mustang Mach 1 into a turn and accelerated to a red light, then braked effortlessly with barely a squeal of the tires.

"Can we not drive like the world is on fire?" Taylor squeaked.

"You're dating *me*, babe. Living on the edge is clearly on your agenda." Julie winked.

Taylor groaned, but Julie slowed down, driving decently for the last two blocks to the steakhouse they both loved.

Taylor ordered a filet mignon with the priciest red wine on the menu. Julie stuck with iced tea and an enormous rump steak with a mountain of fries. She plowed through all her fries and most of the steak before she realized Taylor was watching her with a crooked smile on his face.

"What?" Julie demanded with her mouth full.

He chuckled. "You've got quite the appetite tonight."

"Saving a mythical bird on another continent will do that to you." Julie slurped some tea. "I'm just glad we've got portals. It would suck to fly everywhere."

Taylor looked away. "I'd probably never see you."

Julie sat back. "What's that supposed to mean?"

"Nothing." Taylor waved a hand. "So, what's on your agenda for tomorrow? I thought we could take a mini road trip since you've been missing Genevieve so much."

Julie shook her head. "Maybe. Sarge says he might have a mission for us."

"Another one?" Taylor stared at her.

"Like I said, honey, I'm a soldier." Julie spread her hands. "What do you expect?"

"You've been running yourself ragged for six months." Taylor stabbed a piece of filet. "I just don't think it's right, that's all."

"You need to stop worrying about me." Julie laughed. "I enjoy every minute, especially when there's moonlight."

"Moonlight?" Taylor nearly dropped his fork. "Julie, do you mean moonlight is having an effect on you?"

Julie stuffed a bite of steak into her mouth to avoid answering. She took her time chewing it. "I-I guess."

"That is *awesome* news!" Taylor almost jumped out of the booth. "You've been waiting so long for your powers to manifest, and it's finally happening! Julie, this is amazing!" He raised a hand. "*Server!*"

He smiled. "I don't know if they've got champagne, but this is worthy of buying a bottle."

"Uh—" Julie began.

The server scurried over, and Taylor ordered the champagne. Julie grimaced as he walked away.

"So, did you realize that during the mission?" Taylor leaned forward eagerly. "Did something happen?"

"Um..." Julie cleared her throat. "Actually, it's been a while."

Taylor shook his head in confusion. "A while? What do you mean?"

Julie winced. "Two months or so."

"Two months?" Taylor leaned back in his seat. "You...your powers have been coming in for two months, and...and I'm only finding out now?"

"It happened gradually, T." Julie shrugged. "And I haven't seen you that much, so..."

"So, you just didn't tell me." Taylor wouldn't meet her eyes.

Julie let out a breath. "I didn't mean it like that."

Taylor set his knife and fork neatly together on one side of the plate. "I'm really happy for you, Julie." His voice was tight. "It's great news. Hopefully, it means that the spell is beginning to lift."

"But you're still mad I didn't tell you." Julie folded her arms.

"Mad?" Taylor finally met her eyes. "I'm hurt. Why wouldn't you share that with me, Julie?"

Julie sighed. "I'm sorry if you're hurt, T, but it's been really hectic, okay? I don't have time to share every teeny detail of my life with my boyfriend."

"That's understandable." Taylor took a deep breath and reached for his wallet. He pulled out a sheaf of notes and tucked them under one side of Julie's plate.

"What are you doing?" Julie demanded.

"I had a really long day. The department's been busy." Taylor got to his feet. "I'm going to head home."

"Come on, babe. Don't be mad." Julie reached for his arm. "I'm just used to being independent, okay? I didn't think this would hurt you."

"I know." Taylor bent and kissed her cheek. "Let me know about tomorrow."

"Okay." Julie squeezed his arm. "Be safe."

"You too." Taylor met her eyes, voice softening. "You too."

He strode out of the steakhouse, and when the champagne arrived, Julie was alone at the table.

Julie's bones ached with weariness when she pushed open the door to Room 707 and stepped into the room. "Hey, guys."

"Hey, Juju." Raven was stretched out on her belly, looking like a teenager in pink pajamas. She wore fluffy socks and was reading a tabloid. Korin didn't look up from the computer at her desk, and on the bunk next to Julie's, Jae gave her a brief wave.

Julie dumped her bag on her nightstand, pausing to touch the leaves of the white lily blooming there. She flopped down on her bunk.

"How was the date with your sexy prince?" Raven asked.

"Pretty good." Julie stretched, and sore joints popped in her hips and ankles. "Any news from Sarge? Are we on leave tomorrow?"

"Who even knows?" Korin shrugged.

"I hope so," Jae murmured. "This book is starting to get good."

"What's starting to get good is Griffin Unit Seven." Raven sat up, grinning. "You guys, did we totally kick ass today, or what?"

"That's what we do." Korin extended a fist to Raven.

The vampire bumped it. "Yeah, we do!"

"It's a good feeling," Jae admitted. "Helping others, like that poor Alicanto."

A high-pitched voice spoke from above them. "I particularly like melting people's faces with faerie dust. It's so fulfilling."

Julie and the others looked up. The three faeries sat on the rafters above their bunks. Three tiny, birdhouse-like homes stood beside them, decorated with gory images and metal spikes. The faeries swung their legs over the drop, passing a chunk of raw flesh between them to suck on.

Jae leaned closer to Julie. "Could you tell your boyfriend to stop doing his job so well that the barracks are overfilled?" she whispered. "They're creepy."

A drop of blood fell on Korin's desk from the faeries' meat. She wiped it away without looking.

"Oh, yes." One of the faeries reached behind her back. "Something came for you, Julie." She tossed it down.

Julie caught it easily. It was a gold parchment envelope that smelled of sandalwood and brimstone. She gave the faeries a long glare. "Did you guys read my mail?"

"Don't worry." Korin grunted. "I wouldn't let them."

"Thanks." Julie opened the envelope and pulled out a neatly folded piece of parchment.

Julie of the Meadows,

New moon approaches. Meet me on the mountaintop tomorrow at nightfall.

Alugon.

Julie folded the letter again, trying to hide the kick of excitement in her chest. "Looks like you guys will be going on your next mission without me."

"Not fair that you've got a dispensation for that," Korin grumbled.

"It's not exactly leave, Kori," Raven corrected her sharply. "It's special training, remember?"

"Don't call me that," Korin snapped. She looked at Julie. "What interest do the Lords of the Deep have in you anyway?"

Julie squirmed inwardly. "I rescued a dragon egg for them once."

Why so uncomfortable? You're not lying, Hat pointed out.

Yes, but I'm not telling them I'm a Lunar Fae with a dragon bond, either. It feels weird. Julie sighed.

Korin turned back to her computer, and the faeries snickered above them while tearing off chunks of meat. Julie grabbed her towel and toiletries and started the trek to the communal bathroom at the end of the hall.

Don't tell them, Julie. Hat's voice turned gentle. *For their safety as well as yours. We don't know what threat you're facing.*

Yeah, yeah, Julie muttered inwardly. *I know. It's just getting old, that's all.*

She left him on her folded pajamas as she stepped into the shower and raised her face to the hot water to wash the day away.

CHAPTER TWO

Julie used to be breathless by the time she reached the Avalonian mountaintop on which she spent every new moon. Now, having jogged up the rough-cut stone steps in the mountainside, she was barely sweating when she strode up to the jagged stones at the very summit of the mountain. A large, flat rock occupied the middle of the open space, and it had flowing runes inscribed around its edge.

Alugon was waiting for her. The soft glow that emanated from him illuminated the scene. The moon was a mere sliver in the sky, veiled by clouds. The tall man's gold, blue and purple robes flowed around his body as he turned toward her, his serpentine features and amber eyes revealing him for what he was: a shapeshifting dragon. He cradled what looked like a glassy black watermelon in his arms.

"Julie of the Meadows," he boomed.

"Hey, Alugon." Julie held out her arms. "How's Eggy?"

Alugon sighed deeply. "I really wish you wouldn't call it that." He tipped the egg gently into her arms.

Julie hugged it to her chest. "Ooh, it's gotten bigger!" She looked up at Alugon. "Heavier, anyway. Is that just me?"

"No, it's not." Alugon smiled. "You've grown stronger, Julie, but the young dragon has also grown." He inclined his head toward the rock.

Julie gently laid the egg on the rock and sat beside it, resting a hand on its surface. Liquid moonlight filled the runes, then trickled toward the egg, and the familiar silver glow pulsed within the heart of the egg.

Julie leaned closer. There was more than light inside the egg tonight, she realized, her breath catching. There was...*a presence.* She thought she saw something within, a vague outline of something small curled up.

"Is that the dragon?" she asked.

Alugon leaned a little closer. "It is beginning to take form."

"Wow." Julie reached toward the shell, then hesitated. "Do you...do you think I might feel its consciousness this time?"

Alugon smiled. "You won't know until you try."

Julie pressed her fingertips to the surface of the egg, taking deep breaths. Hyper-awareness spread through her body. She felt the stirring of the grass on the mountainside, the breath of wind across the treetops in the woods below, and the slumbering of sheep in their barns in the surrounding fields. She felt the rush of water in a stream at the foot of the mountain and the rattle of the tram line to Avalon Town. She felt the steady thud of Alugon's heart within his chest and the soft motions of her innards.

As always, she felt the rocking of the fluid inside the shell, as well as something else—a deep *thump-thump.* The beating of the baby dragon's heart. Smiling, Julie listened to the heartbeat for a few moments.

Are you in there? she whispered.

For a moment, she felt a stirring. It might almost have been an awakening.

Hello! she gasped.

There was no response. Julie tried to touch the feeling again, the stirring, but it was gone. A pang of disappointment ran through her. She stroked the egg, listening to the heartbeat while feeling the patter of rain on her skin.

Wait. *Rain?*

Julie opened her eyes, her hyper-awareness fading, and her ears filled with Alugon's laughter. The glowing dragon stood with his hands uplifted, rain splattering on his face and arms, his deep laugh rumbling like thunder. Water poured across the mountainside. Julie shivered, her shirt sticking to her body and drops kissing her cheeks.

"I felt it!" Julie cried. "Just for a moment, but I felt it. I felt someone in there." She paused. "When did it start raining?"

"When your connection with the dragon deepened." Alugon grinned.

Julie stared at him. "What? You mean, I did this?"

"You did, Julie of the Meadows." Alugon held out his hands, catching rainwater in them. "You called moisture from the clouds. It is a power as ancient as the Lunar Fae."

A shudder coursed down Julie's spine, and her mind flashed back to Tintagel. To Morgan Le Fay and the king who slumbered there. "Whoa."

She lifted her hand and held it out to the rain. It slowed, then stopped, leaving behind a petrichor scent that painfully reminded her of Taylor.

Alugon tipped his head to one side. "Your true nature manifests slowly, young one, and the baby grows more slowly still. Both would happen more quickly if you could spend more time here."

A jab of fear rushed through Julie's chest. She pulled the egg into her lap, cradling it. "Is the baby okay?"

"It's fine." Alugon put a hand on her shoulder. "There's no detriment to the egg if it grows slowly. However, your powers would manifest much more quickly if you could spend more time here—and the egg would hatch sooner."

Julie gazed down at the egg's smooth, shiny surface, which

was dotted with raindrops. She wiped them off with her sleeve. "I love coming here, Alugon, and I love the egg already, even if I don't know the baby yet." She took a deep breath. "But I'm bound to the OPMA. I have to honor my duty to the paras who need my help."

Alugon inclined his head. "I respect your dedication, Julie of the Meadows. You have a dragon's heart."

He strolled away across the wet stone. Julie slipped off the rock, still cradling the egg, and followed him. "Hey, Alugon? I have a question."

"Yes?" Alugon rumbled.

"We were in a fight yesterday against a bunch of dwarves holding an Alicanto prisoner. There were thirteen of us, and we succeeded, but it was hard." She scrambled to keep up with him. "I've seen you in your dragon form. You could have taken out those criminals with one puff of fire."

"Your point?" Alugon asked.

"I don't understand why the dragons sit apart from the rest of the world when you could be helping." Julie scrambled up the last few stone steps.

They had reached the entrance to the Deep, which was guarded by two stone dragons who watched Julie with wary eyes. Alugon turned to her, his smile patient. "When we take sides, it is devastating for everyone."

"You mean nuclear-level war," Julie guessed.

Alugon shrugged. "I know little of human lore, Julie of the Meadows, but I can flatten an entire town with a breath of fire. I prefer not to do so. It causes destruction on an unthinkable scale."

"Makes sense," Julie conceded. "But you *were* part of the Second Pendragon War, weren't you?"

Alugon cocked his head to one side. "You have done your reading."

"All I know is that all seven of the Royal Families joined

together to send Mordred underground. Since you're one of them, your people must have been there." Julie stroked the egg.

"Perceptive." The corners of Alugon's lips quirked up. "We had long avoided the matters of other paranormals, choosing not to fight the battles of others, but when Mordred forged the dragon-killer, he made it our battle, too. He had to be stopped."

The dragon's eyes grew distant. "There was so much death. Destruction on a scale your young mind has never dreamed of. I pray that we will never again find ourselves in a situation so desperate that we almost have to end the world to save it."

Julie trembled. "Yeah, so do I."

"Contrary to what the human mythologies say, dragons are peaceful beings." Alugon spread his hands. "We use our fire to warm our children. We will do everything in our power to keep it that way unless our people are threatened."

Julie handed him the egg, then folded her arms. "I get where you're coming from, but it seems harsh to take care of only your own species and not others."

"It is our way." Alugon's face was unreadable. "It has been our way for thousands of years." He inclined his head. "I will see you again next new moon, young one."

"Thanks, Alugon."

The stone covering the entrance to the Deep rolled back, and Alugon was swallowed by the mountain.

***

Julie leaned her head against the window of the tram, staring sightlessly into the dark night. Hat, in his now-habitual form of a navy-blue service cap, lay in her lap. She squeezed him like a stress ball.

Hey! Cut that out, Hat complained.

Sorry. Julie sighed and pulled him onto her head.

You're pensive, Hat noted. *Boy troubles?*

Julie glanced at her phone, feeling a faint stab of guilt at the sight of three new texts from Taylor. Grimacing, she opened them, expecting more of his overprotective bullshit. Instead, there was a gif of a baby goat jumping on a trampoline. **Enjoy the Deep**, he'd typed and added a string of kissy faces. The texts had come in nearly four hours ago. Julie replied hopefully.

Done at the Deep. On the way back to Avalon portal. Want to grab dinner?

Extending an olive branch? Hat asked.

I don't know. He seemed pretty chill when we had lunch together earlier today. He even apologized for walking out on me last night. Julie tucked her phone back into her pocket. *I just wish he'd accept that I have a life of my own. He's been cool about me disappearing on missions. I really hope that's not going to change.*

That's not what was on your mind earlier, Hat pointed out.

Julie sat back against her seat, trying not to jostle the large, hairy person of indeterminate species sleeping in the seat beside her. *No. I was thinking about my conversation with Alugon. I mean, I understand why they don't engage, but I can't help thinking there must be a better way. Maybe they could—*

The tram jerked to a halt so sharply that Julie almost ended up in the lap of the dwarf sitting opposite her. She gasped and grabbed her seat. The hairy person sat up with a snort. A baby cried, and a mutter of fear ran through the passengers.

"What's happening?" a fae near the back shouted.

Something cold and sinister slithered over Julie's senses. She rose to her feet. *Hat, what is that?*

Trouble, he muttered darkly.

"Everybody just stay calm." The tram operator's voice trembled. "Just stay calm."

Julie strode down the aisle toward the front, relieved that she'd worn her uniform, even if her armor was at HQ. As she grew nearer, she saw a bluish glow coming from the windshield at the front of the tram.

The driver was fumbling for his radio, hands shaking, when Julie reached him. "What's happening, sir?" she asked, touching her Griffin arm patch. "I'm OPMA Special Forces."

"Oh, thank Merlin!" the operator gasped. He was a wide-eyed faun, and he was tapping his cloven hooves nervously on the floor. "Look!"

The blue glow came from Sylthana fire. A wall of crackling, magical flame had engulfed the tram tracks just ahead of them. She squinted around the blue fire, trying to spot anyone nearby. In the dim light, the fire was blinding, but she could feel someone escaping across the fields.

"Stay here. Keep the doors closed once I'm out," Julie ordered.

She reached for the two pistols she wore on her belt and slipped out of the doors when they were still half-open into the chilly night. There was the soft thump of the doors closing behind her and the continued crackle of the flames. She kept the pistols balanced in her hands as she circled around the fire, glancing left and right.

There! Hat called out. *Ten o' clock!*

Julie spotted a distant figure fleeing across the fields with a blue glow in their hands. *This isn't right. I'm going to follow them,* she told Hat. *We can't be far from Avalon Town.*

As she spoke, the flames dwindled, then winked out. Its instigator must be out of range to maintain the magic. She hurried back to the tram, holstering her pistols, and knocked on the door.

The driver opened it. "What happened?"

"Turn back," Julie ordered. "Go back to your last stop and stay there until you hear from Avalon."

"What's going on?" the driver asked.

"I'm going to find out, but it's safer for you not to be here right now." Julie didn't wait for his response. She sprinted across the countryside after the distant figure of the retreating arsonist.

Her feet thudded on springy turf, and sheep fields stretched out around her, bordered by wooden post-and-rail fences and dotted with grazing golden-fleeced sheep. The animals shied nervously as she pounded past them, arms swinging, pace and breathing steady.

She grabbed the top rail of the fence in front of her and swung over it, landed running, and kept up her pace as she reached the top of the hill. A jolt ran through her. Avalon Town was a furlong away, a collection of glittering lights at the bottom of the hill, and smoke hung against the cloud-veiled stars. The fleeing arsonist was halfway down the hill, flames still burning in his hands. She saw blue fire silhouetting the castle on the outskirts of town, and her gut clenched.

Avalon North OPMA. They're under attack!

Run, Julie! Hat cried.

Arms pistoning, she thundered down the hill, ignoring the ache in her lungs.

When the fleeing Sylthana Elf heard her coming and whirled, it was too late. Julie tackled him to the ground with a bone-jarring thump. He squealed and threw up his blazing hands, but Julie slapped them aside, then pinned his arms to the ground with a knee on each bicep. The elf roared with pain.

Shit. Shit! Julie yelled internally.

The elf's face was painted black. On his left cheek, there was a sliver of white crescent moon splashed against the dark paint.

"What are you doing?" Julie shouted. "What are you planning?"

The elf grinned up at her. "It's too late, Bluey," he hissed. "Your precious castle is burning."

A roar of flame dragged Julie's attention away from the elf. OPMA Avalon North towered above them, an imposing fortress, all battlements and banners. As she watched, plumes of flame burst up the nearest tower, engulfing the battlements. The people within were screaming.

"Son of a bitch," Julie snapped. She rolled the elf onto his face and ripped Hat off her head. "Cuffs!" she barked.

"On it." Hat hummed, and when Julie reached into him, her fingers closed on magic-nulling handcuffs. She slapped them on the elf and left him face-down on the ground, then ran toward the main gates.

The sight of those streets made Julie's stomach flip over. When grass changed to cobblestones under her feet, the night was lit by blue fire. A family of fae clung to each other in the street, weeping, surrounded by wide-eyed soldiers as their home burned. A group of paras, their faces painted with the symbol of the Dark Moon League, roamed unchecked through an empty clothing store on Julie's left, smashing windows and burning merchandise.

What do I do? Julie staggered to a halt. *Do I stop them?*

No! There's no one inside. There's a burning home just down the street. Get to it! Hat yelled.

Hooves clattered on stone. Bursting through the smoke, a gray stallion plunged toward Julie, saddle empty and stirrups flapping as he galloped. His shoulders foamed with sweat, and his eyes were white and wild with fear. Eight hooves rang on the street, and eight legs churned with every stride.

"*Sleipnir!*" Julie shouted, stepping in front of him.

Sleipnir's gallop slowed to a panicked trot, his hooves beating a staccato on the stone.

"Sleipnir, whoa." Julie kept her voice calm. "Here, buddy." She groped in her pocket for a sugar cube. "It's okay."

The stallion halted beside her, blowing hard, and grabbed the sugar cube out of her palm with hasty lips. Julie seized his reins. They were broken, and the left side of his saddle was scuffed and damp. He'd gone down and lost his rider.

"Come on, Slippy." Julie knotted the broken reins and swung up onto Sleipnir's back, an easy movement after a two-week training camp at a centaur's ranch in Montana. "Let's do this!"

She wheeled the stallion toward the burning house and clapped her heels into his sides. In response, Sleipnir reared, four front hooves pawing at nothing. Julie gasped and grabbed his mane, and the stallion landed with a toss of his head, ripping the reins out of her hands.

"Sleipnir, no!" Julie squealed, grabbing for the reins.

Sleipnir plunged into a gallop. Clinging to the single rein she had managed to retrieve, Julie tried to haul him toward the burning house, but Sleipnir plunged right past.

"What are you doing?" Julie shrieked.

Sirens wailed behind her—actual sirens, driving a firetruck—and she glanced back to see them racing to the burning building. Sleipnir didn't slow down. Head low, ignoring Julie's desperate tugs at the reins, he galloped toward the burning fortress.

The portcullis was wide open, and panicky civilians streamed out of it, coughing and retching in the smoke. Magic fire crackled over the stone walls, and the inner ward was a maelstrom of fire and fleeing paras.

Julie put an arm over her face, eyes streaming, as Sleipnir jogged under the portcullis and into the inner ward. The smoke was too thick for her to see anything. She heard screams but no fighting. OPMA infantrymen in navy-blue uniforms were trying to evacuate the civilians, and all the doors were open.

"We need to help with the evacuation!" Julie turned Sleipnir toward the main doors and squeezed his sides with her legs.

Sleipnir stopped, throwing up his head so sharply that Julie's chest slammed into his neck.

"Dude, not now!" Julie squeezed again. "Come *on!*"

Sleipnir squealed, tossing his head, and furiously kicked at her leg with two of his hind feet.

Something's not right, Hat told her. *This fire is a diversion. The League doesn't want to burn down the fortress. They want to take it.*

No one can see anything with this smoke. Julie looked at the cloudy sky. *Hat, how do I call the rain?*

That seems a little ambitious, Hat hedged.

There was a scream from inside the fortress. Coughing, Julie squinted through the smoke. A terrified figure appeared at the window, silhouetted by blue flames.

Now, Hat! Julie yelled.

Okay, okay! Reach inside yourself. Feel the power of the new moon. Hat's voice trembled. *Julie, be careful. If you reveal yourself...*

If I don't, people will die. Julie closed her eyes and breathed deeply. Sleipnir was motionless underneath her. Power surged through her veins, still fresh from the mountaintop. She felt the heartbeat of the dragon within her own chest, and she felt the moisture in the clouds. She made it rain.

The heavens opened. Rain poured from the sky in thick sheets, splashing Julie's face and soaking Sleipnir's mane. She looked up at it, laughing. The smoke dissipated, and the magic fire sputtered, flickered, and went out. The crackling of the flames ceased, and the screaming stopped.

Julie gasped. *That was so cool!*

The gates! Hat cried.

Julie looked through the wide-open portcullis. Peering past the curtain of rain, she saw an army of paras with black-painted faces coming down the street, filling it from edge to edge, weapons flashing in their hands.

"The Dark Moon League!"

Sleipnir reared. She clung to him as he turned on his hind legs, pinned his ears to his head, and charged.

"Dude, whoa!" Julie squealed, grabbing at the reins. The street was packed with paras, and as Sleipner neared the portcullis, they rushed forward, weapons raised. A Sylthana Elf led them, his blue eyes blazing behind the black paint. He held a vicious pike in his hands.

Julie threw her body back, hauling on the bit with all of her strength, but she might as well have been trying to stop a steam train.

"Move! Move! Move!" a deep voice yelled from behind Julie.

She risked a glance over her shoulder as infantrymen rushed from the fortress, singed and spluttering. Some hustled the civilians back to the safety of the walls. The rest rushed for the portcullis, forming a defensive line.

"We're going to *die*, Sleipnir!" Julie squealed.

Sleipnir reached the portcullis, stuck his eight legs out straight, and slid to a halt, his shoes striking sparks on the stone. He pawed the air with two of his forelegs and let out a ringing neigh—his battle cry.

Julie drew both pistols and fired into the charging Dark Moon League. A crackling ball of magic smacked into the chest of a troll near the front, and he went down hard. Two others tripped and sprawled over him. The pike-bearing Sylthana Elf ducked Julie's shot and slashed at Sleipnir's legs. The stallion snatched his forelegs out of the way and reared, and as the elf jabbed at his belly, Sleipnir came down hard, four hooves crushing the pike as the elf rolled out of the way, bleeding.

Julie kept firing into the group, which was so tightly packed that it was almost impossible not to hit something. Glowing balls of magical water flew from her pistols and into the Sylthana Elves, dousing their fire. Crackling stun ammo sent the trolls sprawling to the ground. She spotted other types of paras in the group, but she shot at anyone with a painted face.

For every attacker that fell, there seemed to be a hundred to take their place. They swarmed closer to Sleipnir, jabbing at him with pikes and swords. He danced under her, kicking and striking, and his square teeth snapped shut on a troll's arm. The troll screamed and Sleipnir flicked his head, flinging the hapless attacker into his comrades. Some fell back, but others sprang over them and slashed at Sleipnir.

An elf sprinted toward them, yelling, brandishing daggers in each hand. A line of blood opened on Sleipnir's neck, and the stallion squealed in rage. Julie fired both pistols into the elf's face, sending him flying. "Hands off my horse, bitch!"

"No. *No!*" Hat cried.

Julie looked back toward the line holding the portcullis. The infantrymen had locked their shields together, forming a wall, but as Julie watched, the line buckled and strained against the continued onslaught of the attackers who slipped past her and Sleipnir. A massive troll at the front of the line swung his club into a blue-uniformed fae's shield, throwing her backward. A dwarf stepped up to take her place, and the club knocked her across the courtyard.

"They can't hold the line!" Hat screamed.

"Hey, asshole!" Julie yelled.

The troll turned toward her, still clutching his club. Julie aimed both pistols at the troll and squeezed the triggers. Twin balls of magic soared toward him, joining to form one.

"Take tha—" Julie began.

Hands closed around her left leg. She swung around, but it was too late. They pulled hard, yanking her off Sleipnir's back. She landed on her back, head cracking against the stone, and was instantly swarmed by painted faces. Yelling, Julie fired into the chaos, hearing Sleipnir's hooves crunching beside her.

She scrambled to her feet, still firing, just in time to see the shield wall crumple. The Dark Moon League poured into the fortress.

CHAPTER THREE

Julie slammed her pistol butt into the nose of the troll beside her. He staggered back, blood bursting across his face, and the rest of the attackers charged toward the open portcullis.

"No!" Julie choked out. Holstering her pistols, she grabbed Sleipnir's mane, stuffed her left foot into the stirrup, and scrambled onto his back, ignoring the pain that lanced through her back and legs.

When he felt her weight settle on his back, Sleipnir whipped around and charged after the Dark Moons, leaping over the unconscious troll. Julie drew a pistol, but when they plunged beneath the portcullis, there was nowhere to use it. The inner ward was a mass of hand-to-hand fighting. Dark Moons and PMA soldiers were tangled in a wild mass of weapons and claws, teeth and blades.

Julie sat back, closing her free hand on the reins. For once, Sleipnir listened and slowed to a collected trot, neck bowed. His four front legs rose so high that his knees almost touched his nose.

We're losing! Julie realized.

It was true. Everywhere she looked, soldiers fell, stabbed and trampled by the wrathful Dark Moons. Most of them rushed for the front doors of the keep. Small groups scrambled up the walls, ripping down the singed and tattered flags of the Eternity Throne. They replaced them with the black banner with a crescent moon slashed across it. Others ran over to the vehicles parked against the walls and cut crescent moon shapes into the paintwork.

What can I do? Julie looked around in panic.

You could flee. The fight can't be won like this, Hat pointed out.

The remaining infantrymen had their backs to the doors of the keep, and they were fighting for their lives. The civilians within kept screaming.

Or I can fight to the death. Julie turned Sleipnir's head toward the fight.

A blue spark appeared in midair on the left side of the inner ward. Julie stared as it spun briefly, opening a gap of shimmering air. Then a huge magic portal burst open, big enough to admit a city bus. Instead, it admitted Captain Jack Kaplan.

He surged through the portal in tiger form, hundreds of pounds of pure predator rage, his orange-and-black coat rippling with muscle. His roar shook the battlefield, rising over the screams and cries.

"Yeah, Cap!" Julie cheered.

Kaplan covered the distance between the portal and the battle in a series of incredible bounds. A knot of elves spun to face him, blades drawn. Kaplan leaped and fell upon them with claws and teeth, giant paws batting swords from their hands like toys.

Feet thundered on the stone, and a sea of navy-uniformed soldiers poured through the portal: yetis swinging heavy clubs, Weres in their animal forms swarmed around their knees, and vampires swooped through the night. The infantrymen at the keep's doors cheered as the PMA soldiers rushed at the attackers.

"Go, Slippy!" Julie yelled.

Sleipnir charged into the battle, hooves trampling, teeth

crushing. Julie pistol-whipped attackers from his back, steering him into the thickest part of the fight. Kaplan was forging a path through the Dark Moons toward the beleaguered infantrymen. A troll swiped at the tiger with a pike, opening a wound on his flank. Kaplan whipped around, roaring, and dealt the troll a killing blow with one massive paw. Behind him, an elf swung his sword. Before the blow could land, Sleipnir trampled him into the stone.

"*Meadows?*" Kaplan demanded, staring up at her.

"Toss me that sword!" Julie pointed at the fallen elf's sword. "Um, *sir.*"

Kaplan reached out with a paw and flicked the sword toward her. Julie caught it by the hilt. "Let's do this!"

She slashed at an elf as he tried to grab her leg. A shrieking goblin scrambled up Sleipnir's other side and clawed Julie's arm, tearing lines of fire through her skin. She slammed her elbow into him and stabbed at the same elf again, and the tip of her blade drove into his shoulder. Kicking hard as the goblin tried to climb her leg again, Julie stabbed an elf in the leg when he tried to attack Kaplan. The tiger was a ball of fury, rolling over and over with his front paws wrapped around a troll, hind claws tearing at its belly.

Julie felt Sleipnir's muscles bunch, so she leaned forward and grabbed a strand of mane in her rein hand just before the eight-legged stallion launched into the air. Julie's neck snapped back with the force of his leap. As he reached the apex, he lashed out with all four hind legs. Bones crunched, and trolls' and elves' shrieks cut off as his hind hooves connected.

Sleipnir landed hard, squashing the goblin as he did. Julie sucked in a breath, but more elves were upon her. She held them at bay with slashes of her sword. The smell of burning hair filled the air, and Kaplan's roar of rage turned into one of pain. A Sylthana Elf had two hands pressed to the tiger's ribs, and smoke rose from his fingers. Kaplan whipped around and closed his jaws over the elf's arm, and blood ran between his fangs.

"There are still too many!" Julie screamed.

An eagle's shriek tore through the night.

Kaplan smiled, revealing bloody canines. "Not for long."

The shriek came again, but it was more than the cry of an eagle. It had a rumbling depth—a leonine roar. Julie looked up as another portal opened on the other side of the inner ward.

"Griffins!" she cried.

The Royal Guard from the Eternal Palace! Hat cheered. *The Eternity Guard!*

They swooped through the portal, wings outstretched, armor flashing on their powerful chests. Diving from the skies, they fell upon the Dark Moon attackers with talons and fangs. The Dark Moons' screams of panic gave way to cries of victory from the PMA soldiers as they pressed forward, pincering the Dark Moons between them.

At last, the Dark Moon attackers' nerve broke. "Retreat!" the pike-wielding elf yelled. One side of his face was a mask of blood, and the paint was gone. "Retreat!"

They broke ranks and bolted for the open portcullis.

"Not so fast!" Kaplan thundered from behind Julie.

She looked up. In human form, uniform slashed and tattered, the captain stood beside a burned-out PMA personnel bus. He grasped the bottom edge of the bus.

Is he... Hat began.

Julie chuckled. *Oh, yes.*

Kaplan hefted the bus over his head, brawny muscles bulging through the bloody rips in his uniform. He threw back his head and let out a tiger's roar, features twisting, fangs lengthening, half-man, half-tiger. The Dark Moons staggered to a petrified halt, and Kaplan threw the bus.

The massive vehicle sailed through the air, scattering broken glass as it pirouetted and then landed over the portcullis with a thunderous crash, effectively blocking the only escape route with a wall of shattered glass and mangled metal.

Silence ensued. The Dark Moons huddled against the bus, meek and wide-eyed.

"Well." Hat cleared his non-existent throat. "That's one way to win a battle."

"Arrest them!" Kaplan thundered, pointing.

The PMA soldiers and palace griffin guards didn't need to be told twice. Brandishing magic-nulling restraints, they surrounded the subdued Dark Moons.

Julie swung down from Sleipnir and gave his withers a rub with her knuckles. "Good boy."

Sleipnir nuzzled her hand for treats. Finding she had none, he snorted, disappointed.

"Slippy? Slippy!" a masculine voice yelled. "Get back here right now! Where have you been?"

Sleipnir whinnied and trotted off toward a limping, one-eyed soldier, tail held high.

"What were you doing here, Meadows?" Kaplan demanded.

Julie jumped. The captain stood a few feet away from her, his giant arms folded, bushy eyebrows butting heads like caterpillars arguing in the center of his forehead.

"I was just on my way back from meeting with Alugon." Julie winced. "Cap, your arm."

Kaplan glanced at the four-inch gash on his left bicep without much interest. "I should have known I'd find you where I usually do. Right in the middle of the chaos."

"I didn't know things with the Dark Moon League had escalated this much in Avalon Town," Julie admitted.

Kaplan sighed as he gently probed an ugly burn on his cheek. "You clearly haven't been in Avalon Town much. Out on assignment most of the time, aren't you?"

"Lots of missions," Julie confirmed. "Lots of them in the human world."

"I saw the report about your unit's work in the Atacama Desert yesterday." Kaplan raised a busy eyebrow.

Julie smothered her grin. *Coming from Kaplan, I'm pretty sure that counts as praise.*

Hat chuckled. *It is.*

"So, they've been getting worse here?" Julie asked.

Kaplan pulled up his shirt, glancing at two huge blisters in the shape of handprints on his ribs. "Much worse. After they tried to burn down the Library, the queen passed a decree outlawing any activities in the name of the Dark Moon League. Even flying the flag carries a hefty fine."

"They tried to burn down the Library?" If Julie had been wearing pearls, she would have clutched them.

"Don't worry." Kaplan chuckled. "They didn't succeed." His smile faded as he looked around the fortress. "But this time, they came much too close."

Julie followed his gaze and saw the Dark Moon flags limp in the steady rain. The wrecked hulk of the bus blocking the portcullis was blackened and fire-gutted. Smoke still trailed out of the doors and windows. Indoors, blue flames still flickered in some places.

Julie's gut knotted. She didn't think she'd ever been in a fight so hard-won before.

"It's now an automatic prison sentence for anyone committing crimes in the name of the Dark Moon League." Kaplan's expression darkened. "And that's right where this lot is going." He nodded to her. "You'd better get back to HQ and your unit. See you next time there's trouble."

Julie watched the weretiger stride away, limping slightly as each stride tugged at the burns in his side.

"What do I do now?" she murmured.

Get back to the portal like Kaplan told you to, I'd say, Hat suggested. *There are more than enough paras here to round up the Dark Moons, and your unit expected you back more than an hour ago.*

Yeah, I guess. Julie brushed the scratches on her arm where the goblin had clawed her. She tugged at her uniform, hoping it would mostly cover the blood, and plodded toward the back gate of the fortress. A contingent of PMA soldiers guarded it, but, recognizing her uniform, they let her through.

The rain stopped a few moments later. Julie trudged through the streets, drying off slowly, trying to ignore the rising pain in her arm.

Are you all right? Hat asked.

Yeah, I'm fine. Just tired now, I guess. Julie stifled a yawn. *There were a lot of Dark Moons back there, weren't there? Easily a hundred.*

Maybe more, Hat agreed.

And they're all being shipped straight to prison? Julie raised an eyebrow. *It's got to be a pretty big prison.*

Oh, yes. It's a separate realm, Hat explained. *Magic-nulling, so no one escapes.*

Julie scrunched her nose. *Sounds barbaric.*

Not really. Hat laughed. *Paras have to live like humans, but there are worse fates. And their natural lifespans are unaffected.*

A realm of exile, Julie mused. *Like para Australia.*

Hat chuckled. *Exactly.*

They were silent for the rest of the walk to Avalon Plaza and the portal that would let Julie out underneath the 110th Street Bridge into Manhattan.

Julie tugged on the bandage on her arm, trying to rub the stitches. After three days, they itched.

Jae slapped her hand away with a white dress glove. "Stop that," she hissed. "It's not good for the healing."

"Sorry." Julie lowered her hand to her lap.

"Stupid. You should know that," Korin snapped beside her.

"Don't be cranky, Korin." Raven leaned over the dwarf's lap to offer Julie a plastic packet of sweets. "Jelly babies?"

"Raven! We're in dress uniform," Julie growled.

"So? I'm snackish." Raven popped one into her mouth. "No one's looking at us, anyway."

This much was true. Julie sat back in her chair, gazing around at the outdoor auditorium. The black sky was almost drowned out by spotlights that surrounded the high grandstands, rising up from the field in the middle like seating at a sports stadium. At the center, a huge stage was covered with scaffolding, holding up cameras and lights that moved with hydraulic smoothness.

The stage was unoccupied for now, except for a series of enormous banners hanging at the backdrop, each a different color and emblazoned with a golden OPMA crest. A firebird sat on a golden perch in one corner, singing softly into a fat round microphone, his voice resounding through the auditorium as it slowly filled.

"Feels like there are a lot more cameras here than for our graduation," Julie whispered.

Raven nodded. "It's being broadcast to the entire paranormal world. Even Avalon."

Julie felt a burst of pride. "Taylor's going up there soon."

"I know! I can't wait to see him," Raven cooed.

"Keep it in your pants, vamp," Korin growled. "He's taken, remember?"

Raven held up both hands. "I'm just planning on enjoying the view."

Hat snickered. *Taylor's going to enjoy hearing about that one.*

Julie pictured her boyfriend's face turning gray with embarrassment and smothered a grin.

The tramp of approaching feet caught Julie's attention. She craned her neck, watching as a set of new recruits in plain navy uniforms marched clumsily to a section of empty seating.

Look at them all, she marveled. *Is it just me, or is there a lot more than there used to be?*

There's a lot more of everyone *than there used to be,* Hat pointed out. *This auditorium was barely half-full for your graduation.*

Now there's almost no space left. Julie stared around, spotting only the occasional empty seat. The royal box, in particular, was crammed. *The PMA's bigger than it used to be.*

Hat chuckled. *Taylor's been working hard.*

A warm burst of pride flooded Julie's chest, and she smiled.

Of course, paras all over the world wanting to do whatever they can to prevent an all-out war might also have something to do with it, Hat added dryly.

Oh, shut up. Let me believe that my boyfriend is single-handedly saving the world. There they come! Julie sat up straighter.

The firebird's voice had risen, drowning out the susurrus of chatter from the audience. His song became a fluting fanfare when Captain Kaplan strode onto the stage, resplendent in his scarlet uniform, his broad chest aglitter with medals. He took his place at the lectern in the middle. Behind him, Julie spotted a shadowy figure gesturing at the cameramen, directing the smooth movements of the giant cameras and spotlights. Malcolm Nox.

He's come a long way, too, she commented.

Hat grunted in agreement.

A hush fell on the auditorium as the department heads of the PMA marched onto the stage after Kaplan. They had shed their red officers' uniforms in favor of their department colors for the occasion. The first, massive and imposing—even taller than Kaplan—was First Sergeant Cadmeus Droppelheimer, wearing navy-blue. The orc's service cap was pulled down low over his bald head, and his massive hands swung by his sides, encased in white gloves. Major Bianca Hartshorn followed him, strutting even in combat boots. Her curving gazelle's horns rose from special holes in her hat, which couldn't conceal her glowing golden hair—contained in a bun, for once. She gave the audience a sassy wink as she sashayed across the stage.

The head of Intelligence was puny in comparison, barely reaching Bianca's knees in his child-sized navy uniform. Then came the heads of Administration and Logistics. These were followed by a tall, green-skinned troll in a white lab coat. Qtana's usual blonde ponytail was a bun for the occasion, and she squinted shyly at the crowd from behind her thick glasses.

Look at her go! Julie grinned as Qtana strode across the stage and took her place beside the administration head.

She's come a long way from the shy troll we met on your first day. Hat sighed. *I suppose I can forgive her for writing the IRSA 4000.*

You seriously need to get over that, Julie told him.

The head of the medical department, wearing royal purple, was next. Then, finally, a willowy figure stepped onto the stage in a forest green dress uniform, buttons shining under the lights. Julie's heart jolted in her chest. She realized she'd clasped her hands under her chin and couldn't seem to unclasp them as Taylor took his place among the highest-ranking officers of the PMA, looking mystical and official and irresistible in his dress uniform. His white-gloved hands hung by his sides, and his soft brown eyes looked straight ahead. They moved to skim over Julie, and she waved. The corner of his lip twitched, and he lifted two fingers in greeting.

"Awwww!" Raven sighed and propped up her chin in her hands. "You two are so adorable."

"Shhh!" Korin hissed. "It's starting."

A few other paras had gathered on the stage. Julie recognized para media, councilors to some of the different royal families, and representatives from the major para groups. When the last had taken their place, Malcolm gestured at Kaplan. The firebird fell silent.

"Today, I find myself delivering the briefing I had hoped I would never have to give." Kaplan rested his massive hands on the lectern, gripping it tightly. On the giant screen behind him, Julie saw that his fingernails were digging into the wood. "It is no secret that OPMA Avalon North was attacked three days ago. Although we have been dealing with scattered unrest throughout Avalon Town in the past few months, this was far more than a mere riot. This was a coordinated and well-planned attack on the heart of the PMA's presence in one of the most important towns in Avalon."

Tension gripped the crowd. Julie thought about the screams in that smoke-filled fortress.

"The attackers," Kaplan went on, "were all from the Dark Moon League."

A mutter ran through the crowd. Julie's gloves tightened over the backs of her hands as her fists knotted.

"Despite being outlawed by the Eternity Throne, the Dark Moon League continues to sow chaos and destruction throughout the paranormal world." Kaplan's sharp eyes bored into the crowd. "They are a plague upon the peace and prosperity that generations of paras have fought and died for. The Eternity Queen has ordered us to confront those bloodthirsty criminals."

Kaplan raised his chin. "The Para-Military Agency has been ordered to put a stop to the Dark Moon League once and for all."

Julie exchanged glances with Jae, Korin, and Raven. The six Weres, sitting in the row behind them, were uncharacteristically silent. When Julie glanced at them, their glittering eyes looked like those of a wolf pack on the hunt.

"First Sergeant Droppelheimer." Kaplan nodded at the orc. "We are going after the Dark Moon League. We are going to stand up for our people and for their safety."

Droppelheimer saluted, a crisp, unhurried motion. "Sir, yes, sir." It was odd to hear deference in the orc's rumbling voice.

The corner of Kaplan's mouth twitched. "Prepare your Special Forces units for rapid-action raids on Dark Moon cells."

"Sir, yes, sir," Droppelheimer repeated.

"Yes!" Korin hissed. "We're going to give those suckers something to think about, am I right?"

There were murmurs of agreement and fist-bumps from the rest of the Griffins. Julie felt excitement rush through her veins like quicksilver.

"To destroy those cells, we need more information about them, like where they are and how they operate. Commander Lapp…oh, for Merlin's sake." Kaplan sighed. "Where *is* he?"

"I think he's still here, sir." Bianca pointed at the empty space beside her.

"Commander Lapp, would you be so kind as to make yourself visible?" Kaplan snapped.

A pair of glowing white eyes appeared beside Bianca, followed by the rest of the kobold commander of Intelligence. His luminous white eyes were set in a wizened face. They turned to Kaplan in silence.

"Commander Lapp." Kaplan cleared his throat, shifting his weight from foot to foot.

Is Kaplan freaked out, or is it just me? Julie wondered.

Hat snickered. *To be fair, Lapp is freaky.*

"You will focus your unit's efforts on acquiring intelligence on Dark Moon cells," Kaplan croaked.

Commander Lapp nodded once, turned into a candle, hovered over the stage, flickering, and then vanished.

Kaplan shuddered before turning to Taylor. "None of these efforts will be possible without the manpower to carry them out." The weretiger folded his arms, and Taylor shrank back. Kaplan's face relaxed into one of his rare, genuine smiles. "In that regard, the recruitment department has shone in the past six months and continues to bring in high numbers of paranormals suited to a variety of roles in the PMA. Keep up the good work, Woodskin."

Taylor's jaw dropped. He stared at Kaplan, and Julie felt like bursting into applause.

Ignoring his flabbergasted CO of recruiting, Kaplan looked at the heads of Administration and Logistics. "We will take numerous steps in order to streamline our operations. Firstly, the red tape is excessive. Travel and requisitions must be converted to a quick, seamless process so our people can get where they need to go with the equipment they need without difficulty. Moreover, Logistics, you will be responsible for ensuring inventory and deployment of resources are up to date and accessible to those in the field at all times. You might be a less glamorous branch of the PMA, but you are instrumental in our function." The two commanders' shoulders straightened at his words. His voice gentled. "We cannot function without you. We cannot beat the Dark Moon League without you."

"Yesss! We get to reorganize the Warehouse!" a brownie hissed a few rows down from Julie. She exchanged high-fives with her companions.

Julie stifled a grin. She'd recruited those brownies last summer at the festival of Beltane in Fernwood Deep. She remembered that even though most of her other memories of that night had vanished into a fog of mead and wine.

Kaplan turned his eyes on Qtana, who stiffened under his gaze, trembling. "Communications and technology have never been as important as they are today. You have carried out a variety of upgrades to our technology since you were promoted to be the head of IT, Qtana, but still more changes need to be made. Your task is to assist all the branches in any way that they need."

He turned to the crowd again, gesturing at Qtana. "In the coming days, the IT department will be visiting every branch to update communications and logistics technology with...what did you call it again, Qtana?"

The troll cleared her throat. "Thaumatech, sir." She pushed her glasses higher on her nose.

"Yes, that." Kaplan nodded. "That is not the only review that will be conducted in the entire PMA. By order of the Queen, all branches will have a budget review with the intention of stream-lining and updating their protocols. Our goal is to cut down on bureaucracy without endangering the paranormals we are working to protect."

High time. Julie chuckled inwardly.

"We are many, but we have a single purpose." Voice rising, Kaplan's eyes swept through the crowd, landing on Julie as though he'd heard her thoughts. She froze. His eyes remained steadily and pointedly on her. "Recent events have shown us that we need to modernize. As technology has grown in complexity, we have ceased to look to human methods for guidance on how to operate in both worlds. Now is the time to spread our wings both metaphorically and literally." He glanced at Bianca, who smirked. "We will adopt and adapt technology to combat this threat to our world."

Julie felt like cheering. Instead, she grinned and gave Qtana an enthusiastic thumbs-up. The troll smiled, blinking behind her glasses.

Kaplan turned to the crowd once more. "The Dark Moon League is a very real, very present, and very dangerous threat." His big hands clenched on the lectern. "But the Para-Military Agency is a united front that stands for peace, and we will not allow that group of troublemakers to divide us, disunite us, or defeat us. The Dark Moon League has the best of the PMA coming for them, and they stand no chance against us."

There was thunderous applause, and Julie joined in with all her might.

CHAPTER FOUR

Bianca's office door was open, and the succubus' strident voice echoed from within.

"What are you *doing*? That's priceless! Don't touch it!"

Julie peered inside. Bianca stood in the center of an ocean of chaos, arms akimbo, fiery golden hair down her back, her leathery wings half-open. Her office furniture had been shoved into the middle of the room. A troll stood on a stepladder in the corner, wearing huge rubber gloves and goggles and holding a length of silver wire. Nearby, a frozen troll had both hands on the seductive painting of a mostly-naked faun that had always hung on Bianca's wall.

"*Put. It. Down,*" the succubus hissed.

"Ma'am, we need to lay the cable here," the troll stuttered. "I was just going to put it aside for a moment."

"Put it aside? *Put it aside?*" Bianca shrieked. She strode over to the troll, snatched the painting from his hands, and very gently hung it on its hook again. "This painting is older than your species! You don't just *put it aside!*"

Julie was enjoying the show, but the poor troll looked ashen, so she stepped forward and saluted. "You wanted to see me, ma'am?"

"Oh, there you are." Bianca turned away from the trolls and flopped down at her desk, then leaped to her feet with a squeal. A pile of computer parts, as well as two brass amulets, a rabbit's foot, a poison apple, and a winged mouse lay on her chair. The mouse flew away with a high-pitched buzz, and Bianca leaned her elbows on her desk and sighed.

"Are you okay?" Julie hazarded.

"Do I look okay?" Bianca thundered. "On top of overseeing the changes to communications between the military branch and others, I have to figure out a rota to give you lot some leave!" She gestured wildly.

Julie squared her shoulders. "I know it's hard, but lately, we've done back-to-back missions."

"I know you have. Of course you need leave. You've been working your sexy asses off." Bianca gripped her horns and sighed again. "Anyway, I called you in here to tell you that you're all getting three days' leave as soon as I figure out the schedule."

She does know you're wearing a magical supercomputer on your head, right? Hat growled.

Bianca glanced at her desk. "Hey! You!"

The trolls jumped. The one on the stepladder clutched the wire. The other gawped at her. "Yes, ma'am?"

"Where's my computer?" Bianca roared.

"That old thing?" The troll laughed. "That wasn't a computer. It was a steam engine."

"Well, I need it for work!" Bianca thundered.

"No, ma'am, you need *this*." The troll stepped forward, eyes shining, and held out a tiny gold object the size and shape of a penny.

Bianca glared at it. "What is this supposed to be?"

"The future," the troll breathed. "You put it behind your ear, and it projects—"

"Excuse me? *Excuse me?*" Hat spoke up, his voice vibrating through Julie's skull.

"Hat!" she hissed, grabbing his brim.

"Don't you think you might want to involve *me?*" Hat demanded. "DUMB LE Dork? A highly sophisticated magical system who's been running half of your comms on missions and could calculate a simple rota in his sleep? Well, if he slept."

Bianca flapped a hand. "It's not my call. I don't have time for this. Spread the word, Julie."

"Will do, Bianca. Sorry," Julie squeaked.

She kept both hands on the wriggling, sputtering Hat until she fled into the hall. Then, after pulling him off, she held him at eye level. "What's your problem?"

"What's *my* problem?" Hat sniffed. "They're upgrading the entire PMA *again*, and no one has so much as thought about me! They might as well put me back in the Warehouse!"

Julie sighed. "Come on, Hat. It's not that bad." She dusted off his crown.

"I'm being overlooked, Julie." Hat's crown squashed down the way he did when he was pouting. "No one appreciates the extent of my power."

"I do," Julie told him, "and working out a schedule isn't the best use of it."

He was silent.

"I get that you want to be involved, but you've got a higher purpose now, remember?" Julie smiled. "You're part of the unit. You're the most reliable comms system we've got, and you can't be hacked. You make the difference between life and death on our missions. Do you want to go back to making schedules and finding recruits or keep making a difference as part of our unit?"

"When you put it that way, perhaps I overreacted," Hat grouched.

Julie gently placed him on her head again. "Now, would you

mind using your amazing and world-shaking powers to find out where the rest of our unit is?"

There was a brief grudging hum. "They're in the armory."

Julie ran a hand over his brim to thank him and hustled through the halls to the armory. Everywhere she went, trolls and brownies ran this way and that. A few times, she had to take detours because trolls were laying cables or because an entire room had been unpacked into the hall, where brownies were labeling and sorting at high speeds.

Finally reaching the armory, Julie stepped through the doors, expecting to walk into the usual cold, quiet concrete room with its endless uniform rows of weapons and armor. Instead, the armory was a mad bustle of activity. Brownies zipped to and fro, their happy giggles filling the air, blurring as they dashed up vertical walls and hustled across the ceiling upside-down. There were trolls everywhere. Julie almost tripped over a line of silver silk ribbon on the floor.

"Careful!" a familiar voice called from the center of the giant room. "Don't hurt yourself."

Qtana stood amid the chaos. Some of the weapons racks had been moved aside and replaced by a giant glass bubble. The inside was covered with fine wires, screens that glowed blue, complicated-looking computer parts, levers, switches, and flashing lights. The silver ribbon stuff spread all over the room from the bubble.

"Hurt myself?" Julie looked at the ribbon. "On some silk?"

"It's not silk." Qtana grinned at her, then pushed her glasses higher on her nose.

"No, and don't try to tear it just to prove it's silk," Korin grumbled. She stood with Raven, Jae, and a gaggle of other gawping soldiers near Qtana, sucking her forefinger.

Qtana sighed. "That was regrettable."

"What is it if it's not silk?" Julie asked, carefully stepping over it to approach the glass bubble.

"It's Gleipnir iron." Qtana grinned. "Originally forged by the dwarves to bind Fenrir. Light as silk but tougher than iron cable, and it conducts electricity amazingly. Our network will be faster than the fastest human fiber internet."

"Cool," Julie murmured.

"And totally unhackable except by magic, so that keeps the humans out of our networks." Qtana's eyes gleamed. "We're laying it all over the PMA to provide the building with the fastest internet in the world."

"What's in there?" Julie asked, gesturing at the bubble.

In the center, a monkey sat cross-legged on a red velvet pillow. His coat was gold and silver, he had a black tuft on the end of his tail, and his eyes were closed. In his arms, he cradled a beautiful golden lyre.

"That's a Satori. They're telepaths," Qtana explained.

Jae pressed her hands against the glass. "That's amazing! What's he doing?"

"Using Amphion's lyre to telekinetically help the brownies move everything around the armory and using his telepathic powers to communicate with them." Qtana grinned. "Pretty cool, right?"

"So, you've supplemented your cutting-edge technology with cables and lyres forged thousands of years ago?" Julie guessed.

Qtana laughed, delighted. "Pretty much. Out with the old, in with the older, right? Hey, *you*! Careful with that!"

She scampered off to yell at one of the trolls, and Jae turned to Julie, her eyes huge. "So much has changed!"

"Yup," Julie agreed, "but it's all to stop the Dark Moon League."

Raven added, "At least we're finally getting free wi-fi!"

Rain pattered on the cafeteria windows, gray and steady. Julie zipped her hoodie a little higher as she looked out at it, shivering, her hands cupping the bowl of mushroom soup in front of her.

"Are you cold?" Taylor asked.

Julie blinked. "Hmm?"

"I asked, are you cold?" Taylor's smile made the corners of his eyes crinkle the way Julie loved. "Also, are you okay? You've been unusually quiet, not that I'm complaining."

Julie punched his arm, which felt good. She still carefully steered clear of conversation about her growing powers, but eating lunch with him mostly felt normal. "No, I'm not cold." She picked up her spoon. "At least, I won't be once I've eaten this."

"Mushroom soup again?" Taylor quirked an elegant eyebrow at his bowl of clam chowder. "You always go for mushroom."

Julie grinned. "Mushrooms were the first paranormally-prepared food I ate, remember? The food that opened my eyes to your existence."

Taylor's eyes didn't leave hers. "How could I forget?"

Heat crept into her cheeks and ran down to the tips of her toes. She ducked her head and took a spoonful of soup.

"Still, that doesn't explain why you're so quiet." Under the table, Taylor pressed his knee against hers. "You look tired. When's your leave?"

"It's going to be a while," Julie admitted. "But I'm looking forward to it."

"Will you send me the dates, please?" Taylor asked.

"Sure." Julie gazed out the window again. "Do you know what I really miss today?"

Before she could finish speaking, an explosion rocked the cafeteria, coming from the lobby. A troll tumbled past the open door, cursing, the front of her white coat black with soot. Two magic rings and a computer motherboard tumbled after her.

No one in the cafeteria batted an eye.

"Peace and quiet?" Taylor guessed. "Given that things are even more chaotic than normal around here with all the new systems being installed?"

"Something like that." Julie managed a smile. "I miss being curled up in my comfy chair in my apartment, reading *Anna Karenina*."

Taylor squeezed her knee under the table. "I bet you do."

"I'm hoping for a mission," Julie admitted.

"Aren't you tired?" Taylor's brow creased.

"Yeah, but I'd rather be out doing something than stuck in the middle of the chaos," Julie confessed. "Even though I know it's for the greater good."

"They took Minesweeper off my computer," Taylor grumbled. "Now I have to find somewhere to play it online."

Julie laughed.

On the table by her elbow, Hat squirmed. "Sorry to interrupt, but your unit is looking for you. Briefing in the conference room."

"When?" Julie asked, tensing.

Taylor's smile slipped.

Hat hopped onto her head. "Right *now*."

Taylor's smile was gone. He scrambled to his feet. "I'm grabbing you a sandwich to take with you."

Julie got up. "I can't eat in the middle of a briefing, T."

"But you're hungry." Taylor's mouth turned down at the corners.

"It's okay. I'll text you." She grabbed his arm and pulled him in for a peck on the cheek that smelled like the first summer rain. "See you."

"See you," Taylor mumbled.

Julie jogged out of the cafeteria, skirted a mass of trolls engaged in mortal combat with the elevator, and headed outside to run across campus to the military wing. Rain splattered her face, cool and refreshing. She slid past the group of harassed three-headed dogs busy with a security upgrade to the front doors and arrived in the conference room slightly breathless.

"There you are!" Raven blurted.

Julie hesitated in the doorway, running a hand over her short wet hair. She'd expected to see her unit and Overwatch or Bianca waiting for her here. Instead, the conference room was full. Seven units of highly-trained paras waited there, facing the stage with trembling anticipation. Each wore a gold griffin arm patch, except the griffins, who wore their insignia on bands around their front legs.

Julie hastily stripped off her hoodie and hung it on the nearest door handle before slinking to a seat next to Jae. "Is this *all seven* Griffin units?"

Jae nodded.

"Something big has to be going on," Raven added. "Maybe we've got our first assignment to hit a Dark Moon cell."

"Griffin Two took one out on their own yesterday," Korin rumbled. "This is much more than that."

"Overwatch will explain, I'm sure." Jae sat back, flicking one of her many thick dark braids over one shoulder.

When the door opened, it wasn't their commanding sergeant who strode onto the stage, however. It was Droppelheimer, his face serious under the traditional orc tattoos that covered his skin. Everyone in the room sprang to attention.

"At ease, soldiers," Droppelheimer rumbled. "Sit."

They sank back into their chairs. Julie's heart thundered against her breastbone. *All seven Griffin units and a briefing from Droppelheimer? What's going on?*

You'll find out in a minute, Hat told her.

The orc's face was stony as he faced the group. "You are being deployed on an urgent mission to Piñon Pines, Arizona. A group of yetis in Intelligence discovered a sizeable Dark Moon League enclave there."

Droppelheimer's brows lowered. "They are destructive and

dangerous enough that they have forced the humans out of the town, mercifully without revealing their paranormal identities, by looting and destroying everything in their path."

Julie winced. *Those poor humans must be terrified.*

"To make matters worse, Piñon Pines was built over a defunct portal to the prison realm," Droppelheimer went on, "and the humans' police and the FBI are already there. No one knows anything yet, but that state will not continue for long." His expression darkened. "Reports indicate that several humans have already died. The death toll cannot rise. Soldiers, it is your objective to capture the Dark Moon members, secure that town, repair it, and bring the humans safely back to their town."

Julie took a breath. *Feels like our training exercise.*

Yes, but with higher stakes, Hat agreed.

"You will have full logistical assistance from the brownies and support from HQ. There are as many as fifty paras active in the town, largely armed with Sylthana fire, blunt weapons, and a handful of pistols."

Droppelheimer noticed the raised eyebrows in the room. "You will outnumber them almost two to one, but that is by design. We need to make this action quick and decisive before we are revealed or any more humans die. You portal out at thirteen-ten from the parking garage. Any questions?"

"Sir, no sir," the soldiers chorused.

"Good. Full details and maps have been uploaded to your communications system." Droppelheimer nodded sharply.

AKA me, Hat pointed out with a trace of smugness.

"Now, move out!" Droppelheimer snapped.

Griffin One exited in an orderly row. Julie and her team members waited in tense silence as the other units headed out of the room. She shot Taylor a quick text to let him know she was leaving.

Then it was go time.

Run through it one more time, Hat. Julie winced as the van, its windows blacked out, struck another pothole in the cracked asphalt. *Shit! Can't you smooth out roads?*

Not without humans noticing my incredible powers, Hat shot back.

Still, he obliged, showing Julie and the rest of her unit—all crammed into the back of this black van—the map of Piñon Pines. It was a tiny town, home to less than two hundred people.

We think they're holed up in the traffic department, Hat added. *Yeti reports indicate movement there. There are no ranged weapons except handguns.*

Piece of cake. Korin grinned, fingering the magic hammers on her belt.

Remember, the first objective is to get the shield up, Hat added. *After that, we'll storm the department. That's where you should make first contact.*

Julie flexed her fingers. It was bright daylight despite the two-hour time difference. *No moonlight,* she told Hat.

No moonlight, he agreed. *You'll have to rely on your wits for this one.*

Don't I always? Julie quipped.

The van slowed, then juddered to a halt. "Weres, Raven, Jae, move out!" Julie ordered. "The rest of you, stay here. I see humans."

Noah opened the back doors and they piled out of the van, cradling automatic weapons. Julie blinked at the expanse of scrubby semi-desert around her. The landscape was almost featureless and eerily flat, and the dry air billowed around her when she moved, making her sweat under her armor. Fortunately, it evaporated instantly.

The faeries and Korin hung back as Julie led the others around to the front of the van. Fourteen PMA vans, two per unit, and two SUVs were parked on the side of the road. In front of them, a couple of FBI vans and a bunch of police cruisers formed a perimeter around the town, which was so small that Julie almost missed it. It was only a handful of streets, hardly any buildings with more than two stories.

A chunky white guy with a handlebar mustache waddled up to them, one hand on the 9mm pistol in his holster, the other thumb in his pocket. "Who're you?" he growled. "The feebies are already here."

Alighting from one of the SUVs, Bianca marched up to him. She cradled an assault rifle to her chest. When she reached him, she cocked an eyebrow. "We're an elite Special Forces counterterrorism unit. The question, sir, is who are *you*?"

The man's cheeks reddened. "Sheriff Hardy. This is my turf."

"Oh, yeah?" Bianca cocked the other eyebrow. "Seems like it's a bunch of criminals' turf right now."

Hardy's mustache twitched. "We're getting the situation under control."

"No, *we're* getting the situation under control." Bianca smiled sweetly. "For that, sir, we need you to move your perimeter back so we have room to work."

"See here, missy! I told you we've got this under control," Hardy spluttered.

Bianca sighed in Julie's head. *Raven, if you please.*

You got it. Raven strode forward, grinning. "Sheriff Hardy?"

"What's this, a Barbie movie?" Hardy snapped.

Raven's smile didn't waver. "No, just some badass chicks about to clean up your mess. Now, you're going to move your perimeter back so that we can do our jobs, *aren't* you, Sheriff Hardy?"

Sheriff Hardy's expression changed from anger to smooth, his brow unwrinkled, mustache motionless.

"You don't have any questions, do you?" Raven murmured.

Hardy shook his head, his eyes not leaving Raven's. "I don't have any questions." He swallowed. "Ma'am."

"Now, who are we?" Raven asked sweetly.

"Some badass chicks who are about to clean up my mess," Hardy repeated.

"What are you going to do?" Raven prompted.

"Give the order to move the perimeter back," Hardy croaked. "And let you do your jobs."

"That's wonderful." Raven kissed him on the cheek. "You're so cooperative."

"I'm so cooperative," Hardy whispered.

He stumbled off, grabbed a megaphone, and yelled at the other cops to move back. Raven giggled and skipped back toward the van.

"You know, that mesmerism shit is very useful, but she creeps the shit out of me," Bianca muttered.

Julie grimaced her agreement, then piled into the van with the rest of her unit.

CHAPTER FIVE

Once the humans had pulled back, the brownies, three driving each of the specially adapted vans, drove past their perimeter and fanned out. Julie peered out the windshield from behind the driver's seat. Through the dusty glass, the town looked terrible. They were moving past a block of stores and fast-food joints. Two were on fire, the familiar blue flames flickering in the windows. All had had their windows broken. A furniture store's doors hung drunkenly on their hinges, shattered glass spread out in an arc around them. Broken chairs were scattered across the parking lot, along with couches with the stuffing ripped out of them.

"This is weird," Julie whispered. "It's destruction for destruction's sake."

"It doesn't make sense," Jae murmured.

"They're Dark Moons." Korin pulled out her hammers. "They never do."

"No, but really." Jae frowned. "It doesn't make sense. Exposing the para world to the humans has never been their agenda. What are they doing?"

The van stopped, so there was no more time for speculation. "Go!" Korin barked.

Julie tumbled out of the van, plucking a tiny leather pouch off her belt. As the rest of her unit covered her, she jogged to the end of the street, two hundred feet from the cops' perimeter. On her left and right, other soldiers were doing the same. She took two tiny objects out of the pouch, a stone and a ring, both inscribed with glowing blue runes. Eluned amulets, imbued with invisibility.

Julie crouched and set the stone and ring a foot apart. *In position!* she barked into their comms system, courtesy of Hat.

Copy, Griffin Seven, Overwatch answered. *Activating invisibility shield.*

With a hiss like a rush of rain, the air changed, shimmering like a mirage as a magical invisibility shield grew from the perimeter of amulets.

Shield is up! Julie barked. *Let's—*

A burly form slammed into Julie, massive arms locking around her body. The air ripped with a whistling thunderclap, and she screamed. Before she hit the ground, she'd ripped a Bowie knife from her ankle holster and almost jammed it into Chester's throat.

Her confusion evaporated as her back slammed into the ground. "Chester, what the f—"

"Down, down, down!" Korin yelled. "Sniper! Get down!"

Julie looked at the enormous bullet hole in the wall where her head had been seconds ago, then at Chester's face, inches from hers.

"Saw the light on the barrel," Chester wheezed.

"Shit, dude. Thank you," Julie croaked.

"Get to cover!" Korin shouted.

Rolling onto her chest, Julie frantically leopard-crawled after Chester. They took shelter behind the furniture store, where the rest of the unit cowered against the wall.

Excuse me, Hat, but what was that? Julie yelled. *You said they only had a few handguns!*

Something's up. I can't sense the sniper rifle, Hat replied.

Well, the sniper rifle almost sensed Julie's face! Korin yelled.

They're using magical cloaking. I don't know how many there are, Hat told them helplessly.

Screams came through the telepathic link. *Contact! Contact!* Bianca shrieked in Julie's mind. *Route 66 West! Backup needed!*

Backup needed? Overwatch barked. *How many hostiles?*

I don't know! Fifty? Sixty? Bianca cried.

What? Overwatch sputtered.

We've got to help her! Julie got to her feet.

Chester grabbed her by the belt and yanked her down. *No!*

There was a roar of flame and glass shattered, then the entire building trembled as it was consumed by Sylthana fire. The wall was blazingly hot against Julie's back. With yelps of surprise, the unit drew back.

It's a trap. It's an ambush! Hat yelled. *We need to retreat. Now!*

Negative! Bianca bellowed. *We're not abandoning this town.*

Griffin Four, Five, Six, assist Griffin One! Overwatch barked. *Griffin Two, Three, Seven, tell me what's going on!*

Julie peered around the corner of the furniture store. Flames and bullet holes peppered the streets. She spotted a glass-bright flash from the building across the street and flung herself out of the way. A sniper's bullet hissed into the wall inches from her, punching a hole through the brickwork and into the sidewalk on the other side of the street.

"Shit," Korin croaked.

The sniper's in the building across the street, Julie reported. *I think that's where the fire's coming from, too. It's exposed all the way around. There's no way to approach without getting picked off from the top story. It looks like a hotel, two or three stories.*

"This is *not* what the yetis told us," Korin grumbled.

We could draw their fire, a familiar voice from Griffin Two suggested. *We're in the building right across.*

Good call, Griffin Two. Prepare to engage. When you can, Griffin Seven, Griffin Three, attack, Overwatch ordered.

A series of affirmatives came through the telepathic link, and Julie hugged her assault rifle to her chest, heart thudding. The six Weres shifted to wolf form. Tiny clicks came from the air above them as the faeries cocked their weapons.

Gunfire exploded across the street as Griffin Two engaged. Julie gritted her teeth as the roar filled the air, punctuated by screams. She rested a hand on the safety of her rifle.

Griffin Three, Seven, engage, engage! Overwatch yelled.

Julie surged forward, the air filled with gunfire, holding her breath. Her unit surged forward in a tightly packed group, weapons at the ready and the werewolves in a tight mass around their knees.

Julie saw a muzzle flash seconds before the bullet whistled through the air. Dirt sprayed inches from her feet. She instantly returned fire and the hotel window shattered, but she knew she hadn't hit anything. Seconds later, more gunfire burst from the other windows.

Austin let out a screaming yelp and collapsed on the ground by Julie's feet. She nearly tripped over him. *Austin!*

Pull back! Pull back! Korin yelled.

Julie grabbed Austin by a fistful of fur and moved back as fast as she could, the rest of her unit closing around her. Blood covered the wolf's front leg, and it wobbled as he bounced over the sidewalk, shattered. The moment they were back under cover, Jae pounced on him, ripping her medical pack off her back.

Is he okay? Korin demanded as Raven and the faeries opened fire from around the corner of the furniture store.

Jae expertly tied a tourniquet around Austin's leg. *He'll live, but he might live with three legs.*

Shit! Korin cursed. *They have too much cover, and there are too many of them! We've got to get into that hotel.*

Crouching beside Austin, Julie leaned to the side, looking around Raven's knees at the hotel. Despite being one of the largest buildings in town, it wasn't very big. Two stories, maybe a quarter of the size of the elementary school in Bay Ridge, where she used to live.

We could take it out with a stun grenade. The whole thing, Julie muttered.

Yeah, but someone would have to get close enough to do it, Korin grumbled.

Julie squinted at the roof. *Hey, does anyone see any shooters on the roof?*

The others peered at the building. Gunfire echoed through the air as Griffin Two continued to engage.

No, but how do you suggest someone gets to the roof? Korin demanded.

The faeries giggled. *Flying, of course.*

You can't arm a stun grenade, Korin snapped. *Your fingers are too small.*

No, but she *can.* One of the faeries pointed her rifle at Julie.

Everyone stared at her. Julie swatted her sweaty hands dry on her pants. *This is what I get for being the skinniest in the unit, isn't it?*

It's risky, Korin growled.

It's happening, so deal with it. Julie unbuckled her utility belt.

What are you doing? Raven asked.

Lightening the load, Julie answered.

Good idea. Keep your armor but no weapons except what you really need, the faerie told her.

Julie stripped off her belt and holsters and set down all her weapons, then took a stun grenade from the belt. She gripped her Bowie knife between her teeth. *Let's do this.*

This is insane! Korin muttered.

There was another blast of fire. This time, heated air rolled around them, and the furniture store let out a long, trembling moan.

We don't have any other options. Julie tensed. *Time to go!*

The faeries fluttered down around her, slinging their tiny rifles. Two grabbed her uniform's shoulders. Two more grabbed her ass.

Hey! Julie squawked.

I'm not enjoying this any more than you are! the faerie growled.

With a mad whir of wings, the faeries rose. Julie's combat boots left the dirt. Suspended in her uniform, which chafed, she floated into the air.

Cover them! Korin ordered.

Gunfire roared beneath Julie. The faeries kept rising, panting with the effort but steadily lifting her higher. She looked down at the roof of the furniture store and swallowed hard, then fixed her eyes on the roof of the hotel instead.

Higher! the leading faerie urged.

When Julie glanced down again, the hotel roof was far beneath her. The faeries buzzed across the street, their small hands slipping on Julie's uniform. She tried to ignore the instability of their grip, instead staring at the roof. It was a tile roof, and no snipers were stationed there. The mesmerizing flash of the firefight taking place below her made it difficult to focus.

The sniper fired out of that window. The southeastern one, Julie rasped. *Drop me right above it. He won't be able to take us out from such close range.*

The Bowie knife still clutched between her teeth, Julie looked at the stun grenade in her hands. It glowed with blue runes.

Remember to close your eyes when you detonate it, Hat told her. *That Sandman dust is potent.*

You're still here? I thought you'd fainted when you didn't try to stop me, Julie groused.

Hat chuckled. *I won't stand in the way of your destiny.*

Whatever that*'s supposed to mean?* Julie grumbled.

Get ready! a faerie yelled.

Julie loosened the pin. The stun grenade contained enough Sandman dust to knock out an entire building full of Dark Moons and only enough explosive to propel the tiny fine particles through walls and ceilings. *Here goes.*

Her outstretched combat boots met the tile roof and she landed with a grunt, then slipped to her knees. The faeries dove under the overhang and into the room below, and someone screamed. Julie knew they only had moments. Scrambling to the edge of the roof, Julie clutched the grenade in one hand and grabbed the edge with the other, then threw herself through the open window and into the hotel room.

The sniper, a Sylthana Elf, lay on the ground, screaming and clawing his face as faerie dust melted his skin like acid. Julie kicked his rifle aside and ran into the hall, almost colliding with a troll. A metal mace swung toward her face. Hugging the grenade to her chest, she snatched the Bowie knife from her mouth and dodged the mace, then plunged the knife to the hilt in the troll's shoulder. He squealed like a pig, and Julie kicked him aside.

Now! she yelled. *Faeries, get out!*

Squeezing her eyes shut, she pulled the pin and flung the grenade down the hallway.

Amid the gunfire, the explosion was almost silent. She barely heard a distant *pop* when the grenade blew. Then, footsteps thundered on the floor. Slamming her back to the wall, she kept her eyes screwed shut until she felt goggles creep over her cheekbones, courtesy of Hat.

Her eyes snapped open as a Sylthana Elf, his face painted black and a saber in one hand, raced toward her. The air was filled with sparkling particles. The elf swatted the dust aside, eyes narrowing, still rushing her.

Julie clutched her knife and tensed.

The elf's eyelids fluttered. Mid-run, his knees buckled and he fell headlong, the saber skittering across the floor. Lying on his face, the elf began to snore deafeningly.

He wasn't the only one. The gunfire had abated throughout the building. Instead, Julie heard snoring all around her. She chuckled and wiped her bloody knife on her thigh. Even the wounded troll, sprawled on the ground, was snoring peacefully.

Julie prodded his motionless body with her toe. "I'm flabbergasted that that worked."

Griffin Seven, report! Overwatch demanded.

It worked, Overwatch. Julie grinned and strutted down the hall, stepping over slumbering bodies as she went. *They're all having a nice nap.*

The comm was silent. When Julie stepped through the front doors of the hotel and onto the street, her unit whooped. They ran across the street to greet her, laughing and high-fiving. Fists pounded her back and Were tongues playfully slopped her hands.

Good job, Meadows, Overwatch told her.

You go, girl! Bianca cheered.

Korin held out Julie's assault rifle. "We're not done yet." She grinned as she flipped her magical hammers off her belt. "There are still a few left, scattered around the town. Let's go teach them a lesson."

"Sounds good to me." Julie grinned.

They set off, armor clanking, boots hitting the ground in a steady rhythm.

Faeries buzzed past Julie's face, carrying an enormous bag of fertilizer between them with some effort. She dodged, her arms wrapped around a heavy bag of chicken feed, and stomped into the feed store in the center of this tiny town.

"Hey! You lot!" Bianca barked. "*Where* are you going with that fertilizer?"

The faeries hesitated. "Nowhere?" one offered.

"Nowhere except straight to the right pile in the back of this warehouse." Bianca jerked her head in that direction.

Sighing, the faeries did as they were told. "She's no fun," one muttered.

Julie dumped the bag of feed on a pallet and headed to where Bianca stood at the door of the storeroom. She paused beside the succubus, watching Korin, who was across the street. The dwarf was in the middle of the parking lot, face creased in concentration, hands stretched toward the ground. Torn-up paving stones gently replaced themselves at her bidding.

A few doors down, Jae crouched in the parking lot in front of a clinic, her Shajara magic shining green between her fingers. Ruined flowers came back to life and replanted themselves in the garden. A unit of griffins in flight was restoring a broken power-line, electricity crackling harmlessly over their talons as their strong wings kept them aloft.

Julie squinted at the red sky. The sun was slipping behind the horizon, and her heart squeezed. Taylor would be waiting for her.

"Where do you want me next?" she asked Bianca.

Across the street, the neon sign over the tire store window flickered to life. Streetlights flashed on, illuminating the clean, tidy town. The griffins landed on the sidewalk, emitting deep leonine purrs and rubbing their heads on one another in congratulation.

"We're done." Bianca grinned. "We can let the humans back in." She cocked her head to the side. *Did you copy that, Overwatch?*

Copy, Major. Pull all unnecessary personnel back to the vehicles and lower the shields, Overwatch ordered.

"You can stay here with me." Bianca grinned down at Julie.

"I've got a strong enough glamor on me that the humans won't see me, or you."

Julie laughed. "Maybe there *are* advantages to this concealment spell."

The rest of the soldiers fell back, and the brownies slowly drove the SUVs around the perimeter, collecting the Eluned rings and stones. The shield finally shimmered and vanished. Police cruisers headed down the main street toward Bianca and Julie. The one in the lead came to a cautious halt a few yards from Bianca.

Sheriff Hardy stepped out, eyes wide. "How did you do this?" he demanded. "It's like nothing ever happened here!"

"Cleanup is our specialty, Sheriff." Bianca tugged the brim of her service cap. "And you don't need to worry about the people who did this. They're in federal custody, and they'll be dealt with accordingly."

"Good." Sheriff Hardy's shoulders slumped. He looked exhausted.

They watched in silence as more cars crept back into the town, ordinary people emerging from them to hurry into their homes and businesses. Cries of relief and delight filled the air. Julie watched as a little girl pushed her parents aside and ran into their home, returning a few moments later with a doll in her arms, squeezing it and laughing.

"Makes it all worth it, huh?" Bianca asked.

"Pretty much," Julie agreed, grinning.

The sheriff turned to them. "Thank you." He cleared his throat. "Really."

Bianca nodded at him, and tires crunched on gravel as a blacked-out SUV pulled up to them, its windshield too dark for the sheriff to see that it was being driven by a trio of brownies.

"Time to go. Goodbye, Sheriff." Bianca turned away.

Julie followed her to the SUV. Her hand was on the door when the sheriff called, "Wait!"

Bianca turned back, one eyebrow raised questioningly.

"I never got your names." The sheriff scratched his head. "*Which* branch of the government did you say you were working for?"

Bianca grinned and waved, then got into the SUV.

CHAPTER SIX

"Man, am I ready for a hot shower." Raven stretched, almost smacking Julie in the face as the van rattled over another bump. "How much longer until we get to the portal, anyway?"

"We've been driving for two minutes. Maybe give it five before you get cranky," Korin snapped.

"Cranky? I'm not cranky. *You're* cranky," Raven countered.

"I'm not cranky. I'm pissed," Korin barked. "They haven't let us know anything about Austin's condition yet."

"Oh, he'll be fine." Chester waved a breezy hand. "He's had worse. Dr. Olena will fix him up in no time. He'll be back at work tomorrow. It wasn't a silver bullet."

"I think so too." Jae smiled. "Don't worry about him, Korin."

"I wasn't worried. I told you. I am pissed," Korin grumbled.

Julie smothered her grin and checked her watch. She was going to be late for dinner with Taylor, but he'd understand.

"It's still the same time as when you checked your watch ten seconds ago," Chester teased.

Julie rolled her eyes. "Some of us have places to be, Chess."

"And hot princes to date," Raven cooed.

There was a communal groan from the van.

Hat spoke up. "Looks like you're going to have to get a rain check on that, Julie."

Korin looked up at him sharply. "Why?"

"I've just heard from Overwatch. We're not going home right now." Hat sighed. "Griffin Seven is the freshest unit left, and there's a time-sensitive mission in Germany that needs our attention."

"Germany?" Julie groaned. "Seriously?"

"Yep. The Black Forest. A village of ogres is being terrorized by goats, and they need our help. Their homes are being destroyed," Hat reported.

Julie pulled him off and stared at him. "You're kidding."

Isaiah was peering through the windshield. "He's not kidding."

Julie looked up. An enormous portal shimmered in the air in front of them, and the other PMA vans headed for it. Julie could see the PMA parking garage through the shimmering air. Their van peeled away from the others, followed by another containing the rest of Griffin Seven. Julie watched as the other vehicles disappeared happily through the portal that would take them back to HQ.

"Portal engaging!" one of the brownies called from up front.

Julie dragged her eyes away from the promise of HQ and pulled out her phone, then tapped Taylor's contact. She held the phone to her ear, tucking herself against the back of the van, away from the throaty banter of the rest of the unit.

He answered on the first ring. "Hey, babe! Where are you?"

"Still in Arizona, T." Julie sighed.

"That's okay. If you're tired, we can just grab some takeout and watch a movie in the common room," Taylor offered.

Julie gritted her teeth. "Actually, I-I'm not going to make it tonight. I'm really sorry. We've been sent straight on another mission in Germany."

"Oh." Taylor paused. "Hey, that's okay. You're doing great

work, Julie. Important work. I wish you could be here, but clearly, someone in Germany needs you right now."

Julie smiled. "Thanks, T."

"Be safe, okay?"

"Okay. Bye." Julie hung up and tucked her phone into her uniform.

From across the van, Korin met her eyes. "You good, Meadows?"

Julie nodded. "I'm good."

The van bumped, and dizziness and nausea gripped Julie. She gritted her teeth and rode it out, clutching the edge of her seat for balance. The rumble of the van gave way to a gentle hiss of tires on grass.

Jae sat bolt upright. "Oh!" she exclaimed. "I like it here."

"It's a forest. You're a tree elf," Korin pointed out. "No-brainer."

"It's more than that." Jae blinked. "There's old magic here. Deep magic."

The van crunched to a halt, and Korin pushed the back doors open. The unit piled out into a cool, dark night that smelled of crushed grass and pine trees. Rich silver moonlight poured over a wooded mountainside, and a thin asphalt road wound its way through the woods. The van was parked on the grassy verge, and only a few distant lights marked pockets of civilization among the trees.

Julie shivered. She wasn't sure if she was sensing magic with her Lunar Fae powers or if her instincts were telling her that this was an old, wild place.

"Welcome to Germany, I guess," Korin quipped.

"I've never been to Europe," Julie murmured, gazing at the starry sky.

"It's better in daylight." Korin cocked her weapon. "Okay, Hat. Where are these ogres who can't deal with a few goats?"

Hat hummed on Julie's head. "They're deep in the woods.

You'll have to go on foot. Head north-northeast. I'll guide you from there." He let out a breath of relief. "No concealment spells."

Chester stepped forward, and his outline blurred in mid-motion. He turned into a giant blond wolf before he finished the stride. "This is our kind of country." His tail waved gently, and he pricked his ears toward the woods. "Let us lead the way."

"Go ahead." Korin gestured.

"I'll bring up the rear," Isaiah volunteered.

Chester threw back his head and let out a long, eerie howl that echoed off the mountainside, making goosebumps rise on Julie's arms. Then he bounded forward with the other were-wolves flanking him, yipping and barking in excitement.

"Well, they're having fun," Julie commented.

"No need to bring the assault rifles. We'll just freak out the locals," Korin decided. "Handguns and knives only."

It was a relief to follow the rest of the unit into the woods without the weight of a heavy assault rifle. They followed a trail —a goat trail, Julie assumed—into the woods. The way was lit by the faeries, who glowed silver. The trail was soft under Julie's tired feet. Jae's eyes shone with excitement. She stretched out a hand as she walked, trailing her fingers through the ferns, touching the trunks of the ancient evergreens. The faeries were giggling, darting among the trees, play-wrestling with one another in mid-air.

Chester, who had trotted ahead, halted. The hackles rose on his back, then flattened. "Hey, look!" he barked. "It's a goat."

Julie peered past him. The goat strolled out of the under-growth and onto the path in front of them. It was a hairy black-and-white billy, his beard stained yellow, horns curving from his intelligent head. He looked at them with unearthly yellow eyes for a moment, then nibbled the nearby ferns.

"Intimidating," Korin commented.

Julie tapped the dwarf's shoulder. "Hey, Korin, can I Facetime Taylor? He loves goats."

"Sure." Korin shrugged. "Don't see why not."

Julie dialed Taylor's number. He answered immediately, his wide-eyed face appearing on the screen. "Julie! Are you okay?"

"I'm fine." Julie giggled and flipped the screen. "Look!"

"A goat!" Taylor's yell startled the goat, which stared at them for a moment, then peed on his beard.

"Well, that's disgusting," Julie stated.

Taylor's voice trembled with excitement. "He does that to make himself sexy for lady goats! Look how cute he is!"

Raven made a retching noise.

"For the record, don't do that," Julie quipped. "You're sexy enough as you are."

"That's just gross," Chester muttered.

"He's so cute! Can you pet him?" Taylor gushed.

"No, T. We're here to *stop* him. These goats have been destroying the ogres' village." Julie flipped the screen back and smiled at him. "I've got to go."

"Okay." Taylor paused. "Please don't hurt the goats."

"I'll do my best." Julie laughed and hung up.

"Piss off, goat," Korin ordered, waving her arms.

The goat strolled off the path in a leisurely manner and disappeared into the woods, and they set off again.

"We can't be far from the ogres since we've seen one of the goats," Korin mused. "Hat, how are we doing?"

"You're close," Hat informed her.

Chester raised his head, black nose quivering. "That's right. I can smell them. The ogres."

They slowed. Julie kept a hand on her pistol and looked around, squinting against the bright moonlight. A breeze stirred the trees, and the tossing branches caused goosebumps to rise on Julie's skin. Was that a pine bough blown by the wind or a gigantic ogre turning to look at them?

"Where are they?" Korin whispered.

"Smells like we're right on top of them," Noah murmured.

A crunch made Julie whip around. Something was moving deeper in the woods. Something huge. She took deep breaths to steady her hands, keeping one on her pistol's grip.

Chester shifted into human form and scanned the trees. "They must be coming," he whispered, taking a step back.

A high-pitched voice squealed from somewhere near the forest floor. "Hey! Watch it!"

Chester jumped, and an ogre emerged from the undergrowth. Julie barely controlled her urge to burst out laughing.

The ogre was about ten inches high and wore thick clothes made of leaves and woven grass. His skin was the smooth gray texture of living stone, and black pebble eyes glittered up at them as he gestured furiously. "You almost trashed my house!"

"Your house?" Julie squeaked.

The ogre grabbed a few fern fronds and hauled them out of the way, revealing a tiny hut made of sticks and dried grass. A slightly smaller ogre, cradling an ogre baby the size of a pebble in her arms, peered up at them from the doorway.

Julie gasped when more ogres appeared out of the undergrowth, none taller than mid-calf. Their huts were tucked among the ferns and bushes. Some were tidy, decorated with wildflowers, with crackling fires visible through the arched doorways. At the center of the village, a mass of cloven hoofprints had churned the little street into mud. Several homes were completely flattened, the grass torn to shreds and trampled into the mud, and a few ogres had fur bandages wound around their arms or heads.

"Oh, you poor l—" Julie bit off the word *little* just in time. "You poor things!" she finished lamely.

"Who are you?" the first ogre demanded.

"Griffin Unit Seven, OPMA Special Forces, at your service." Korin's bow was only slightly sarcastic.

Jae stepped forward. "I can help your wounded."

"OPMA?" The ogre's eyebrows, or the craggy bits of stone

above his eyes that served as his eyebrows, rose. "You came to help *us*?"

"We received your distress call," Korin told him.

The ogre glanced at the rest of the villagers, who were silently staring at the unit. "They came," he muttered.

Julie crouched down. "What's your name, sir?"

The ogre studied her with his pebble eyes. "Wilhelm. Chief Wilhelm of the Black Forest."

"It's good to meet you, sir." Julie bowed her head just slightly. "We're here to help. What can we do?"

"These goats have been terrorizing us for generations." Wilhelm waved his arms. "They come here and destroy our streets and eat our homes and the food we store for the winter. They trample our children!"

"Why would they do that?" Julie asked.

Wilhelm snorted. "They're goats. They don't need a reason to sow chaos. And these are wild goats, wily things that get past us every time, even if we post sentries." He tugged his fur hat. "Lately, the herd has grown, and things have gotten worse."

The ogre lady cuddled her baby closer, grains of sand filling her eyes like tears.

"Last week, they killed one of us." Wilhelm's shoulders slumped. "When they trampled our houses again this morning, we decided we had no choice but to call for help. But, well, we didn't think you'd come." He paused. "We are so small."

"Size doesn't matter." Julie smiled. "What matters is that you need help."

"I have an idea." Jae was standing a few yards away, her hands pressed against the trunk of a gigantic old oak. The tree was gnarled and leafless, its branches twisted and dead in contrast to the deep green of the pines surrounding it.

"Spit it out, Jae." Korin fingered her hammers with some disappointment.

"This could be a perfect new home for the ogres." Jae turned to them. "I could shape it into houses for them. They'll be safe from the goats here, especially if we build a fence around the bottom of the tree."

"We'd have to rig up a system to get food and supplies into the tree." Julie rubbed her chin. "But I think it's a good idea."

"It *is* a good idea." The faeries swarmed the tree, touching it. "Our folk have been building this way for generations. It's safe and strong."

"What do *you* think?" Jae asked, looking at Wilhelm.

The female ogre was crying trails of sand, and Wilhelm put an arm around her shoulders, smiling. "We have long thought that. If we could get up the tree, we'd be safe, but we weren't able to do it on our own."

"Well, we can help you." Julie felt a fresh wave of energy crackle through her muscles.

Korin nodded. "Let's do it. Faeries, you're in charge of advising everyone. You know how this works. Jae, do your thing with the tree. Raven, Julie, sort out that pulley system you were talking about. The Weres and I will build the fence."

In a matter of moments, the clearing was a bustle of activity. The presence of the Weres alone was enough to keep the goats away for the moment, and the ogres' happy, high-pitched chatter rose into the night as they bustled around, carrying things, giving input, and getting in the way.

Three ogre children were almost flattened by Chester before Isaiah was assigned the important mission of keeping them out of the way. They climbed onto his back and clung to his long gold fur, and their giggles filled the night as Isaiah bounded through the trees with them.

The rest of the ogres swarmed over the fence that Korin and the other Weres built from dry wood. Jae leaned against the tree, her hands pressed to the wood. A staircase was slowly appearing, winding around and around the trunk.

Korin fashioned smooth stones into pulley wheels for Julie and Raven. The vampire mostly got in the way while Julie figured out how to hang the pulley. "We need something strong but light," she murmured.

"Spidersilk is good for that," one of the faeries told her. "Do you have giant spiders around here?" she asked Wilhelm.

Wilhelm shook his head. "Not anywhere we'd dare to venture."

"It's okay. I've got the perfect thing." Julie unzipped her pack and pulled out a spool of Gleipnir iron.

"Where did you get that?" Raven asked, wide-eyed.

Julie grinned. "I asked Qtana for some. Figured it'd be useful."

"You know that stuff is *really* expensive, right?" Korin demanded. "Those mountain roots are impossibly difficult to mine."

Julie shrugged. "Seems like this is a good use."

"How did you get Qtana to give it to you?" Raven asked.

Julie unwound some Gleipnir iron ribbon and ran it through the pulley wheel. "We have a history."

"Is there anyone important you *don't* have a mysterious history with?" Raven asked.

Jae chuckled.

Julie rigged counterweights to make the pulley operate smoothly, and Jae fashioned large baskets out of branches. The ogre children clambered off Isaiah, who was panting with exhaustion, and took turns riding in the baskets, shouting "Whee!" in delight. In the meantime, the adult ogres lined up in front of the trunk with requests for the homes Jae was making for them.

"A roof over my head and a safe space for my family is all I want," Wilhelm told her, grains of sand seeping from his eyes.

The next ogre was a curvaceous female. "Two bedrooms and a balcony over the woods, please."

The tiny ogre clinging to her hand removed a stone thumb from its mouth. "I want my room to be Paw Patrol," it lisped.

"Paw Patrol?" Julie raised her eyebrows.

Wilhelm sniffed. "We're ogres, not barbarians."

When Jae finished the last of the homes, the old dead tree was beautifully transformed. The staircase wound around its trunk, and hundreds of tiny bark doors opened onto the broad steps. Captive fireflies glowed in the windows. Ogres wandered up and down the stairs, their happy voices echoing from within their new houses. An army of young ogres worked to load their furniture, all mushrooms and sticks and nests of grass and feathers, into the baskets, and the pulleys rattled cheerfully as they worked.

Wilhelm stood at the base of the tree, gazing at it in awe. Korin and the Weres strode up, followed by the faeries.

"The fence is all done, sir." Korin slapped her hands clean. "I doubt the goats will get in now, and even if they do, you're safe in your tree."

"We covered the fence with animal-repellent faerie dust." One of the faeries fluttered down beside Willem and held out a little leather pouch. "There's more in here, and you should be able to buy some at your next faerie market."

"Thank you." Wilhelm reached out to Korin. She offered him her forefinger, which he gripped with great solemnity. "Truly, thank you. We will never forget what the PMA has done for us."

Korin cleared her throat. "It's what we do."

"I will be sure to tell everyone I know in the Black Forest about what you have done," Wilhelm added.

Julie reached into a pocket on her utility belt. "We're also always looking for paras to join us. *All* kinds of paras." She held out a PMA business card with Taylor's details on it. "This is our recruitment department, in case you know someone who'd be interested."

"Thank you. Thank you kindly." Wilhelm took the card.

Once a recruiter, always a recruiter, huh? Hat quipped.

"Come now, Willie." The female ogre took his arm. "Let's look at our new home."

They mounted the staircase together, gazing at their safe new home.

CHAPTER SEVEN

Julie slapped more chocolate spread on her French toast. "This is *soooo* good," she moaned, stuffing it into her mouth.

"Yes, but I'm not sure it's meant to be eaten in multiples of ten." Taylor discreetly moved the chocolate spread a few inches away from her. "You're going to throw up."

"No, I'm not." Julie moved it back. "I missed lunch *and* dinner. I need more breakfast."

"That's what you said the last time. You threw up after eating half the jar," Taylor pointed out.

Julie shrugged. "Worth the risk." She took another slice.

Taylor chuckled and squeezed her knee under the table. The cafeteria was bustling at this time of the morning. For most of the PMA, work started in ten minutes. Julie had dragged herself out of bed a few minutes ago, exhausted and bleary-eyed after yesterday's back-to-back missions. She felt disheveled in her sweatpants beside Taylor, who was immaculate in his emerald green uniform.

"Thanks for making the time to have breakfast with me." He smiled, eyes crinkling. "I know you're tired."

Julie returned his smile. "Thanks for being cool about missing dinner."

"You were out saving the world." Taylor winked. "I can take second place to that when I need to." His eyes widened. "Did you hurt any of the goats?"

"No goats were harmed in the saving of the ogres, no," Julie reassured him.

"Good." Taylor's expression softened, and he touched Julie's cheek with his fingertips. "I missed you," he whispered.

She leaned into his touch. "I missed you, too."

"I can't wait for your leave." Taylor's eyes shone. "I have the best time planned for us both, even though I know one of your leave days will be with Alugon."

"Two whole days are all yours," Julie confirmed. "Ernesto surprised Mom with a trip to the Palisades for the weekend, so I won't see her. Just you."

Taylor's grin widened. "I'm counting on it."

In the hustle of the cafeteria, Julie was pretty sure no one was watching. She leaned over to him, felt the tip of his nose brush against hers, and heard his intake of breath in the instant before their lips met—

"Sorry to intrude," Hat blared, "but there's a situation."

Julie groaned, sitting back, and Taylor shot Hat a furious glare. "Could you have waited thirty seconds?" he snapped.

"No. Sorry." Hat jumped onto Julie's head in a bound. "Griffin Seven is being deployed immediately."

"Deployed!" Julie straightened him on her head. "Where to?"

"You've barely gotten back from your last mission," Taylor protested.

"Avalon Town. It's in an uproar," Hat told her grimly. "Prince Lotan of the Sylthana Elves has published a rebuttal to Kaplan's address at the briefing. He feels Sylthana Elves are being unfairly attacked as a result of the discrimination against the Dark Moon League."

"Discrimination? The League is full of violent criminals!" Julie spluttered.

"That's what he said. Queen Esmerelda didn't take it well. She's ordered to have him detained on treason charges, and Avalon didn't take *that* well, either." Hat winced.

Taylor grimaced. "I can only imagine."

"It's not just the Dark Moons. Ordinary paras are rioting in the streets, and the council members are under threat. PMA is being deployed to support the Eternity Guard." Hat tightened on Julie's head. "We need to go. Now!"

"Okay, okay." Julie grabbed a last slice of French toast and bent to kiss Taylor on the forehead. "See you."

"Julie—" Taylor grabbed her hand.

She looked into his wide brown eyes. "What?"

"Please. Be careful." His eyes searched hers.

"Always. I need to go." Julie plucked her hand out of his grasp and left the cafeteria at a dead run.

***

Avalon was in chaos.

Briefly disoriented after jogging through an emergency portal, Julie stared out an elegantly arched window at the town at the bottom of the hill. Smoke rose from the once-quiet buildings. Blue and yellow flames flared in the sunlight, and every street was either empty or filled with a mass of bodies, jerking in violence.

Barricades blocked the broad streets, some of them burning. Protestors flung themselves against others. Groups of griffins—real griffins from the Eternity Guard—struggled to maintain tiny islands of peace. Even from this distance, Julie could hear the screams and clashes, the angry chanting.

"You with us, Meadows?" Korin barked.

Julie turned away from the window, hugging her assault rifle.

"I'm with you."

The portal had taken them directly into the Eternity Palace. Julie had seen it from a distance, all towers and flags and glorious architecture, and she wished that she had less adrenaline coursing through her veins so she could take her time and look around the vast room they were in.

The great round hall had pillars rising from its edges, and the floor was polished marble with threads of sapphire and gold. Massive windows punctuated the walls between the pillars, and statues on small plinths stood at the foot of each pillar. Julie spotted one that had to be King Arthur Pendragon.

There was no time to admire the room. Droppelheimer strode toward them, brow knotted, his hand not straying far from the broadsword at his side.

"Griffin units, the Eternal Palace is under threat," he snapped. "Queen Esmerelda has been moved to a safe secret location, and the heads of the Royal Families are in their own homes. However, the council must be evacuated safely to HQ via OPMA Avalon North. Each unit will be assigned one council member to evacuate to HQ as quickly and safely as possible. Am I clear?"

"Sir, yes, sir!" the Griffin units echoed, their voices shaking the room.

"The rest of OPMA and the entire Eternity Guard are in the streets, trying to control the situation. That is not your task. Remain focused on getting your charges safely to HQ," Droppelheimer ordered.

Footsteps sounded in the hallway, and a chaos of griffins spilled into the room: Eternity Guards. They accompanied seven wide-eyed councilors, one from each of the Royal Families.

Overwatch spoke into Julie's mind. *Griffin Seven, you are assigned to the Aether Elf Councilor.*

"There's no time to waste." Korin turned to the unit. "Meadows, you've met the Councilor. You wrangle him. Weres, flank us all."

Julie spotted two griffins escorting a slender male Aether Elf toward them. He was middle-aged, with a sprinkling of salt-and-pepper in his close-cropped black hair, and had the same nose as Taylor, though his eyes were sharper. Right now, they darted around the room nervously.

"Don't worry, sir." Julie stepped forward. "We'll get you to HQ safely."

The Weres, in wolf form, prowled at her feet, hackles raised, ready for battle. Faeries buzzed over their heads, and Raven, Korin, and Jae stood at Julie's back, weapons at the ready.

The elf's eyes narrowed. "I know you. Aren't you the one who helped Taylor to free me from the Haunted Hill?"

Julie grinned. "See, sir? I've saved your ass once. I can do it again. You've got nothing to worry about."

The elf's eyes froze, and Julie thought she'd committed an appalling faux pas. Then he relaxed, a laugh bubbling from deep inside his chest.

"Just call me Arion," he told her. "Come on. Let's get out of this mess."

"Couldn't agree more, Arion." Julie grasped his arm in her left hand, keeping the rifle in her right. "Stay close."

We're leaving via a secret exit at the side of the palace that will take us into the back streets of Avalon, Hat instructed as Julie hustled Arion toward a small door in the back of the room.

Can't we just take the portal? Julie glanced at it.

It only goes one way, HQ to Eternity Palace, for security, Hat explained.

The door opened onto a narrow spiral staircase. Below, Julie could hear the clatter of boots as Griffin Five moved the Lunar Fae councilor downstairs at speed. A pang ran through her. She wished she'd seen the councilor, another person from her species. She pushed it aside.

"Just stick close to me, and we'll be fine." Julie kept her grip steady on Arion's arm as she went down the stairs with the Weres surrounding them. Raven, Korin, and Jae brought up the rear with the faeries.

Arion was already panting. "Can't we take a car?"

"It'll draw too much attention to us. We'll slip through the streets quickly and quietly and hopefully unnoticed." Julie steadied Arion when he stumbled. "The Guard is doing their best to keep the trouble out of the streets we'll be using."

"Doing their best? Reassuring," Arion muttered.

Julie grinned. "You're surrounded by six giant wolves, sir. You'll be okay."

"Besides, the real fighters are focused on the Eternity Palace," Korin added from behind them. "The rioters in the street are just regular people. We're Special Forces. We can handle them."

"I hope you're as competent as you are confident," Arion remarked.

"Trust me. We've got you." Julie tightened her grip on his arm.

The staircase took them to a long, narrow hallway, almost a tunnel, lit by flaming torches. Julie got serious Lara Croft vibes as they jogged down it as quickly as Arion could go. The councilor panted beside Julie, his fitness no match for hers.

"You're all putting me to shame," he grumbled sheepishly. "I've had plenty of combat training, but clearly, I missed boot camp." He fingered the Aether daggers in the sheaths at his waist.

"Good to know, sir." Julie flashed him a grin. "Let's hope you don't need any of that training today."

The tunnel dead-ended at a wall with a series of iron rungs set into the stone. Raven scrambled up them and opened the barred metal grille at the top. She climbed out cautiously, rifle first. "All clear," she called.

The Weres shifted to human form to negotiate the rungs. Julie kept a hand on Arion's back as he climbed out of the tunnel ahead of her and took his arm again as soon as she was out of the hatch.

She glanced around. They were in a small, quiet alley that

smelled deliciously of the fish-and-chips shop on the adjacent street, and there was no one in it except the unit. The air also smelled of smoke. Distantly, Julie could hear chanting.

"Justice for Qbiit! Justice for the Sylthana Elves! Equality for all trollkind!"

"Are they really still beating that dead horse?" Arion sighed. "It's his own fault his head got exploded."

"Let's not think about exploding heads right now," Julie suggested.

"This way!" Korin barked. "Weres, mark us. Chester, you're with Meadows and the councilor."

Chester stepped forward, sinewy muscles rippling under his thick blond coat. "I've got you," he growled, his brown eyes meeting Arion's.

They moved out of the alley and into the street, their feet quick and silent on the stone. Korin led the way, flanked by the faeries. Julie and Arion followed. Jae and Raven were at the back of the group, and the Weres surrounded everyone. Julie had abandoned her heavy assault rifle in favor of her pistol, and it was in her hand as they went. Her eyes darted around.

Korin turned left up ahead, and as she stepped forward, a blast of blue flames roared into the street in front of her. She gasped and staggered back, her hammers pulsing with magic as she searched for their attacker. A Sylthana Elf burst out of a wrecked store, flames blazing in his hands, grinning.

"Running away, are you?" he yelled, raising both burning hands. "That's what the Royal Families always do. You abandoned the Sylthana Elves to their fates, even though—"

Julie shot him in the face. The crackling ball of stun magic slammed into his nose and sent him tumbling backward, twitching and out cold.

"I'm not in the mood for monologues," she snapped.

Korin eyed the wall of fire in front of them. "We'll need to take a detour."

"It's okay." Arion stepped forward and flicked his wrist, and wind roared across the street, blowing the flames out like candles.

"You can do that?" Julie asked.

Arion's eyes sparkled. "Our telekinesis is really an affinity for air," he told her. "So, yes, I can do that."

"Can Taylor do that?" she blurted.

"Nobody cares, Meadows. Move out!" Korin ordered, striding down the street with a hammer in each hand. The Weres stayed close to her.

Arion leaned over as they hurried after her. "He will be able to in time."

Julie flashed him a grin.

They jogged through the streets, hearing yells and flames roaring and the pops of guns in the distance but managing to dodge the edges of the riots. The noise lessened as they approached Avalon OPMA.

The fortress towered over the streets, neatly restored after the attack a few weeks ago. Soon, the only sound was the jingle of weaponry, the panting of the Weres, and Arion's heavy breathing in Julie's ear as they turned down the last block to the fortress. Smoke filled the air, low and black. They all coughed periodically.

"Almost there!" Julie exclaimed.

Arion's pace quickened at the sight of the fortress looming through the smoke. Julie allowed herself to let out a breath of relief. They'd made it. They were almost there—

Behind her, she heard someone shifting. When she whipped around, Chester was in human form, rifle raised to his face. The shot echoed down the street. From a second-story window just yards from them, a Sylthana Elf tumbled to the ground with a sickening crack, a grenade rolling out of his lifeless fingers.

"Contact!" Korin bellowed.

They were everywhere, and they were more than monologuing rioters. Paras, their faces painted with the Dark Moon symbol, came pouring into the street, brandishing clubs and blades and fistfuls of fire. Trolls, Sylthana Elves, dwarves, fae...

Julie's pistol buzzed and clicked as it changed from one type of ammunition to the other when she swept it across the approaching enemies.

"Keep going. Keep going!" Korin yelled.

She charged forward, swinging her hammers, and the attackers closed in. Julie kept Arion on her left side, sandwiched between her and Chester. The Were fired his rifle into the crowd as they drew closer. Julie did the same with her pistol, but when one Dark Moon fell, two took their place.

"Shit. Hat, we need backup!" Julie yelled, firing into a troll's chest. He fell to the ground, screaming and writhing.

"I'm trying!" Hat yelled.

Julie felt a stirring somewhere to her left, a presence, and she whipped around and shot an elf in the shoulder when he was inches away from firing an arrow at Arion. As weak as she felt under the midday sun, some of her Lunar Fae senses were still with her. She fired into the crowd again, but they were closing on the unit.

You can sense the water in their bodies. Pretty cool, Hat told her.

Stop with the fun facts and get us some backup! Julie yelled.

Chester let out a roar, fired a final barrage into the chaos, and flung his gun at a charging elf, sending her flying. He shifted into wolf form and sank his teeth into a troll's calf, then shook him like a rag doll. The troll's screams filled the air. Fairy dust glittered, and Korin's hammers flashed in all directions. Julie kept firing, enemies just feet from her, dodging clubs, maces, and swords when she could.

Jae let out a roar, and two sets of roots burst from the ground, shattering paving stones. They surged up to the nearest Sylthana Elf and wrapped around his waist, then threw him into the air. He screeched and sent a blast of blue fire into the root, which shriveled and collapsed. The other root slapped him across the face. He staggered back and held up both hands, and wind rushed over his palms, blowing out the flames.

"Give me room!" Arion demanded, ripping his arm from Julie's grasp. "We need every blade we've got."

Julie didn't argue. Arion whipped both daggers from his belt and stood ready. Chester's haunches were pressed against Arion's knees as he snapped at the approaching Dark Moons. His coat was singed and smoking from a brush with Sylthana fire.

Julie felt something coming from her right and dodged a troll's club that whistled inches from her gun arm. She used her momentum to snap the butt of her pistol into the troll's face. He stumbled back, squealing, and Julie fired into his chest and holstered the pistol.

They were all much too close now. A Sylthana Elf thrust at her with a curved saber. She stepped back and let the blade go past her, then grabbed his wrist in one hand and the hilt in the other. She twisted the blade up and back, hearing the crack as his fingers shattered. The elf stumbled back, screaming, and melted into the crowd. Julie slashed the saber across an attacking were-moose's face, and the creature fell back.

"On your left, Arion!" Julie shouted, half-turning.

The Aether Elf jumped back as a troll stabbed at him with a dagger. Rising unnaturally into the air, Arion backflipped six feet off the ground, and his boots slammed into the head of a charging dwarf. The dwarf fell, and as Arion landed, he slashed at the troll with both daggers, felling her.

"Whoa! Where did that come from?" Julie shouted, blocking a blow from a troll's mace.

Arion flashed her a smile. "Telekinesis. I can move my own body too, you know."

"Cool!" Julie returned, slashing the saber across the troll's wrists.

The others in the unit were fighting hard. The Weres stayed

in a tight circle around them, keeping the Dark Moons from breaking them apart. Julie's back pressed against Arion's, and Chester's furry form pressed against their knees as he sank his teeth into the thigh of a nearby elf.

The elf screamed, and Arion's dagger slashed his sword from his hand. Julie felt a blow coming and lunged to block a troll's sword, shoving Arion to the side. He fell to the ground in a full split, and the mace floated harmlessly over his head. He then leaped into the air like a kung fu hero and slammed both heels into the nearest enemy's face.

The club didn't come out of nowhere. Julie felt it, but as she was nose to nose with an orc, she had nowhere to go. It crashed into her armored side, and she skidded over the cobblestones on her side, her saber spinning out of her hand. Dizzy, she stared up at the troll who strode toward her, the club raised over his shoulder like a baseball bat to smash her face in.

Julie! Get up! Hat screamed.

Julie tried, but her limbs felt like lead. Her breath hitched in her chest. The troll raised the club, and Chester's roar shattered the bright day. Coat streaked with blood and burns, the blond wolf filled Julie's vision as he leaped over her. His outstretched claws slashed into the troll's belly. The attacker fell, with Chester a ball of teeth, fur, and fury on his chest.

An unseen power grabbed Julie's arm and raised her to her feet. She looked up at Arion, who had a bloody streak on his forehead. His daggers were scarlet in his hands. "Look!" he shouted, pointing at the sky. "Griffins!"

Julie looked up. Through the smoke, three silhouettes cut through the sunny sky, wings spread wide. She saw the flash of armor and the symbol of the Eternity Throne, then the griffins were diving toward them, the thunder of their wings sending Dark Moons flying in all directions.

"Quick!" the nearest one rumbled as she landed, her head swinging back and forth. "Get on!"

The Dark Moons were already regrouping.

"Arion, go!" Julie shouted, shoving the Aether Elf toward the nearest griffin.

Arion grabbed the edge of the griffin's breastplate and hauled himself onto her back in one smooth movement. Julie scrambled up behind him. Raven, Korin, and Jae did the same with the other two griffins.

"Hold on!" the griffin rumbled.

Julie threw an arm around Arion and tightened her abs, pressing her weight into the griffin's back. She spotted the flash of a sword being raised, whipped out her pistol, and shot the nearest Dark Moon in the face with a stun ball. She swung the pistol to aim at another, and the griffin flung her wings open and leaped into the air.

Gravity yanked her down. She gasped and clutched at Arion, who clung to the griffin's breastplate. In seconds, they were soaring above the fight, and the battle cries of the Dark Moons turned to yells of indignation below them.

"Wait, wait!" Julie exclaimed, looking back.

The Weres were a tight-packed mass of fur in the center of the fight, moving as one, each pack member heedless of his safety as he fought to protect his brothers. Chester's coat was streaked with blood.

"I'll stay low. Cover them!" the griffin roared. "They need to get into the fortress!"

The griffin swooped, talons outstretched, and Julie fired into the fight as the screaming Dark Moons fled from the griffin. It opened a brief gap in their ranks.

Go, go, go! Korin bellowed at the Weres.

Isaiah surged forward, claws scrabbling on the cobblestones. He snapped and snarled his way through the closing ranks of Dark Moons. The rest of the Weres followed, Chester bringing up the rear, scrambling backward, his teeth and claws keeping the pursuing Dark Moons off the flanks of his brothers.

An elf aimed a crossbow at Noah. Chester pounced on him and sank his teeth into the elf's wrist. Blood sprayed the thick fur of his neck. A troll raced to the elf's rescue, club raised. Twisting on the griffin's back as she flew ahead, Julie fired three shots that punched into the troll's back. He sprawled to the ground.

Chester, go! Korin yelled.

Julie looked ahead. The OPMA portcullis had been raised just high enough for a wolf to slip beneath it. The battlements bristled with bows and rifles.

"Almost there!" Julie cried. "Keep going!"

Stones uprooted from the street, pelting the attackers as they harried the Weres' flanks. Korin leaned down from her griffin's back, her face twisted in concentration. Beside her, Jae's hands reached for the ground, and roots burst from the street, tripping Dark Moons and grabbing their legs.

Isaiah barked encouragement to the others, forging on.

Then they were within range of the defenders on the battlements. The thin hiss of arrows came first, followed by the meaty slap of bodkins striking flesh and the staccato roar of gunfire. Beams of magic and plumes of flame arced from the fortress' walls. The Weres doubled their speed and bolted into the safety of the defenders' cover. Chester, limping, broke away from the fight and scrambled under the portcullis.

CHAPTER EIGHT

The order thundered from the battlements. "Lower the portcullis!"

The portcullis thudded to the ground, and Julie let out a breath. She holstered her pistol and hung onto Arion as the griffin flew over the battlements, then spread her wings and swooped in a slow arc to the courtyard.

"Are you guys okay?" Julie jumped down from the griffin, keeping one hand on Arion's shoulder. The sounds of battle still echoed around them, and the air tasted of smoke.

"We're fine." Isaiah's chest heaved, and his tongue lolled over his white teeth.

Korin hopped down from her griffin. "Merlin's balls, that was close."

"Korin!" Raven gasped in horror. "*Language!*"

"Calm down, bitch. It's not like—" Korin began.

"*GET DOWN!*" the griffin roared.

Julie seized Arion, threw him to the ground, and covered him with her body. A blazing ball of blue fire sailed over the battlements, hissing and crackling. For a moment, Julie thought it was heading right for her. Soldiers scattered in all directions. Chester leaped in front of Julie, hackles raised as if he could fight it. Then it roared over their heads, its heat singeing her face, and smashed into the pavement feet away.

"Get inside!" Korin shouted. "Go!"

Julie dragged Arion to his feet. The doors to the keep were open, and she put her head down and sprinted for them, dragging the elf behind her. Another fireball punched into a row of vehicles parked yards away. She raised an arm to shield her face from the explosion and kept going.

They burst through the doors and into the main hall. Normally elegant, composed, and silent, with balconies adjoining the offices overlooking the floor, it was now a sea of grimy-faced soldiers, griffins with singed feathers, and wide-eyed councilors sandwiched between them. The crush of bodies made Julie's heart race, though they were all allies. She kept a firm grip on Arion's arm.

"How are we going to get them all through the portal without anyone being trampled?" Jae asked.

"Order, soldiers." The voice of Overwatch soared over the chaos.

Everyone looked up. A pair of doors banged open on a balcony on the far side of the hall, and a moon-white centaur strode between them, his pace steady and measured, armor flashing. Eyes the blue of a frozen lake scanned the room, taking in everything.

Sergeant Levin Shulme's voice was as calm and decisive as ever. "Exit the main hall in numerical order. Griffin One, go. The rest of you, wait for my command."

Palpable calm filled the hall. Almost tranquilly, Griffin One and their charge left the room.

"Griffin Two, proceed," Shulme purred.

Outside, flames roared, and Julie heard the thud of something massive striking stone. She pushed the thoughts aside and focused on Arion. He dabbed the cut on his forehead with the back of his hand, but it had stopped bleeding.

Finally, Shulme called, "Griffin Seven, proceed." Korin led them out of the hall and down a silent passage with the portal to HQ crackling at the end of it. The rush of relief that ran through Julie's veins as they stepped through it was almost as powerful as the portal dizziness. She shook her head to clear her vision, and they stepped safely into the comfortable lobby of the HQ.

"You're here!" Taylor cried.

Julie looked up. Taylor shoved his way through the chaos of soldiers and councilors and hurried toward her. For a horrified moment, she thought he was going to hug her in front of everyone. Instead, he seized Arion's arm. "Uncle! Are you okay?"

"I'm fine." Arion smiled. "Thanks to your girlfriend and her unit."

Julie's toes curled inside her boots. She was acutely aware of everyone else in the unit staring at her.

"Julie! I was so worried." Taylor turned to her and grabbed her hands. "I saw the riots on TV. They were so violent, and so many buildings were burning. Knowing that you were in the middle of it—" There were tears in his eyes, and he took a trembling breath. "I don't know if I've ever been so scared. I thought I might never see you again. I thought—"

"Taylor, relax." Julie pulled her hands out of his grip.

The faeries floating above her head tittered, and her cheeks burned.

"I-I was just afraid for you." Taylor swallowed, wringing his hands. "I couldn't imagine you in the middle of all that."

"Why not? I'm a trained soldier, remember?" Julie shot back.

Down, girl, Hat cautioned.

Shut up! Julie snapped.

"I know. *I know.*" Taylor took a deep breath. "I'm sorry. I've just never seen one of your battlefields live, and it scared me. I'm sorry."

"It's okay." Julie smiled and touched his arm lightly.

"*WOODSKIN!*" Kaplan thundered from the back of the lobby.

"I'd better go." Taylor backed away. "Come on, Uncle."

Arion gave the unit an elegant bow. "You have my gratitude, soldiers." He followed Taylor into the crowd.

Hat hummed on Julie's head. *The unit's been stood down. Mission accomplished. Well done, chaps.*

"I need a drink," Korin announced. She hung her hammers on her belt and strode to the nearest door.

Raven scampered up beside Julie, giggling. "Your boyfriend is *sooooo* cute!"

Korin groaned. "Ugh, Raven! Don't be such a fangirl."

Raven stuck out her tongue. "He *is* cute! He's so caring."

Chester shifted into human form and fell into step beside them. "Yeah, *so* caring!" He clasped his big, bloodied hands under his chin and batted his eyelashes. "He wuvs you *sooooo* much."

"Stop it." Julie elbowed him in the ribs.

"Oh, Julie, I was so *worried!*" Chester cooed.

Teddy, also in human form, joined in. "I thought I might never see you again!" He draped his arms around Julie's neck. "Oh, Julie! My poor little princess!"

Julie grabbed his thumb and twisted him into a painful arm lock.

"Ow, ow, ow!" Teddy squealed.

Julie let him go. "Ass." She forced herself to laugh.

"We're just messing with you." Chester slapped her on the back. "I'm first in the showers!"

"No way!" Teddy shoved him aside.

"I saved your life, asshole!" Chester thundered, and the Weres poured down the hall, yelling and pushing like teenagers.

Julie rubbed her cheeks as if that would make the blush go away. Her stomach was knotted.

Jae stepped up beside her. "He really cares about you."

"Yeah, I guess." Julie forced a smile.

She's not wrong, Hat murmured.

Maybe not, but he's going to hear about it when we go on leave. Julie pulled him off and ran a hand through her sweaty hair. *I had a helicopter mom for my whole life. I don't need a helicopter boyfriend, too.*

<hr>

A flutter ran down Taylor's spine as he walked across the lawn at HQ. There was a garden tucked away at the back of the building near the barracks, containing fragrant rosebushes and a fountain shaped like a leaping hippocampus with water spilling over its stone body so it flashed like the skin of a real one. Perched on a bench in one corner by the rosebushes was Julie.

She hadn't noticed him yet. She sat sideways on the bench, her phone to her ear, her eyes raised heavenward in the special pose of exasperation she reserved for her mother. It was good to see her wearing something other than her military sweatsuit or uniform. She was in the form-fitting studded black jeans that hugged her shapely figure while reminding him that she was a total badass. Her flowing white blouse left much to the imagination, even though the top button was undone, offering a glimpse of her smooth collarbones.

He paused at the entrance to the garden, hands shoved into his pockets, and gazed at her for a moment, drinking her in. Her skin had always been smooth, but the way the sunlight struck it made it look like silver—almost as though he could see the Lunar Fae in her. Maybe that was just her Julie-ness, the light within shining through.

"Mommmmm." Julie slouched on the bench, leaning her head against the back. "Stopppppp."

She closed her eyes, listening. "I'm pretty sure that's not true, Mom. And besides, I *really* don't want to hear about the effects of aloe vera juice on your libido. That's gross."

Julie opened her eyes and spotted Taylor waiting for her. She sat up, a grin bounding onto her face. His heart squeezed at the sight of it. It seemed like she'd forgiven him for the faux pas he'd committed in front of her unit last week.

"Taylor's here, Mom. I gotta go. Yeah, I love you too. Bye." She tucked the phone into her pocket and leaped to her feet. "Hey, T!"

No one else called him that, and he loved it. He strode up to her and wrapped her in his arms. She giggled, and he felt it ripple through her body as she pressed against him. It seemed like an invitation. Pulling her closer, Taylor sought her lips. She kissed him back, her arms twining around his neck, and his heart thundered. His arms tightened around her—

"Hello? I'm still here, you know. Can you two engage in hanky-panky somewhere else?" Hat demanded.

Taylor instantly let go, his face burning. "Hat! What are you doing here?" He whirled to glare at the innocent-looking black fedora on the bench.

"Oh, yeah. Sorry." Julie grinned. "He's coming too, but only for a little while."

"Coming with us?" Taylor stared at her, dismayed. "Why do we need him on our romantic getaway?"

"About that." Julie grimaced.

Dismay flooded through Taylor's chest like tepid bathwater. He stepped back, hands falling to his sides. "You can't make it?"

"No, no!" She rested a hand on his chest, her eyes searching his. "Of course I can. I wouldn't miss it. I know you've been planning it for ages, even if you won't tell me what it is."

"Okay." Taylor let out a breath, his smile returning. "I just thought..."

"No. It's okay. But there's something I want to do first." She squared her shoulders, and there was a gleam in her eye.

Taylor groaned. "Oh, no. You've got that look again."

"You bet I do. There's something we have to do before we go."

Julie planted her hands on her hips. "And you're not going to like the idea."

"Do I ever?" Taylor raised his eyebrows. "Go on."

Julie took a deep breath. "There's still a leak in the OPMA."

Taylor nodded. "That much has been obvious since the drama with your rifle cert."

"More than that." Julie folded her arms. "I think the leak is directly from the OPMA—or the Eternity Throne—to the Dark Moon League."

Shock rippled through Taylor's chest, and his mind flashed back to the images he'd seen on the TV in the lobby at HQ on the day of the riots. The smoke, the violence, the way ordinary paras had turned into monsters in the street, beating each other with beer bottles and brandishing steak knives. "Are you sure?" he croaked.

"It's the only explanation that makes sense. How else did the League know that the council was in session that day? How did they know we were smuggling your uncle through the back streets? That wasn't part of the riots, T. That was a targeted attack." Julie's brow creased. "More than that, the League's been prepared for us on our recent ops. They set the ambush in Piñon Pines to cripple the Special Forces."

"I'm guessing you have a crazy plan to do something about it." Taylor raised an eyebrow.

Julie huffed. "Bianca won't give me the authorization to do this as a Special Forces soldier."

"I wonder why," Taylor remarked dryly.

She poked him in the abs, rolling her eyes. "So I'll have to do this the old-fashioned way. As Julie Meadows, civilian, while I'm on leave." She smirked.

"And 'this' is?" Taylor asked.

Julie raised her chin. "I think the leak is Prince Lotan. He's been standing up for these Dark Moon assholes. I hear he's been released, and I want to question him."

Taylor felt his jaw drop. "*Question* him? You? Julie, do you have any idea what you're saying?"

Julie grinned. "Crazy enough for ya?"

Taylor shook his head sharply. "They won't let you into the Sylthana Palace, Julie. They won't let *me* into the Sylthana Palace. You have to go through endless royal protocols to meet with someone of that rank. Setting up an appointment could take weeks or months if you even get one, which I doubt you will. I doubt I could."

He paused. "Besides, Lotan's an asshole. I don't know what he'll do to you." The familiar worry gnawed at his chest, and he stopped.

"That's all great, but I'm not a royal." Julie grinned. "No one can blame a human for being ignorant."

Taylor's guts knotted. "But you're not human, Julie. You're a fae. A *Lunar* Fae. What happens if Lotan figures it out and—"

"How would Lotan know what I am?" Julie threw up her hands. "He probably gets his news from the same rag the rest of the Dark Moon League reads. As far as he's concerned, I'm a human sticking my nose in where it's not wanted. Hopefully, he'll slip up and give something away that we can use to put an end to this."

Taylor sagged onto the bench. "This is dangerous."

"I'm a soldier." Julie chuckled. "Dangerous is kind of my thing."

"What are you going to do, walk up to the palace and demand to see him?" Taylor asked.

"I'm pretty sure Hat can get us inside." Julie patted his crown. "I think it will work."

Taylor groaned. "It's not that I don't think it will work. I just worry."

Julie raised her chin and met his eyes. "Quit worrying, T. We're doing this. You owe me for treating me like a damsel in distress in front of my unit. Do you know many 'Oh, Julie, I was so worried' jokes I've had to put up with?"

Taylor winced. He'd seen the shame in her eyes that day. "Okay." He sighed. "Let's get this over with so that we can still make our reservation."

"Fantastic." Julie grinned. "I knew you'd come around. Let's go!"

She looped her arm through his and dragged him across the campus toward the parking garage. He tried to ignore the prickle of excitement that ran through his body.

"This is going to be fun!" Julie announced as they strode into the garage.

Taylor permitted himself to grin. "I guess."

They dodged the parking spot containing a huge black hearse with a skeletal fire-breathing horse harnessed to it and approached Genevieve's usual spot. Taylor spotted a gleam of pewter past Sleipnir's stall and felt a pang of nostalgia. Julie must have had Genevieve cleaned and detailed for the occasion. He hadn't seen her out from under her dust cover in weeks.

Sleipnir put his head over the door and whinnied.

"Hey, Slippy." Julie reached into her pocket for a sugar cube and froze. "What are you doing here?"

A Sphynx cat sat on Genevieve's hood, his bare tail curled around his paws, contentedly kneading the black paintwork. "Hello," he purred.

"What *are* you doing here, Horusiris?" Hat repeated.

"Calm down, old man." Horusiris raised a paw and licked it unhurriedly. "I'm just here to help with your little...secret mission."

"Help? *Help?*" Hat thundered. "What makes you think we need a two-bit psychic cat? We've got *me!*"

"A two-bit psychic cat who can open portals in the aether." Horusiris lowered his paw and fixed Hat with a steady amber gaze. "I could portal you into Lotan's office. Unless..."

Hat let out an exasperated grunt. "All right, then. Just don't expect to be treated like royalty."

Julie waved her arms. "Break it up, you two!" She pulled out Genevieve's keys, eyes gleaming. "Get in the car, all of you."

Taylor hastily slipped into the passenger seat, the leather bucket hugging his body, and buckled his seat belt. Horusiris climbed over his lap and stretched out on the back seat with a purr of delight. Julie tossed Hat onto the seat beside him and started the engine. Genevieve's three hundred seventy-five horses rumbled in eager response, and Julie touched the accelerator just enough to make her roar.

"Oh, yeah." Julie grinned, flexing her fingers on the steering wheel.

"Oh, no," Taylor whimpered.

Tires squealing, they peeled out of the spot at slightly less than the speed of sound. Taylor groaned, clutching the handle above the window as they skidded sideways out of the parking garage and headed for the main gate. Julie let out a whoop, like the adrenaline of battle didn't provide the same exhilaration as driving the Mustang.

"You're taking up the whole seat. Move your naked tail," Hat complained.

"At least I *have* a tail," Horusiris purred.

"You think I couldn't have one if I wanted? You think I couldn't take on any shape I wanted?" Hat snapped.

Taylor leaned back in his seat and closed his eyes, letting out a sigh. This wasn't what he had planned.

Avalon Plaza wasn't the same. Julie's heart clenched as she remembered the way it had been the first time she'd stepped through the portal: the glittering multi-colored cobblestones, the happy bustle of shoppers moving down the sidewalks, the restaurants and stores lining the plaza, and diners sitting under umbrellas on the street. Now, some of the stores were closed, their windows dusty. There were new iron bars on many of the windows, with blue protection runes glowing on them. Very few of the doors were open. Instead, iron grilles barred the way.

She clenched her fists by her sides as Taylor followed her through the 110th Street Bridge portal with Horusiris in his arms. Genevieve was safe in a parking garage after they'd driven here from Staten Island in a fun but unbelievably short time.

"I can't believe the Dark Moon League's done this to Avalon," Julie growled.

Taylor looked at her. "If Lotan really is the leak, we might make a real difference."

"That's the idea," Julie muttered. "Let's go!"

She took a few steps before she realized that Taylor wasn't following. She turned around. He watched her with a lopsided smile on his face, his chocolate-brown eyes warm.

"What?" she demanded. "Why are you looking at me like that?"

"So, do you know where the Sylthana Palace is?" Taylor asked.

She felt her cheeks redden. "No, but Hat does."

Hat snickered.

"What are you not telling me?" Julie yelled.

"It's an hour's drive out of town, with no tram lines heading there," Hat admitted.

"Dude! You couldn't have mentioned that earlier?" Julie squawked.

Taylor strode up to her and draped an arm around her shoulders. "Don't worry. I arranged transport on the drive over. Booked and paid for, courtesy of my officer's salary, *not* the Aether Throne." He grinned.

Julie snuggled under his arm. "So *that's* what you were doing on your phone on the way here."

"Yep." Taylor kissed the side of her head.

"You like my mad schemes." Julie wrapped an arm around his torso. "Admit it."

"I try to support them, anyway." Taylor chuckled. "Come on. The rental garage is this way."

Just down one of the side streets branching off the plaza, the rental garage was a flat, blockish, utilitarian building. The front desk was manned by a large, lumpish orc of indeterminate gender who grunted at them, held out a form for Taylor to sign, and nodded them through.

"Don't we need keys?" Julie asked, following Taylor across the office toward the door that led to the garage.

Taylor grinned. "You'll see."

The parking garage smelled of diesel, straw, manure, and the strangely electric aroma of magic. A pair of skeletal oxen glowered at Julie with red eyes from their stall, munching on hay that fell between their jaws. Something suspiciously police box-shaped lurked under a dust cover.

"Ooh!" Julie turned toward it.

"Nope." Taylor gripped her arm. "We're not going there."

They passed a pair of pegasi, saddled and ready, their eagle wings rustling as they gazed toward the door. Finally, Taylor stopped in front of a parking spot that looked empty at first glance. It took Julie a moment to spot the dusty rug lying on the floor. It looked like a Persian rug, but the patterns and embroidery were so faded and the tassels so worn that she was pretty sure even Mom would have thrown it out. It might have been maroon and purple once. Now it was brownish and gross.

"Um…" Julie glanced at Taylor.

He grinned, crouched beside the rug, and pressed a palm flat on its nasty surface. "Wake," he whispered.

The rug stirred, and motion ran through its fibers like nerves sparking to life. The tassels twitched, and with a lurch, it rose into the air and hovered at knee height, rippling steadily.

Julie burst out laughing. "You have got to be kidding. Is that a flying carpet?"

"It is absolutely a flying carpet!" Taylor beamed. "Hop on!" He clambered onto the carpet, which barely sank under his weight, and held out a hand to her.

"I have reservations," Hat announced.

Horusiris smoothly leaped onto the carpet, sat down, and began to knead it, purring.

Julie took Taylor's hand. "Yeah, baby! Let's Aladdin this shit."

Taylor chuckled and helped her onto the carpet. It felt like climbing onto a gently bouncing trampoline.

Julie ran a hand over the coarse, worn fibers. "Does this thing have seat belts?"

"It's okay. You can't fall off. It's part of the magic," Taylor assured her.

Horusiris curled up in her lap, and Taylor cleared his throat. "Forward," he ordered.

The carpet jerked forward.

"Slowly!" Taylor squealed.

Julie almost pitched onto her nose as the carpet braked.

"Dude. Do you know how to drive this thing?" she squeaked.

"It's been a while, but don't worry. I've got this." Taylor cleared his throat. "Onward, carpet!"

The carpet smoothly cruised forward, then rose through the large hatch in the roof. In moments, they were sailing over the streets of Avalon, the homes and streets looking like a painting below. From this height, it was impossible to see the iron doors and the silent barred shops. Avalon was a tapestry of wood and stone, brick and concrete, glass and steel.

Julie leaned over the edge of the carpet, eliciting an unhappy squawk from Hat, and gazed down at the city. A stone tower with a pointed roof stood beside a high-rise office building, all metal and shimmering glass. The building beside it was a thatched longhouse with thick black smoke rising from its chimney and the distant shapes of dwarves carousing in front of it.

"I love Avalon," she murmured.

"Pretty from up here, isn't it?" Taylor smiled.

"It is." Julie grinned. "Still looks like fairy puke, though."

"We even have music." Taylor grinned. "Carpet, play Folk FM."

A weird combination of bagpipes, fairy flute, and rock oozed into the air, apparently out of nowhere.

"What *is* this?" Julie asked.

"Noise," Hat grumbled.

"This is traditional. This is *culture!*" Taylor spluttered.

Once they'd left the edge of the town, Taylor muttered, "Haw," and the carpet arced smoothly to the left. Julie spotted the blue line of the ocean on the horizon.

"I don't think I've been to this part of Avalon before," she admitted.

Taylor's smile faded. "We're going to the Sylthana Lands."

Silence fell, and Julie's stomach clenched. She scooted closer to Taylor, and they sat side by side in silence as the carpet soared nearer to the Sylthana Palace and whatever awaited them within.

CHAPTER NINE

The Sylthana Palace was built into the clifftops at the edge of the broad golden beach. Spire upon spire rose from the sandstone as though they had grown from the rocks, glittering with copper and broad sheets of glass that dizzily reflected the bright sunshine over the sea.

Julie squinted up at it. "This is not what I was expecting."

"What were you expecting?" Hat asked. "Alcatraz?"

"Something like that," Julie admitted. "It's…well, *tasteful*. I like it."

"Sylthana Elves love glass and metal. Stuff that can be refined in fire." Taylor rubbed the back of his neck. "Unfortunately, they also love security."

That much was obvious. Apart from arrow slits, there wasn't a single window in the lower part of the cliff. The first windows were three stories up, with no way of reaching them apart from scaling the sheer cliffs. Balconies jutted from the cliffs, and guards in shining copper armor stood on each one, armed with rifles. There was only one door, ornately carved and made of burnished copper, at the foot of the cliff. A broad paved driveway led up to it, winding slowly down the cliff half a mile away.

"Okay, so we fly up to Prince Lotan's window and go in through that," Julie suggested.

Horusiris yawned. He was curled up on the carpet, which Taylor had rolled up and stashed behind a rock. "Don't be ridiculous. You'll be butchered by the guards. That's what I'm here for."

"Well then, go ahead," Julie told him.

"I still don't like this," Hat muttered. "This *is* the cat who got trapped in Tintagel Castle for being annoying."

"Better than being trapped in the Warehouse for being redundant," Horusiris purred.

"Dude!" Julie exclaimed. "Why would you go there?"

The Sphynx ignored her and lazily looked past her left shoulder. Taylor's eyes widened, and Julie turned to see a portal shimmering open. She caught a glimpse of an opulent room, all draped silk and engraved metal.

"See you later," Horusiris purred. "The old man can let me know when you're ready to come back."

"Shut up," Hat snapped.

Julie squared her shoulders. "Let's do this!" She stepped forward before she could second-guess her choice, and after a moment of dizziness from the portal, she stood with Taylor in the chambers of Lotan, Prince of the Sylthana Elves.

The sandstone floor was bare and cool. On one side of the room, the sandstone wall was inlaid with brilliant streaks of copper in flowing patterns like flames. The other wall was glass, with white silk curtains blowing gently in the sea breeze, offering a breathtaking view of the flat, shimmering ocean. A bed that would have taken up half of Julie's old apartment stood in one corner, crisply made up and draped with white linens.

"What the... *Who are you?*"

Julie whipped around. The voice came from the hot tub in the corner of the room, or more specifically, from an athletic Sylthana Elf currently scrambling out of the hot tub and throwing a fluffy white robe around himself. Prince Lotan's long silver hair was a damp curtain down his back, and his flawless sand-colored skin rippled with muscle. He would have been attractive except for the permanent sneer tugging at one corner of his broad mouth and the glittering arrogance in his pale blue eyes.

"Guards!" Lotan shouted.

"No, wait!" Julie stepped forward, holding out her hands. "We're unarmed. We're not here to hurt you."

Lotan stopped but glared from Julie to Taylor and back.

"I mean, if you want to shout for the guards to come and save you from two unarmed people, that's cool, I guess." Julie folded her arms.

The prince's eyes narrowed. "Who are you?" He looked at Taylor. "You seem familiar."

"Taylor, Prince of the Aether Elves," Taylor supplied.

"I'm Julie Meadows. Human troublemaker." She smirked.

"Oh, yes. Taylor. The sixth in line." Lotan tied his robe and strolled over to an elegant glass table by the hot tub. He selected a grape from a large bowl and popped it into his mouth. "I'd forgotten you existed."

"Unsurprisingly," Taylor muttered.

"I can understand that, in your position, you're looking for someone of power to support you." Lotan waved a hand. "But my family has no interest in the Aether Elves. Besides, there's not much you can do about your birthright. You'll just have to accept that you're unimportant. Now go away and stop annoying me."

"Excuse me! I am *not*—" Taylor spluttered.

"We're not here for your favor, Prince Lotan." Julie arched an eyebrow. "We're here to find out why you're so determined to prove you are the dumbest heir alive."

Lotan whirled. "*What?*"

"You heard me." Julie laughed. "Supporting an illegal terrorist group? That's insane. Do you really think the Dark Moons can overthrow the Eternity Throne? Even if they do, what do you think happens next? How is a war going to benefit your people?"

"I don't think they can overthrow the Throne," Lotan snapped. "I'm not stupid."

"Uh-huh. Sure you aren't, babe." Julie yawned.

Lotan's eyes narrowed. "You're insolent and uneducated."

"Better than being as dumb as a box of rocks," Julie commented.

Taylor audibly swallowed. Hat snickered.

"Don't you see that the Dark Moon riots have done nothing but destroy infrastructure and make you even less popular with everyone else in power?" Julie demanded. "You're inches from being rejected as heir to the Sylthana Throne, let alone heir to the Eternity Throne."

"The Eternity Throne is my birthright!" Lotan barked. "I *will* have it."

Julie burst out laughing. "You know no one believes that, right? Not now that you've been imprisoned. Birthright!" She chuckled, shaking her head. "You'll never see the Eternity Throne if you're stupid enough to think terrorism is the way to get it. There'll be a Dark Moon leader on the Throne if their coup succeeds. They're playing you, moron."

"Silence!" Lotan thundered, taking a step forward. "That throne is mine by right! None of that pathetic rabble will ever so much as breathe upon it!"

"Pathetic rabble?" Julie raised an eyebrow. "I thought they had your support."

"Of course they do. They're my tools, don't you see? They're how I will reach the Throne," Lotan spat. "*I* am using the Dark Moons. They are not using *me*!" His hands were clenched by his sides. "I will be the Eternity King. I will have that throne, just as my parents promised. It's mine!"

Something snapped in Julie's chest. She took a fierce step

forward, and felt Taylor's hand close to her arm, not quite holding her back.

"Power? That's what this is all about?" she asked. "You don't believe in the Sylthana cause?"

Lotan snorted and leaned on the glass table, then ate another grape. "What, all that bullshit about the Throne being stolen from my people? Not really. I mean, the test is there for a reason." He shrugged. "But the Lunar Fae are dying out, and someone's going to have to take that throne. It's going to be me, and the Dark Moon League is going to help me get it."

"Personal power." Julie's hands trembled with rage. "That's all you care about. Having what you want."

Lotan considered that, then shrugged again. "Pretty much."

Julie wrenched her arm out of Taylor's grasp and strode toward Lotan, jabbing a finger into his face. "How can that be worth the pain you're causing *your innocent people*?" she yelled.

Lotan blinked. "What are you talking about? Everything I'm doing is for the good of my people." But there was a tremor in his voice as he spoke.

"Oh, yeah? When did you last talk to an ordinary Sylthana Elf?" Julie challenged. "When did you last ask an everyday elf their opinion of the Dark Moon League and the unrest they've caused? Have you seen the prejudice they're experiencing? Do you know that everyone treats them with suspicion and they can't get or keep jobs anymore?"

Lotan opened his mouth, then slowly shut it. He paused before speaking. "I'm ushering in a golden age for Sylthana Elves everywhere." The words fell flat.

"You don't really believe that, and with good reason, because it just isn't true." Julie put her hands on her hips. "You don't know about Dr. Olena, who runs the para-ER in Staten Island, and how paras demand to be seen by any other doctor because she's a Sylthana Elf."

She remembered the hollow look in the doctor's eyes when

she'd accompanied Chester to the ER after the riots. "And you haven't seen how the Sylthana Elves in the cafeteria at the PMA all sit in one corner because no one wants to be associated with them. You haven't seen all the Sylthana-owned businesses in Avalon that have closed down because no one supports them anymore."

Lotan was silent.

"Come on, Lotan. You're smarter than you look. You've suspected this all along, haven't you?" Julie asked. "You know that this isn't a 'golden age' for Sylthana Elves. It's a curse."

Lotan met her gaze, his eyes steely. Then he let out a rush of air.

"You'd better sit down," he mumbled.

The prince strode over to a smooth white couch near the window and flopped down on it, gesturing at the opposite couch. A copper coffee table stood between them. Julie sat, arms folded. Taylor perched on the edge.

Lotan stared out of the window for a few moments before speaking. "I know my parents want me on the Eternity Throne. And yes, I want that power. I have to want that power. That's what my parents demand." He looked at Julie. "But I didn't know about stuff being hard for the Sylthana Elves. I didn't know they were losing their jobs and businesses."

Julie stared at him. She'd seen that same helpless expression on Taylor and his sister, Crown Princess Ilsa.

"You've been locked in an ivory tower all your life, Lotan." Her voice was gentle. "You're an only child, right?"

Lotan shifted uncomfortably and rearranged his robe. "I am. What does it matter? My parents would have kept all of their focus on me anyway. I'm the Crown Prince." He dropped his gaze to his bare toes.

Julie sat back. "Do you really want to be nothing except what they expect of you?"

Lotan folded his arms and scowled at her. "It's not like I have a choice."

Julie glanced at Taylor. His eyes were intent, hands clasped on his knees.

"I think you do." Julie nudged Taylor with her knee. "Tell him, T."

Lotan raised his eyebrows. "Tell me what?"

Taylor leaned forward. "I might only be sixth in line to the Aether Throne, but I'm close to my sister Ilsanthia." He took a deep breath. "So I know about the pressures you face, Lotan, and how inevitable it must feel. I've seen my sister labor under what my parents demanded of her during her entire life.

"She was just a little kid when she was pulled out of tutoring with the rest of us and sent to all these different finishing schools. She didn't play with us, didn't go to lessons with us, didn't get to ride horses in the woods or shoot slingshots or swim in the river with us. All Ilsa ever did, from morning until night, and still does, is prepare to become the Crown Princess."

Lotan gazed out across the ocean, but he said nothing.

"Ilsa wants to be a leader. A good, fair leader. My parents, for all their faults, brought her up that way. Your parents raised you to desire power, Lotan, and they've taught you that it's okay to hurt people to get it."

Taylor's eyes didn't leave the Sylthana prince. "Are *you* okay with that? Are you okay with our doctor friend crying in a corner after a twenty-four-hour shift because people ask her to take the next elevator like she's got a disease? Are you okay with Sylthana Elves locking up their businesses and taking their kids out of school because of how relentlessly they're being bullied?"

Lotan rubbed the back of his neck. "No. No, I'm not okay with it."

"You're trying to be what your parents want you to be. *I* think you can be better if you try to be who *you* think you can be. If you stand up for what *you* believe in." Taylor took a breath. "You could be free, Lotan, and you could still be a good king. A better king than your father, even."

Lotan shot him a glance.

"You have it in you to be brilliant, but by living up to your parents' expectations, you're not growing to *your* potential. You're just trying to live their dream. You can do better, and your people deserve better!"

Taylor slapped the coffee table. "Your people deserve a prince who can lead them through a time that's already hard for them. Your people deserve somebody to advocate for them, not oppress them. They deserve a hero, and you're the only one who can be that for them!"

Julie realized that her jaw had dropped. Taylor's eyes blazed, and his jaw was set. She didn't think she'd ever seen him look so tall.

Look so much like a prince of his people.

Lotan had shrunk and looked like a little boy in his sagging fluffy robe. He wrapped his arms around himself, eyes distant. "I might not know my people well," he whispered, "but I've always told myself that I'm doing right by them. I *want* to do right by them."

He snuck a glance at Julie. "And I think…well, I've suspected for a long time that what we're doing isn't right. My parents keep telling me we're helping them." He inhaled sharply. "But we're not."

"No. You're not." Julie folded her hands in her lap. "But you can fix it, Lotan. It's not too late. If you stand up now, you can make a real change for Sylthana Elves everywhere."

There was a long silence. Lotan stared at his feet some more. Finally, he sat up straight, and the former steeliness was back in his eyes when they met Julie's.

"You're right." His voice rang around the chamber. "I *can* set things right. I am the Crown Prince of the Sylthana Elves, and I will not be controlled any longer." He raised his chin. "I'm going to make this right."

Julie grinned widely. "Yes, you are."

"Yes, I am." Lotan cleared his throat and rose to his feet. "Right now!" He turned and strode toward the door.

"Uh, Your Highness?" Julie hazarded.

He stopped. "What?"

"You're still in your robe," Julie pointed out.

"Oh." Lotan looked down. "Yes. That. Well, piss off so I can make some changes!" He stomped toward a door that presumably led to his walk-in closet.

That's our cue, Hat, Julie murmured.

I've already given the kitty his command, Hat sniped.

A shimmering spot appeared in front of the window. Julie and Taylor rose, and she reached for his hand. "Ready to go, Mr. Inspiring Speech?"

Taylor grayed in embarrassment. "Ready."

They clasped hands and stepped through the portal.

The flying carpet soared over the long stretch of golden beach that shone like a ribbon of light beneath them. The salty breeze ran its fingers through Julie's hair as they left the Sylthana Palace far behind them.

"Hey." Julie looked at Taylor. "You were brilliant in there, by the way."

Taylor's cheeks grayed. "Thanks. I think we actually got through to him."

"I think *you* got through to him." Julie squeezed his arm.

"I've been waiting to say those words for a long time." Taylor smiled. "Just not to Lotan."

"To Ilsa?" Julie guessed.

Taylor nodded. "I never could because I'm too afraid of what might happen to her if she goes against my parents. She could be disowned or banished."

"Do you think your parents would do that?" Julie asked, surprised.

Taylor shrugged. "My parents will do anything for what they think is in the best interests of the Aether Throne."

Julie leaned her head against his shoulder, the rustle of the wind and the weird folksy rock music filling her ears, and missed Rosa. She was pretty sure her mother would do anything for her.

"Hey, T?" she murmured.

"Yeah?"

"Thank you." Julie looked up at him. "For humoring me. I mean it."

Taylor's lips curled, and he kissed the top of her head. "I'll always go along with your crazy ideas, silly. They make life interesting, and they mostly lead to good being done for all paras involved."

Julie snorted. "My ideas are *not* crazy."

"Uh-huh. Sure, babe," Taylor mocked.

"Shut up." Julie poked him in the ribs, laughing.

The music stopped abruptly, and a masculine voice spoke into thin air. "We interrupt your favorite Fernwood Rock for a special announcement from Lotan, Prince of the Sylthana Elves, who has called an emergency press conference at the Sylthana Palace."

Julie sat up. "That was quick."

"Let's hear what he has to say." Taylor cleared his throat. "Carpet, volume up."

Lotan's voice was stronger and steadier than it had been in his chambers. "Thank you all for coming so quickly." They heard the muted snap of cameras behind his deep voice. "I have an urgent announcement to make. One I should have made a long time ago, even though I know there will be consequences."

Julie glanced at Taylor, whose mouth was a grim line.

"As of this moment, I withdraw my endorsement of the Dark Moon League. I entirely renounce the League, its members, and its ideals." Lotan's voice got stronger. "The Dark Moon League is a terrorist organization. They sow destruction and mayhem for their personal gain, not for the good of Sylthana Elves.

"It has been brought to my attention that my people are suffering due to the actions of the League. I find that utterly unacceptable. I apologize for my previous stance on the League, and I will lend my support to the Eternity Throne and the Para-Military Agency to put an end to their despicable actions."

"Strong words," Julie murmured.

"I don't think he knows any other kind," Hat commented.

"Sylthana Elves, I have failed you, but I stand for you now. If I am going to reach the Eternity Throne, I want it to be for the good of my people, and I want it to be done fairly, with the support of my people. If there are any of you listening who support the Dark Moon League as I did..." Lotan took a deep breath. "If I can admit my mistakes, so can you. I endorse the Eternity Queen's edict outlawing the League."

Julie and Taylor exchanged glances.

"Those who abandon the League now will face no further consequences," Lotan went on. "However, anyone who continues to support the terrorist group won't make it to the Locker because I will have them executed for treason."

"*Executed?*" Julie squeaked, staring at Taylor, who looked shocked.

"Baby steps," Horusiris purred. "He *is* still the Sylthana Prince."

The music resumed, and Taylor sat back, laughing. He put a hand on Julie's shoulder, then let his fingers wander down to her hand and intertwine with hers. "You did it again."

"*We* did it again," Julie corrected him, smiling into his eyes.

Horusiris gagged, retched, and produced a slimy hairball, which landed on the carpet with a sad little slap.

"Mature," Hat remarked.

Taylor laughed, squeezing Julie's hand. "Don't worry. We'll drop these two at HQ, and we should *just* make our reservation.

Then we have two days to ourselves."

"You'll never make it," Hat announced. "Not if you still have to take us back to HQ. You have to check in by sunset."

Taylor's shoulders sagged.

"Have you forgotten you have a Sphynx with you?" Horusiris enquired. "I can take DUMB LE Dork back to the Ware—"

"No!" Hat shrieked.

Horusiris chuckled. "I'm joking, old man. I'll take you to Julie's barracks for a peaceful weekend on the foot of her bunk."

Julie ran her fingers around Hat's brim. "Will you go with him, Hat?" She glanced at Taylor, who was staring down at the carpet, not looking at her. "Please?"

"Please?" Hat spluttered. "Did you just say 'please?'"

"There will be no funny business." Horusiris wrapped his tail around his paws. "I promise."

Hat sighed. "Very well, then."

Taylor's eyes brightened, and he grinned at Julie. "Is it possible that we're going to have some time alone after all?"

She wrapped an arm around him and pressed her lips to the smoothness of his cheek. "It's happening, babe."

CHAPTER TEN

Taylor's hands were pressed over Julie's eyes. She giggled, clutching his wrists for balance. He'd made her close her eyes shortly after they stopped on a random country lane to let Horusiris and Hat leave. They'd flown for ten more minutes after that, and she was fairly sure that she'd stepped off the flying carpet onto grass. It crunched under her feet, and she smelled pine and something earthy.

"Can I open my eyes now?" Julie asked.

Her back was pressed against his chest, so when Taylor chuckled, she felt the rumble. "Not yet."

The grass turned into something softer and deeper. Sand. The seashore? Julie hoped it wouldn't be swarming with tourists. She listened hard, but she couldn't hear anything but the crunch of her feet and the lapping of water. No traffic, no people. Did high-end hotels in Avalon have muffling spells cast on them?

"A few more steps," Taylor instructed.

"You know this is *super* cheesy, right?" Julie asked.

"I'm your boyfriend. I'm allowed a few cheesy moments." Taylor stopped. "Ready?"

"Yes!" Julie exclaimed.

"Okay." Taylor dropped his hands to her shoulders. "You can open your eyes now."

Julie braced herself for the huge, fancy hotel and did so. She was looking at a beautiful sweep of wild forest bordering a lake so still that it perfectly mirrored a sky full of scattered clouds. The woods were motionless and had an ancient stillness in them. The landscape was composed of giant ferns as tall as redwoods. They were ancient dryads, Julie knew, so old that time passed differently for them.

The lake's shore was composed of golden sand, unblemished except for a series of delicate glittering hoofprints going down to the water. A flock of gold geese paddled across the lake, their rippling wakes the only wrinkles on the smooth surface.

It was so old, so wild, and so quiet that it took Julie a few moments to notice the cabin tucked between the roots of one of the dryads. The log structure was a little bigger than her apartment in Brooklyn, with a fire pit out front and a little wooden pier running into the lake. Apart from that, this wilderness felt as though it had been untouched for centuries.

"Well?" Taylor's voice trembled. "What do you think?"

Julie realized that her hands were pressed to her mouth. "Oh, T, it's amazing!" She gazed up at him, laughed, and glanced at the cabin again. "It's perfect!"

Taylor's shoulders relaxed, and a smile spread over his face. "Come on." He took her hand. "Let me show you the inside."

"Wait." Julie kicked off her boots and socks, tied the laces together, and picked them up. She sank her bare feet into the warm sand and sighed. "Let's go."

They crossed the shore, stepping carefully around the glittering hoofprints. "We might see the unicorn come down to drink at dawn," Taylor told her. They reached the cabin, and he unlocked the door and pushed it open. There was a pot-bellied cast-iron stove in one corner, its chimney jutting through the roof, with a rustic kitchenette arranged around it. Two doors led to bedrooms and the bathroom, and one wall was a big window with a leather couch facing it.

Julie sagged onto the couch and gazed out at the lake, unable to utter a word.

"Coffee?" Taylor opened the stove's firebox and peered into it, puzzled.

"That would be great. Let me help you with that." Julie got up.

"Thanks." Taylor laughed sheepishly.

There was a matchbox in a nearby drawer, and in a few moments, wood was blazing happily in the stove, filling the air with the smell of woodsmoke and the hum of the kettle.

Taylor rummaged in one of the cabinets and discovered two tin mugs. He set them on the counter and shooed Julie away. "You sit and allow yourself to be spoiled."

Julie sank onto the couch and stared at the lake.

"So, is it okay?" Taylor handed her a mug of coffee.

She carefully took it by the handle since there was steam rising from the liquid. "Okay? Taylor, I love it. It's perfect." She checked her phone. "And I have no cell reception. No Hat. No work. Nothing. Just you and me."

Taylor's eyes crinkled in a smile.

"It's not what I was expecting, I'll admit." Julie sipped her coffee.

Taylor sat beside her. "Oh? What were you expecting?"

"Something more high-end, given your tastes," Julie admitted.

Taylor scooted closer to her on the couch. "You and me together is all I need to be happy," he murmured. "I know you've been missing the peace and quiet of your apartment."

Julie put her head on his shoulder. "Thank you."

He kissed the top of her head, and blissful, perfect silence fell.

They ate breakfast the next morning at the table by the firepit, listening to the birdsong that filled the woods and watching the gold geese waddle across the shore to the lake. Julie couldn't remember the last time she'd slept this late. She was wearing her favorite pink pajamas, the ones with little purple hearts on them in which she would not be caught dead in the barracks, and her unicorn slippers, even though the sun was high in the sky.

Biting the corner off a piece of French toast, she let out a sigh of contentment, swinging her slippers over the sand. Opposite her, Taylor was pleasantly rumpled with sleep as he sipped his coffee.

His eyes widened. "There!" he whispered, pointing.

Julie slowly turned. At the edge of the woods was a splash of brilliant white—a doe, her coat the color of ivory. She stepped onto the sand with the floating delicacy of all deer, her big ears flicking this way and that. A moment later, a magnificent stag followed, his proud head bearing antlers that shimmered like they'd been carved from diamonds. They walked across the shore side by side, then lowered their heads to drink, perfectly reflected in the mirror-smooth surface.

"Amazing," Julie whispered.

She kept her voice low, but the stag's big ears twitched and he leaped to attention, blue eyes wide. With a snort of alarm, he took off over the shore, leaping effortlessly. The doe followed, and they melted into the woods.

"Oops." Julie grimaced. "Sorry."

"It's okay. They'll be back." Taylor smiled. "So, how are my cooking skills coming along?"

"They're good!" Julie laughed. "This was actually edible. Sort of rubbery, but edible."

"Hey!" Taylor swatted at her. "You've got to cut me a little slack. It's only been a few months since I started trying."

"You're doing great." Julie touched his arm. "Seriously. I'm proud of you."

The words made Taylor grow six inches. He ran a hand through his hair, smoothing some of the ruffles, and gathered their plates. "Hey, do you know what today is perfect for?"

"Reading?" Julie suggested.

Taylor chuckled. "Well, yeah. I figured you'd say that." He got up. "I've got something for you."

"Ooh, what is it?" Julie scampered after him as he strode over to the cabin.

They headed inside, and after he put the plates down, Taylor opened one of the suitcases that had been delivered by mysterious (and expensive, Julie supposed) magical means. "This." He pulled out a well-thumbed book and laid it in Julie's arms.

Tears stung her eyes. "*Anna Karenina.*" She blinked, hugging the book to her chest.

"I asked Jae to pack it for you, but she couldn't find it. I figured you'd left it at your apartment, so with your mom's help, I fetched it for you." Taylor twined his fingers together. "I hope that's okay."

"There wasn't room in the barracks for that many books." Julie blinked again. "Thank you, Taylor."

"I figured it could stay with me after this weekend since you don't have room. I could bring it to you whenever you want it." Taylor's voice was gentle.

"Thank you." Julie put the book aside and wrapped her arms around him. "Thank you so much. I know it's a little thing, but..."

Taylor returned the embrace, pulling her close. "The little things are the big ones."

Julie blinked away her tears, feeling silly, and looked up at him. "So, were you really going to say that today is perfect for reading?"

"No." Taylor chuckled. "I was going to say swimming."

"Oh." Julie bit her lip. "I don't have a bathing suit. Well, except for the standard-issue one in the barracks."

A wicked gleam crept into Taylor's eye. "You do now!" He produced a gift bag from the suitcase and held it out.

"Taylor! You shouldn't have." Julie took it and peered inside. "Wait, did my mom help you buy it?"

"She did, but don't worry. I rejected the skimpy one she suggested." Taylor grayed. "She called it the Grandchild Encourager."

"Ewwww," Julie moaned. She reached into the gift bag and pulled out a piece of silky-soft fabric, expecting a silly two-piece. Instead, Taylor had chosen a plain emerald-green one-piece with an open back. Julie gasped. "It's so pretty!"

"Am I going to get to see you in it?" Taylor raised an eyebrow.

Julie gave him a playful shove. "Only because it's green. Reminds me of our recruiter days."

Taylor laughed. "I'll meet you in the water."

Julie scampered to the bathroom to change, giggling like a little girl and not caring how silly she felt.

***

The time Julie had spent in the pool in HQ's gym had paid off. Her body sliced through the water, which felt pleasant and natural against her skin compared to the chlorinated pool. She was several hundred feet out before she stopped to tread water and look around for Taylor.

He popped up a few yards away, shaking his hair out of his eyes. "You're fast!" he panted.

"My body is a military machine." Julie ran her hands over her arms, enjoying the new sturdy curves of her shoulders and biceps.

Taylor laughed. "I can see that."

"Hey, are there magical alligators in this lake or anything?" Julie asked.

Taylor shrugged. "I don't think so. The website said it was safe for swimming."

"Safe for swimming if you're a fae, or safe for swimming if you're a magical alligator?" Julie raised an eyebrow.

"It didn't clarify." Taylor came over to her and trod water, close enough that she felt the way he stirred the water. "I don't think magical alligators exist, just FYI."

"Good to know." Julie kicked her feet and turned onto her back, allowing herself to float. The sunlight was hot on her skin, which was deliciously cooled by the water when it lapped against her.

Taylor did the same next to her. "So, are you having fun?"

"This is perfect," Julie murmured sleepily. "Next leave, it's my turn to spoil *you*, okay? I'll take you to a goat-petting zoo or something."

"There are goat-petting zoos?" Taylor shot upright, flailing at the water. "With only goats? Like, different colored goats? Different breeds of goats?"

Julie burst out laughing.

"I'm serious!" Taylor spluttered. "Is it a thing?"

"I have no idea, but if it is, I promise I'll—"

Her words died in her throat, and she began to tread water again, dread in the pit of her stomach.

"What?" Taylor asked.

"There's something in the water," Julie whispered. "I can *feel* it."

Taylor came closer. "With your Lunar Fae Spidey senses?"

"Yes." Julie swallowed. "Taylor, it's big. Huge."

They stared around the lake, but Julie couldn't see anything. "Maybe we should—"

"There!" Taylor gasped, pointing.

It was several moments before Julie could see what his elf eyes had picked out. A shadow in the water. It moved toward them, ripples stirring the surface above it, and it was massive. It was the size of a shark. It was the size of a—*horse?*

"Get behind me!" Julie yelled, grabbing Taylor and shoving him aside. She lifted herself in the water, feeling appallingly naked and unarmed in her bathing suit, her fists clenched in front of her face.

The equine head broke the surface of the lake in a spray of glittering droplets. Something huge soared into the air over Julie's head, leaping over them like a dolphin. For a moment, she thought it *was* a dolphin. It had the long tail of a dolphin, its silver skin shimmering in the sunlight. However, it had the head, neck, shoulders, and chest of a pure-white mare.

She floated over their heads, front hooves tucked tight to her chest, and sliced back into the water head-first. Julie only caught a glimpse of a massive dorsal fin before the creature was gone.

"Where is it?" she roared, her head whipping left and right. "*Where is it?*"

"It's okay!" Taylor was laughing. "Julie, it's okay. It's just a hippocampus."

"A hippo-what now?" Julie demanded.

Her training belatedly kicked in as the adrenaline began to fade. *Hippocampus,* it told her. *Common in the Mediterranean Sea. A curious, playful, and harmless horse-dolphin hybrid bred by Poseidon and excellent for sea travel. Small feral groups exist throughout Avalon.*

"Did your training catch up?" Taylor asked.

"It's *not* going to eat us?" Julie lowered her fists.

"It's not." Taylor grinned. "Here it comes again! Come on. Dive down, and it'll swim with us."

"If we get eaten, it's on you." Julie was still shaking.

"Come on." Taylor grabbed her hand, sucked in a breath, and dove. Julie followed him, plunging into the unbelievably clear blue water. The lake's floor was far below her, sandy and motionless. Sunlight stabbed through the surface in daggers of gold.

The hippocampus swam toward them in strong, graceful

movements, her mane rippling. Her face looked like a horse's, delicately dished like an Arabian's, but she lacked nostrils. Instead, two blowholes occupied the crest of her neck. They parted, and bubbles burst from them as she let out a strange sound of greeting, pitched as high as a neigh but broken up with dolphin chatter.

Julie glanced at Taylor, who grinned at her, his hair a dark cloud around his head.

The hippocampus circled them, chattering and snorting, her front hooves pawing at the water as her strong tail drove her forward. Julie reached out and trailed her fingers through the soft mane, the wet hairs curling around her fingers.

Taylor struck out for the surface. Julie followed him, sucking in a long breath of cold air and shaking her short hair back when she broke through. "Wow!"

Beside them, the hippocampus' head broke the surface, water spraying from her blowholes. She studied them with big brown eyes, then dove again and disappeared into the clear water.

"Okay." Julie turned to Taylor. "This is officially the coolest place ever."

Taylor laughed and paddled closer to her. "I'm so glad you like it."

Julie wrapped her arms around his neck, and their legs brushed as they trod water. Her world filled with his smell, the fresh earthy aroma of rain. "I like *you*, my petrichor prince," she whispered.

This time, when Taylor pulled her in for a long kiss, there was no one to interrupt them.

They stretched out on the warm sand, Julie's muscles pleasantly tired from swimming, and lay watching the hippocampus play with the gold geese. In the woods, a flock of tiny firebirds sang, their flaming feathers not harming the green leaves.

Julie's arms were tired from propping up *Anna Karenina*. She lowered the book to her chest and sighed.

"You okay?" Taylor asked, stirring beside her.

She allowed herself to gaze at him for a few moments. He was only wearing his swimming trunks, and she hadn't noticed how much muscle he'd put on until now. "Mmhmm," she murmured. "Wondering if you're going to go get us some lemonade."

"Sure, you can get your petrichor prince some lemonade." Taylor lay back, grinning.

Julie poked him in the ribs. "I knew I shouldn't have said that."

"Ow!" Taylor curled up. "Hey, I liked it."

"You've repeated it six times since I said it an hour ago." Julie poked his belly this time. "You're being insufferable."

"Your insufferable petrichor prince." Taylor grinned.

"Fine. We'll make it part of your title." Julie lay back on the sand, smirking. "Commander Taylor Woodskin, Petrichor Prince of the Aether Elves. I'm sure your parents will love that one."

"Noooo," Taylor moaned.

"We can put it on a plaque on your office door." Julie spread her hands, visualizing it. "Taylor Woodskin, Julie's Petrichor Prince."

"Stop it." Taylor tickled her armpits.

Julie grabbed his index finger and twisted it deftly, stopping before causing actual pain. "You stop it!"

"Ow, ow, ow!" Taylor tapped her arm, breathless with laughter. "I yield!"

Julie giggled and let him go, and they flopped down on the sand again. Fluffy white clouds obscured the sun, and there was a distant rumble of thunder, promising a rainy afternoon of reading.

"Seriously, though." Julie rolled onto her elbow, looking at him. "What *do* you want, ultimately, on that plaque?"

Taylor ran a hand through his damp hair. "I don't know. I've already exceeded my own expectations, and I love my job as it is." His eyes slid to her. "It's my home life that I want to change."

"Oh?" Julie propped her head on her hand. "How so?"

"I don't know. I feel like I've outgrown my suite in the Aether Compound. It's a bachelor pad for a spoiled prince working a nothing job to stay out of his family's way," Taylor admitted. "Which was exactly who I used to be."

Julie smiled. "I think you always were the person you're becoming. Smart and strong and independent. It was just hiding back then."

Taylor's eyes met hers. "You saw it in me, though. You were the only one who did."

"Oh, stop it, you." Julie flapped a hand at him, her cheeks coloring.

"How about you?" Taylor asked. "Are you planning to be a soldier for the rest of your life?"

"I'm happy where I am, and I love it." Julie rubbed her chin. "Although I think my meeting with Lotan showed me that I do want more. Maybe I'll get it when I start slowly climbing the ranks in the military. I hope to be an officer someday. My fae powers could change a lot of things, so maybe it'll be possible."

"I think almost anything is possible for you," Taylor murmured. "Lieutenant Julie Meadows, Commander of the Military. Ooooh!" He grinned. "*Captain* Julie Meadows."

Julie burst out laughing. "Don't let Kaplan hear you say that. He'll kill us both."

Taylor grimaced. "Kaplan's been wanting to kill us since the day I romantically carried you into his office when you passed out after eating mushrooms."

"Romantically?" Julie grinned. "Oh, yeah. That was when you fell for me. At first sight."

Taylor scoffed. "Uh, no way. *You* were the one who fell for *me*.

The day that I saved your life when you nearly fell out of the Statue of Liberty."

"You did not save my life." Julie snorted. "I was fine. I had it under control."

"You were three hundred feet above the ground. *I saved your life*." Taylor lay back, interlacing his hands behind his head. "Then you looked into my heroic eyes, and you fell for me."

"Fine. Maybe you saved my life a little, but I didn't fall for you then." Julie grinned. "You fell for *me* right after that when we were fighting yetis and you saw my amazing warrior power!" She flexed her biceps. "You were head over heels for me when I fainted in the alley from my concussion and nearly face-planted onto Genevieve."

"Oh, you mean when I had to sit through a night of your mom and Lillie ogling me?" Taylor raised an eyebrow. "Romantic stuff."

"Face it. You were wild about me from that moment onward." Julie smirked.

"Nuh-uh. You fell for *me* when we fought the undead army at Haunted Hill. You were crazy about how majestically I shot Robin's bow." Taylor mimicked the movement, tipping his head back.

Julie rolled her eyes. "Sure I did, babe. I especially liked the part where you nearly got strangled by a banshee. *So* sexy."

"I had that under control." Taylor rolled onto his side and propped himself up on one elbow. "I had her right where I wanted her."

"Of course you did," Julie teased.

Taylor reached out and traced the outline of her cheek and jawline. "Okay, fine," he murmured. His voice was deep and soft. It gave her goosebumps. "Maybe I did know you were special from the moment I stepped into the cafeteria and saw you sitting there, staring at the buffet like you hadn't eaten in weeks."

Julie met his eyes. "I know the moment I fell for you."

"Oh?" Taylor's smile crinkled the corners of his eyes.

"It was when Lillie was sick." A lump formed in Julie's throat. "We were in the hospital. I'd been with her for hours, and I was so cold and so hungry. You appeared out of the blue with gyros."

Taylor lowered his eyes but let his fingers roam down her neck to her shoulder and arm. "I remember," he murmured.

"I'll never forget that," Julie managed.

Taylor wrapped his arm around her and pulled her closer. "I'll never forget *this*." He pressed his lips to hers, his big hand spread out over her lower back, her chest tight against his. Their feet tangled together, warm and sandy, their damp arms draped over one another, and his lips were slow on hers, luxuriant, rejoicing.

As kisses went, Julie admitted to herself, it *was* pretty unforgettable.

CHAPTER ELEVEN

"Eggy!" Julie held out her arms.

Emerging from the darkness, Alugon let out a deep sigh. He cradled the dragon egg in his arms. "I *wish* you wouldn't call it that."

"I've missed it." Julie looked up at him expectantly.

"Oh, all right." Alugon lowered the egg into her arms.

They stood between the two animated stone dragons at the entrance to the Deep, the sky clear yet black and moonless above them. Alugon regarded her with amber eyes, his glow illuminating the patterns of gold, blue, and purple on his bald head and bare hands. "You look well, Julie of the Meadows."

"Aw, thanks, Alugon. I just had the best weekend with my boyfriend." Julie smiled fondly. "He's just gone back to HQ."

"Good." Alugon chuckled.

Julie hugged the egg to her chest. "Oh!"

"What is it?" Alugon asked.

"I-I can feel its heartbeat," Julie whispered. She gazed at the obsidian egg, feeling the soft thump of the dragon's heart within. "Even without being on the stone."

Alugon's smile flashed. "Come. Let's see what progress we can make this day."

He strode down the narrow path, and Julie followed him to the great flat stone with its flowing runes. Alugon gestured to it and stepped back. Julie laid the egg in its usual spot and sat beside it.

"Take your time," Alugon rumbled. "Breathe slowly."

Liquid moonlight poured into the runes as Julie crossed her legs, rested her hands on her knees, and took slow, deep breaths. Awareness crept across her skin. She could feel the rattle of the tram at the bottom of the mountain far below, the soft touch of silver starlight on her skin, and the steady thump of the unborn dragon's heart.

"Good," Alugon murmured. "Very good."

Slowly, Julie extended her hand to the egg and lowered her fingertips to its smooth surface, then gasped. She'd felt more than a heartbeat, more than movement.

A presence.

Trembling, almost too scared to breathe in case she made it disappear, Julie pressed the egg's surface harder. Something stirred, both within the egg and deep within her chest. It was incoherent, but there was curiosity and familiarity in it. She could feel the slow movement of fluid inside the egg and the baby dragon's heartbeat—and a flicker of consciousness reaching for her.

"I can feel it," Julie whispered. "Alugon, *I can feel it!*"

Inside the egg, the dragon flinched. Startled, Julie snatched her hand back with a gasp. Horror clawed at her chest. "I frightened it," she cried. "Alugon—"

"It's all right." Alugon smiled. "You did no harm."

"I felt it. More than its heartbeat. Its mind, almost." Julie's eyes widened. "It was reaching out to me. It felt like it was inquisitive about me."

"Of course it is. Its bond with you is strong if it has matured in a single moon to the point where you can feel its presence." Alugon's grin widened. "The unborn heir is developing well."

Julie's shoulders sagged in relief. She rested her hand on the egg, palm flat, feeling the thud of its heart. "I'm glad to hear it. I know I should spend more time with it."

"There is no need for haste." Alugon spread his hands. "I have spoken to the mother of the egg."

Julie's eyes widened, and she shifted closer to the egg. "Does she have a bond with it too?"

Alugon chuckled softly. "There is no need for jealousy, Julie of the Meadows. The bond between dragon and fae is unique."

Julie's cheeks heated. "I wasn't jealous. Okay, maybe a little, but I know it's silly. Anyway, what did she say?"

"She is prescient," Alugon told her. "She has looked into the future and seen that the longer it takes for the egg to hatch, the more powerful the heir will be. We must take our time and allow the egg to develop slowly and completely. Our monthly schedule has been working well."

"Wow." Julie blinked at the egg. "That's good news." She stroked its surface. "You hear that, Eggy? Take all the time you need. Cook until you're done!"

"I *wish* you wouldn't call it that," Alugon grumbled.

Julie watched the faint light of the new moon soak into the surface of the egg, which drew it in as thirstily as dry ground draws rain. "The heir," she whispered. "I keep forgetting that this is more than just a baby dragon. It's a baby dragon who will be the king or queen someday."

"That is correct, Julie of the Meadows." Alugon came closer, gazing at the egg. "It is royalty of the highest order."

A shudder ran down Julie's spine, and she looked up at the adult dragon. "Can I ask you something?"

Alugon arched an eyebrow. "When did you start asking for permission?"

"It feels like everywhere I go, I run into royalty." Julie bit her lip. "Malcolm Nox and I became friends totally by accident. Taylor happened to sit next to me on my first day at the PMA, and now the dragon egg."

She glanced at it. "I just want to understand why that keeps happening to me. It's not like I seek out royals to hang out with. It makes me wonder who I am and why I feel connected to royalty. I'm a nobody. Why does this keep happening?"

Alugon folded his arms with a rustle of robes. "The lowliest Lunar Fae is capable of the most incredible feats," he rumbled. "Your inner magic is inexorable, like the tide. What you choose to do with your lives—all of you—has an impact, whether it be for good or ill."

"Poetic, yet cryptic." Julie sighed. "I just want to know who I am now, Alugon."

The dragon laughed. "Julie of the Meadows, you have always known exactly who you are."

"Who I was born as, then." Julie returned his smile. "Isn't there anything more you can do to break the concealment spell?"

"Your spell will break when it is time, young one." Alugon's tone was gentle. "Until then, you must make use of your bond with the egg to access your magic."

"Okay." Julie hesitated. "Last time I was here, I could call down rain afterward. It's not consistent."

"You will gain more control over your power as you strengthen your bond with the egg," Alugon told her. "Try again now. Concentrate on the feeling of the moonlight flowing through you. Focus on its energy. You draw your strength from the moon. Keep your eyes upon the source of your power."

Julie nodded and took several slow breaths. "Okay. I can do that."

She pressed her palm to the egg again, bowed her head, and focused. The presence was discernible, but she could sense timidity in it. Instead, Julie listened to the heartbeat of the dragon, then tipped her head back and felt the faintest touch of moonlight on her skin from the sliver of moon that hung in the sky. She felt its power coursing through her and its energy in her veins.

Now to *do* something with that energy. Call down rain? No, there wasn't enough moisture in the sky. Something else, then. *Anything* else. Julie gritted her teeth, feeling the energy and willing it to do *something*, but it felt like pressing against a giant cobweb: pliable yet impenetrable. She pressed against it again, frustrated by the block. Power built in her chest, but it couldn't break through the invisible wall that held her magic back.

Inside the egg, the unborn dragon stirred. There was caution but also empathy. Julie clung to the power building in her as she felt its consciousness gently nudge hers. She could almost feel the sinuous curves of the dragon wrapping around her as it pressed against the spiderweb wall that was holding her magic back.

It was time to try again. The knowledge seeped into her from nowhere and everywhere at once. Mustering her strength, Julie threw her willpower against the invisible wall, and this time, she was not alone. There was a surge of strength from the dragon egg, and the wall snapped like a thread.

Julie's eyes flew open and she gasped, throwing her hands forward as though she was falling.

"I have you!" Alugon grabbed her hands. "I have you."

"What happened?" Julie stared up at him.

Alugon chuckled. "I'm not sure, but *something* did." He nodded at the egg.

Julie stared at it. The egg was glowing silver, every inch of its black shell covered in light.

"Eggy?" Julie whispered, extending a hand toward it.

Her fingertips brushed it, and a brief sense of elation rushed through her before the glow faded and the egg went back to being obsidian.

"What happened?" Julie asked.

"You unlocked some part of your power with the help of the dragon egg," Alugon explained.

"What part?" Julie looked down at her hands, turning them this way and that, but they didn't look any different.

Alugon smiled. "That is for you to find out, Julie of the Meadows. Give it time."

"It feels...it feels amazing." Julie wiped the sweat from her face. "I feel flushed."

"That is the magic." Alugon smiled, but it quickly faded. "There will be consequences for this."

"Consequences?" Julie asked.

Alugon gathered the egg in his arms and turned to go. Julie slipped off the stone and followed him, her body still trembling.

"It will be obvious to some that you are a Lunar Fae." Alugon spoke over his shoulder as he walked. "Be prepared for their reactions. Not everyone will be glad to see one of the Lost returned."

A shiver crept down Julie's spine. She instantly thought of Morgan Le Fay, who had told her that she could be in grave danger.

They reached the entrance to the Deep, and Alugon turned back to her with a soft smile playing on his lips.

"Fear not, young one," he murmured. "Whatever faces you, you have the strength within you to stare it down."

"Thanks, Alugon." Julie smiled at him, then brushed her fingertips across the surface of the egg. "Bye, Eggy. Be good."

Alugon turned and disappeared into the Deep. "I *wish* you wouldn't—"

The rumbling of the stone rolling closed over the entrance cut off the end of his sentence.

After paying an exorbitant fee for parking her car for three whole days in Manhattan, Julie drove back to HQ in Staten Island unusually slowly and in silence.

"I don't get it, Gennie," she told the Mustang out loud as she turned down the broad street leading to HQ. "I *felt* something happen, but I'm not shooting lightning out of my ass or anything. How can I have unlocked something, but I don't even know what it was?"

Genevieve answered with a throaty roar as Julie revved the engine at the gates of HQ. The guard, a Copper Dwarf, gaped through the window of the gatehouse as the gates swung open.

"Morning, Fred!" Julie called, waving.

Fred stared after her.

"Okay, then," Julie muttered. "Be unfriendly."

She steered Genevieve into the quiet, empty garage and pulled her dust cover on. After giving the Mustang a friendly pat goodbye and handing a sugar cube to Sleipnir, Julie made for the military wing.

She pulled out her phone and shot Taylor a quick text.

Safely at HQ. See you for lunch, assuming no mission?

She added a string of goat emojis. Before she could return her phone to her pocket, it buzzed, and Rosa's name popped up on the screen.

Julie stifled a sigh and answered. "Hey, Mom."

"*Juliaaaaaaaaaaaa!*" Rosa squealed in her ear. "How was the weekend with Taylor? Tell me everything. Every detail!"

Julie felt her cheeks warming. "I'm pretty sure you don't want *every* detail, Mom."

Rosa let out a throaty chuckle. "That good, huh?"

"*Mom!*" Julie moaned. "I didn't mean it that way!"

"Don't worry, baby. Momma's not going to pry. I just wanted to know if you enjoyed it," Rosa assured her.

The memories made Julie's lips curl into a smile. "It was amazing, Mom. And thanks for everything. I know you helped him plan it."

"Anything for you, honey. Do you still have aloe vera juice?" Rosa asked.

Julie wondered how many dusty boxes of juice had piled up on the front step of her apartment by now. The thought sent a pang of sorrow through her belly. "Yeah, I'm good," she mumbled.

She passed a gaggle of new recruits in plain navy uniforms as she approached the front door. As one, they turned and gawped at her. Annoyed, Julie flipped them off. What were they staring at?

Rosa prattled on about their weekend in the Palisades. "And let me tell you, honey, the effect that that juice had on Ernesto's ability to get a—"

"I don't want to know, Mom." Julie held up a hand. "I seriously don't. I've got to go now. You have a good day, okay?"

"You too, baby. Let me know when you're in town again. I miss you." Rosa's voice was gentle.

Julie let out a breath. "Yeah, I miss you too," she admitted. "Love you."

"Love you, sweetie." Rosa hung up.

Julie stuffed her phone back into her pocket and stepped through the front doors, then made straight for the hallway to the barracks. A trio of Logistics brownies hustled past her, turning their heads to gape at Julie as she passed.

"Why is everyone staring at me?" Julie glanced after them. "Do I have something in my teeth? Or… Oops!"

She'd almost crashed into Ellie Feathertouch, the PMA agent who'd been Julie's first recruit.

"Oh, hey, Ellie!" Julie grinned and stepped back.

"Hi, Julie!" Ellie looked up from the open file in her hands. "How are…" Her voice trailed off, and her huge amber eyes widened. The file dropped from her hands to the floor, papers scattering everywhere.

"What? What is it?" Julie ran a hand over her hair. "*Is there something in my teeth?*"

"Wh-what happened to you?" Ellie gasped.

"What?" Julie looked down at herself: purple slacks, black shirt, boots. Same as ever. "What do you mean?"

"Julie, you're *glowing.*" Ellie blinked. "You probably can't see it, but you're projecting a fae aura. It's silver." Her eyes widened. "Like moonlight."

"Moonlight?" Julie's heart thudded, and she remembered Morgan's words at Tintagel about how the concealment spell was keeping her safe. *Not everyone will be glad to see one of the Lost returned.* Alugon's words also echoed in her mind.

"Are you okay?" Ellie asked.

"Yeah, I-I just…I need to get to Hat," Julie blurted.

She ducked her head and bolted down the hall, dodging everyone she saw, her heart racing. She'd never felt so naked. Nausea churned in her gut when she finally reached her room and hauled the door open, then tumbled inside and slammed it shut behind her. Pressing her back to the door, she stared into the room, faintly hoping that Jae would be there. However, all four bunks were empty. Even the tiny faerie houses in the rafters were silent.

"Hat," Julie croaked.

The navy service cap dotted with gold insignia on her nightstand stirred to life. "Oh, hello, Julie," Hat began. "How was—"

He stopped. "No, no, no, no!"

Julie stumbled over to Raven's nightstand, on which an extravagant gold-edged mirror took up most of the space, and peered into it. It felt as though the ground had dropped out from under her feet.

She *was* glowing. Soft silver light oozed from her skin, and there was something else. She had always been pretty, but there was a new sharpness to her features, and her eyes seemed to be changing color as she stared at them.

"What's happening?" Julie stumbled back from the mirror, heart racing. "Hat, what's going on?"

"It's too soon," Hat moaned. "*It's too soon!*"

"Everyone can see that I'm fae." Julie's gut lurched. "I-I can't pass for human anymore. Everyone will know I've been hiding something."

"Never mind that!" Hat snapped. "Whoever your parents hid you from… Whoever was so dangerous that you had to be disguised as a human and smuggled out of the paranormal world and kept hidden even now, they might be able to find you."

A shudder ran down Julie's spine, and it didn't stop there. It felt as though the floor itself juddered under her feet. Julie yelped and glanced around as Raven's Malcolm Nox poster fluttered loudly against the wall.

"Julie, you need to calm down," Hat ordered.

"Why? What's happening?" Julie cried, and this time there was no doubt. The floor trembled under her feet, the entire building quaking with a terrible moan that rose from its tortured foundations.

"*Calm down!*" Hat yelled unhelpfully.

The floor bucked wildly. Julie fell forward, and her hands slammed down on the floor. Dust puffed off the walls. Raven's mirror fell and shattered, fragments of glass scattering across the floor.

"Julie!" Hat cried.

"*Help!*" Julie yelped, shaking uncontrollably.

Cracks spread on the walls, black and ominous, and the faerie houses rattled on the rafters. Julie tried to get up, but the floor was shaking too much. She fell back to her hands and knees.

The door banged open and Bianca leaped into the room with a broadsword in her hands, red magic glowing between her fingers. Her golden curls were wild around her head, and her blue eyes were filled with fire.

"Help!" Julie squeaked.

Bianca's jaw dropped. She stared around the room, then at Julie.

"Bianca, please," Julie sobbed.

"Well, shit," Bianca stated. "We need to go to the ER." She strode over to Julie and gripped her arm. "It's okay. I'm here."

Bianca's steady grip allowed Julie to take a deep breath for the first time in what felt like hours but had likely been less than two minutes. The quaking under her feet subsided.

"That's it, girlfriend," Bianca soothed. "I've got you."

The building's rocking slowed, then stopped. Julie blinked at the floor, its surface cracked and dusty under her feet, then stared at Bianca.

"Did…did *I* do that?" she quavered.

"Looks like it." Bianca grinned cheerfully. "Let's get you checked out. And the captain needs to know about this, as well as Droppelheimer."

"Bianca, there's something I need to tell you," Julie began.

Bianca raised an elegant eyebrow. "Something the Lunar Fae aura glowing in your skin hasn't already told me?"

Julie hesitated. "Uh, no."

"Good!" Bianca grabbed Hat from the nightstand and rammed him onto Julie's head. "Let's go."

Before they could set off, an elegant, pale-skinned elf with pitch-black hair stepped into the room, wearing the purple jumpsuit of a PMA medic. "Oh, hey, girl." She grinned at Bianca, then at the destruction in the room. "Did you do this?"

"Not exactly." Bianca nodded at the star of life symbol on the medic's chest. "Can you get us to the ER right away? We don't need anyone to see us. Then keep looking for any injured, though I doubt anyone was hurt."

"Sure." The elf touched the star of life, and a shimmering

portal appeared in the air beside Bianca, offering a glimpse of a hospital bed. "See you around, B."

"See ya." Bianca gave the elf a jovial high-five before leading Julie through the portal.

They emerged beside one of the ER beds, as crisp, white, and clean as the rest of the large room. Two nurses in purple scrubs stood chatting beside the reception desk just across the room, and they both turned to stare at Julie.

Bianca grabbed the curtains and drew them shut around the bed. "Get me Olena stat!" she yelled at one of the nurses, then grinned at Julie. "I've always wanted to say that. Isn't it a great word? I have no idea what it means, but it lights a fire under any medical ass."

Julie perched on the edge of the bed. "Am I still glowing?"

"Magnificently," Bianca told her. "It suits you."

Yes, but it also endangers you, Hat murmured.

Do you want me to cause another *earthquake, Hat?* Julie demanded. *You're not helping.*

Hat winced. *Sorry. You're not the only one who panicked.*

It's okay. I just hope we can figure out a way to stop this. Julie hesitated. *What did you mean when you said it was too soon?*

Before Hat could answer, the curtains twitched aside, and Dr. Olena stepped in. The pretty Sylthana Elf had dark rings under her eyes and a coffee stain on her usually spotless white coat, but she managed to smile at the sight of Julie.

"Julie! Wow! You're—"

"Glowing, I know." Julie grimaced. "I'm not supposed to be."

Dr. Olena studied her, head to one side. "You don't seem happy or surprised that you are a Lunar Fae?"

"I've known for a while," Julie admitted. "It's supposed to be a secret to keep me safe."

"I see." Dr. Olena smiled and rested a hand on Julie's knee. "Still, I'm glad you finally know what you are. I know it was bothering you."

"She also accidentally caused an earthquake," Bianca interjected.

"Oh, that was you?" Dr. Olena raised an eyebrow.

"Yes." Julie lowered her head to her hands. It was aching. "I'm sorry. I didn't mean—"

"You're not the first person to nearly knock the building down with accidental magic, girlfriend." Bianca slapped her on the back. "Don't worry about it. Engineering will have it fixed in a matter of minutes."

The curtains flew aside, and Kaplan strode into the tiny space, filling it with his broad-shouldered presence. "Meadows!" he barked.

Julie straightened. "Sir!"

"Did you just nearly bring the barracks down?" Kaplan thundered.

"Sir, I—" Julie began.

Droppelheimer appeared beside Kaplan, somehow squeezing into the last drop of space. "Major, what is the meaning of all this?"

"Can you two boys calm down?" Bianca planted her hands on her hips. "We're going through a little crisis here, and your blustering isn't helping."

"You'll both need to wait outside." Dr. Olena put a protective hand on Julie's shoulder. "I need to run a few tests on Julie. *Then* you can get all your questions answered."

Grumbling, Kaplan stormed off to the waiting room. Droppelheimer followed more serenely. Dr. Olena opened a nearby drawer and pulled out a fistful of blood tubes. "Remember these?"

Julie grimaced. "Yeah."

"Sorry. I just need to check a few things." Dr. Olena wrapped a tourniquet around Julie's arm. "Sometimes, a sudden burst of magic can cause physical damage."

"I feel okay now, except for a headache," Julie admitted.

"Let's make sure you *are* okay before we throw you to the wolves," Dr. Olena quipped.

Julie winced. "They're not wolves. They're an orc and a huge guy who can turn into a tiger."

"Don't worry, sister. We've got you." Bianca patted her on the back.

Julie managed a grateful smile.

CHAPTER TWELVE

Dr. Olena kept Julie hidden with a lab coat around her shoulders for the short trip across the ER to the private rooms at the back of the medical unit, although, when they went inside, this room was anything but private. Kaplan paced the floor, muttering to himself. Droppelheimer leaned against the back wall, and Taylor sat in an armchair.

He shot to his feet at the sight of Julie and rushed over to her. For a moment, she thought he'd grab her hands and give another heartfelt panicky speech, but to his credit, Taylor stopped a few feet short of her. "Uh, I brought you this." He held out a navy PMA hoodie.

"Thank you," Julie murmured. After handing Dr. Olena's coat back to her, she took the hoodie and pulled it on, then zipped it up to her chin. It hid most of the silver glow.

Taylor rested a hand on her shoulder. "You okay?"

Julie nodded. "I'm fine."

"Is she?" Kaplan demanded of Dr. Olena.

The elf smiled. "Julie's in excellent health, Captain. She was lucky this time. The uncontrolled magic outburst didn't do anything to harm her or anyone else."

Taylor let out a breath, and his shoulders sagged.

"That *is* good news, Doctor." Droppelheimer straightened. "Although surprising, considering Private Meadows is listed on our system as human." He raised an eyebrow.

Kaplan turned to the orc. "Cadmeus, we've known for some time that Meadows here is not human. She is fae."

"Lunar Fae," Julie added quietly. "I've kept that secret."

"*Lunar* Fae?" Droppelheimer's composure slipped, and his hands dropped to his sides. "Really?"

"Yep," Bianca confirmed. "She's been under a concealment spell all her life. Thanks to her bond with the dragon egg, it's weakening."

Julie flashed her a grateful smile, glad she'd shared the whole story with her while Dr. Olena had been conducting her tests.

Taylor stepped forward. "She had to keep it secret, sir. It's to keep her safe." He squared his shoulders. "I was the only person who knew."

Kaplan waved a hand. "I'm aware of the risks Lunar Fae run, Woodskin." His bushy eyebrows drew together like bulls locking horns in a fight. "I'm just surprised that Meadows didn't consider that if we *had* known, we could have taken steps for her protection."

"Perhaps that is why we weren't told, Jack." Droppelheimer smiled faintly. "We all know how Meadows feels about being protected."

Kaplan rounded on Julie. "Is that true, Meadows?"

Julie squared her shoulders. "I'm not interested in being caged, sir. I want to serve the PMA, and I've been doing a good job of it as a human." She tipped her chin up.

Kaplan's eyebrows were in danger of getting seriously tangled, and his massive hands curled into fists. Julie gritted her teeth, ready for a shouting match, but after a moment, Kaplan's shoulders sagged.

"I understand that, Meadows." His voice was unexpectedly soft. "But you have put yourself at risk by not taking the advantage of training to get your new powers under control."

Julie sat on the edge of the bed, her body aching with exhaustion. "I'm sorry," she admitted. "I thought I was going to get wings, not the ability to bring the building down around me!"

Kaplan sighed, pinching the bridge of his nose. "You have no idea what Lunar Fae are capable of or the dangers that face them." He looked up sharply, his eyebrows butting heads again. "The only people who know what Meadows is are standing in this room, correct?"

"Well, and Alugon," Julie added.

"Fine. *Apart* from cryptic dragon shifters, we are the only people who know she is a Lunar Fae." Kaplan swept the room with a burning glare. "No one in this room will divulge that to *anyone*. Understood?"

Everyone murmured their agreement at once.

"Private Meadows, you're not wrong when you say you've been doing well in your Griffin unit." Droppelheimer sighed. "But I will have to suspend you from active duty until you get your powers under control. You understand why. You place your entire unit and the objective of every mission in danger by emitting uncontrolled bursts of magic."

Julie wanted to protest, but she knew he was right. "I accept that, sir."

"We need to get you trained *now*," Kaplan barked. He raked a hand through his hair. "There are so few Lunar Fae left. I could ask Penelope—"

"I have a better idea, sir." Bianca stepped forward, grinning. "An old friend of mine will be able to help."

Kaplan gave her a long look, then nodded. "Very well, Hartshorn, but there is the little matter of your role as the commander of our military branch to deal with."

"I'll have the time to help Julie if I can have an assistant take over my managerial duties for a few weeks, sir." Bianca tossed her horns.

Kaplan grinned, showing off rows of sharp white teeth. "That works for me. I think Malcolm has been getting bored on the recruitment floor." His grin widened. "He needs to experience every branch of the PMA."

Bianca burst out laughing. "Don't you worry, sir. I'll make sure he gets the *full* experience."

"Poor Malcolm," Taylor whispered to Julie.

She managed a slight chuckle, and a relieved smile blossomed on Taylor's face.

"The matter is settled." Kaplan nodded sharply at Julie. "Meadows, you will train with Hartshorn, get your powers back under control, and rejoin your unit as soon as possible. Your training starts immediately."

"Not quite *immediately*." Dr. Olena crossed her arms. "Julie will need a few days of rest and more tests to be sure she's fit to begin training. Hopefully, her aura will also fade during that time since all Lunar Fae have the strongest auras at the new moon."

"Do I have to stay here?" Julie asked, dismayed.

"It's the safest place for you right now, Private." Droppelheimer's voice was gentle. "No one will see you here, and until your aura fades, you need to stay hidden."

"I'll visit." Taylor squeezed her shoulder. "All the time."

"Enough." Kaplan waved a massive hand. "Meadows, you will not leave this room without permission, do you understand? And Hartshorn, speak to your friend. I need Meadows back in Griffin Seven *now!*"

Kaplan stormed out of the room, followed by Droppelheimer and Bianca. Julie glanced at Taylor. "Was that a compliment?"

Taylor laughed and put an arm around her shoulders, then planted a kiss on her cheek. "Maybe."

She leaned into him. "Thanks for being here."

"Any excuse to spend time with my beautiful, smart Lunar Fae girlfriend." Taylor winked.

Julie stared down at her hands. "Lunar Fae," she murmured. "It feels so real now."

"I should hope so," Hat interjected, "considering that you *are* a Lunar Fae."

"Yeah, but I've always *felt* human." Julie turned her hands this way and that, inspecting them. "Now I feel like everything is about to change."

She couldn't decide whether that was a good or bad thing.

Julie sat cross-legged on the hospital bed in her pink and purple pajamas, her chin cupped in her hands as she looked at the board in front of her. A series of tiny green plots of land lined the board, with a dungeon in one corner and a starting flag in another. Her token, a tiny dragon, sat down and scratched its ear with a hind paw.

"Are you ever going to make your move?" Taylor enquired.

"I'm still deciding," Julie shot back. "Should I put a village on this square or a castle on this one?" She pointed at a square with a tiny wooden fort on it.

"I'd go for the castle. That way, if I land on it, you'll ruin me." Taylor grimaced. "Considering I've already ended up in the dungeon three times, and somehow I keep missing the starting line to collect two hundred gold shekels."

Julie narrowed her eyes. "Are you just saying that because it's a bad strategy so you'll have a better chance of winning?"

"I'm your loving boyfriend!" Taylor pressed a hand to his chest. "What do you think of me?"

"Yeah, he's definitely trying to trick you," Hat opined. He was a beanie today, lying at the foot of the bed.

"I concur." Julie built a village on one of her undeveloped plots.

"Okay." Taylor took the dice. "Let me run the gauntlet." He rolled them, and his token, a prancing unicorn, trotted happily onto the plot where Julie had just built the village.

Laughing, Julie looked up at him as he sorted through the sacks of gold and silver game money. "Hey, T?"

"Yeah?" Taylor flicked a pair of silver coins in her direction.

"Thanks for spending time with me." Julie smiled. "I know you had to put in for leave to do it."

Taylor grinned. "I thought it was in the entire world's best interests not to let you sit around here getting bored in case something exploded."

"Ass." Julie prodded him with a toe.

There was a knock on the door, and Julie straightened. She was expecting Dr. Olena, hopefully to tell her that her aura was now invisible. Instead, Bianca stepped into the room, resplendent in her armor and carrying a jingling armful of Julie's uniform and weapons.

"Here you are!" She dumped the pile on the floor at the foot of the bed. "Put these on and pack for a few days' travel. Leave Hat with your hot boyfriend."

Taylor turned gray. Julie eagerly leaped out of bed, almost overturning the board. "Where are we going?"

Bianca winked. "You'll see. Meet me in the military wing. Oh, and put this on." She lifted a full-length hooded navy cloak from the pile. "You're still glowing a little."

The succubus was gone before Julie could thank her. She grabbed Hat, squeezing him in excitement. "T, could you take care of Hat?"

Hat snorted. "Take care of me? I'm not a puppy."

"Of course." Taylor beamed and reached for the beanie.

"Thank you." Julie kissed him briefly but tenderly. "I'll kick your ass in Castleopoly when I get my next leave, okay?"

Taylor wrapped his arms around her and gave her a long, heartfelt squeeze. "Go, babe," he whispered. "Go live up to everything you are."

Julie held him for a moment longer before hurrying into her uniform. Her excitement grew with every heavy piece of armor she donned.

***

After she followed Bianca through the portal, a jolt of wild joy pierced Julie like a lance.

They stood on a beach below a cave-pocked cliff. At the top of the cliff, two vast towers rose from the green hills, connected by a bridge. Banners hung from both towers, displaying a golden dragon rampant on a red field, and the crackle of pure magic in the air made a shudder run over Julie's body.

"Tintagel," she murmured. "I didn't know if I'd ever see it again."

Bianca grinned at her as the sea breeze combed her mass of curls. "Something tells me you'll be seeing a lot more of this place. Come on! Oh, and you can take your cloak off now."

Julie had kept the hood over her face as she'd hurried across campus to meet Bianca in the military wing. Dodging around a corner to avoid her unit had sucked, especially since she hated keeping her species from them. Now, with the cloak stuffed into her backpack and the breeze playing with her hair, all of that fell away as she followed Bianca along the narrow path up the cliff.

It was impossible to be anything but awed in the face of the sandstone castle that glowed upon the hills in the fading light of the setting sun. As they hiked across the hillside, feet crunching on grass and heather, Julie gazed up at the battlements and arrow slits and gates and towers.

"Pretty, isn't it?" Bianca commented, grinning at the look on her face.

"It's more than pretty." Julie glanced at her. "It feels more familiar than it should."

Bianca shrugged. "You're Lunar Fae. Tintagel's always been important to your species. Maybe that's why."

"I don't know if I like being Lunar Fae," Julie admitted.

"Well, you are one, so I guess you'll have to learn to like it," Bianca pointed out, not unkindly.

The wooden gates at the foot of the first tower were open, and the portcullis raised itself when they were a few yards away. Julie stepped beneath the iron spikes and into the inner ward, pausing to gaze at the statue of King Arthur Pendragon clutching the hilt of Excalibur.

The portcullis clanked down behind them, making Julie jump. A door in the tower swung open and a hooded figure stood silhouetted in it. The soft voice emanating from it felt as though it was shaking the stones beneath Julie's feet. "I am Morgan Le Fay, Steward of Tintagel Castle and Keeper of the Quest."

Julie bowed deeply in respect to the greatest presence she had ever seen.

Bianca threw out her arms. "Bestie!" she squealed.

A happy shriek rose from the hooded figure. Throwing back her cloak, Morgan rushed forward, arms outstretched. "Bee!"

The succubus and the fae embraced, dancing around each other with yelps of delight like little girls. Julie straightened from her bow and stood staring at them both.

"Merlin's beard, your hair's gotten so *long*!" Morgan gasped, touching one of Bianca's curls. "Are you using something new?"

"Wyvern urine. Who knew, right?" Bianca picked up one of Morgan's hands. "Bestie, this shade of polish on you is *fire*! I dig it!"

"Thank you!" Morgan blushed prettily, to Julie's shock. "I thought you'd like it. I'm so glad you came. Did you bring some new Christmas movies?"

"It's April?" Julie hazarded.

"Oh, shhh, you." Bianca waved a hand. "It's never a bad time to indulge in Christmas movies. And yes, bestie, I did bring some."

"Bee-Bee, you are the best." Morgan grinned and hugged her again. "I see you brought our Lost with you."

Bianca's eyes turned serious. She stepped back and put a hand on Julie's shoulder. "Actually, she's the reason I'm here. Julie's had a little trouble controlling her powers lately."

"My bond with the dragon egg got stronger," Julie explained. "I pushed against some kind of wall inside myself, and the dragon helped, and the next thing I knew, I was glowing and nearly knocked the HQ building down by accident."

Morgan's eyebrows rose. "I see how that could cause some difficulty."

"We're here for training, Morgs," Bianca explained.

Morgan nodded. "I can help, of course." She grinned. "But first, a banquet! My best friend is here! The wine and gossip will flow in equal measure!"

Bianca and Morgan strode into the castle arm-in-arm, and Julie followed, bemused. She'd been expecting to jump straight into training, but she could roll with this.

***

The wine *did* flow spectacularly. It was vastly different from the occasional half-glass Julie had shared with her mom since she was a teenager. That was cheap supermarket stuff, sweet and white. Morgan's jugs, which magically refilled themselves, poured forth a frothy liquid as dark as blood. It tasted wild and spicy, and it made Julie's head spin almost immediately, though Morgan and Bianca seemed capable of drinking endless amounts.

Bianca quaffed another gobletful and plopped it on the long table that ran the length of the Great Hall. The table was currently strewn with the debris of a feast that had begun with deviled eggs, continued with roast peacock and vegetables, and was slowly ending with bread pudding. This, Julie discovered as she tucked into hers, was a lot more appetizing than it sounded.

"Any development on the Kapelope front?" Morgan asked, waving a hand. One of the jugs rose into the air and poured Bianca another goblet of wine of its own accord.

Bianca picked up the goblet. "Oh, *yes!* You should have seen him when we brought Julie in, and he found out she was Lunar Fae. He immediately wanted Penelope to train her."

"Penelope, train a warrior?" Morgan chuckled. "She's a great judge, but that's not her role."

"Eh, I don't know. I wouldn't screw with her." Bianca sipped her wine.

Julie raised her eyebrows. "Kapelope?" she enquired thickly, even though she'd stopped at one goblet.

"It's their couple name. You know, Kaplan and Penelope," Bianca explained.

"Are they a thing?" Julie asked, shocked.

Morgan lolled back in her chair. "They should be."

"We ship them," Bianca announced.

Morgan cackled. "To shipping!" She raised her goblet.

"The ship will sail!" Bianca roared, clashing her goblet against Morgan's.

Julie retreated to bed after another hour and more wine. With her belly full and the quiet sound of the sea coming in through her bedroom window, she fell asleep almost instantly on the huge canopy bed.

When she woke up, it was pitch-black, and she had a dry mouth and an overwhelming need to pee. Scrambling to her feet, Julie clutched her aching head with a groan and scurried down the hallway, her bladder complaining with every step. She was so desperate that it was only on the way back from the bathroom, thankfully far less medieval than the rest of the castle, that she realized Morgan and Bianca were still at it.

She hesitated at the door of the Great Hall, steadying herself on a cast-iron candlestick, amused and ready to hear more Kape-lope theories. Instead, the first name she heard was Ilsa's.

"Ilsanthia was a more than worthy candidate." The voice belonged to Morgan, and she sounded far soberer than she had earlier in the evening.

Bianca's voice was clear and steady too. "You shouldn't have passed her if she wasn't the one who led."

"What was I supposed to do in that situation?" Morgan asked.

"Fair enough." Bianca sighed. "It's a conundrum, to be sure. Julie *has* shown command of two elements."

Morgan grunted in agreement. "So far."

Two elements? What did that mean? Julie leaned closer, hoping to peer through the crack in the door, and accidentally knocked over the candlestick. It crashed to the floor with a deafening clatter of iron on stone.

"Crap!" Julie squeaked.

She heard the scrape of chairs in the Great Hall and bolted for her room, her bare feet slapping on the stone. If she got to her room in time, maybe they'd think it was a castle ghost or some-thing. Castles had ghosts, right? As long as they didn't realize she'd been—

"Eavesdropping, were we?" Morgan appeared in the hall in front of Julie with disconcerting suddenness.

Julie's cheeks burned. "Uh, maybe a little."

The fae's beautiful features were very still, and her hazel eyes searched Julie's for a long moment before creasing into a smile. "Well, we might as well begin."

"Begin what?" Julie asked.

Behind her, Bianca chuckled. "Training, of course."

***

Julie's head hurt. She thrust a hand through her hair, trying to get rid of the ache, and peered at her two trainers. They were in the lists at the back of the castle, a sand-floored arena with a barrier down the middle for jousting that had grandstands surrounding it. The Pendragon banner snapped merrily on flag posts at the top of the grandstands, which were occupied only by Morgan and Bianca. Rich silver moonlight poured down from the full moon above.

"Access my magic?" she echoed. "How am I supposed to do that without the dragon's help?"

"We know you can do it since you caused that earthquake." Morgan sipped from a mug of hot chocolate with tiny marshmallows floating in it, looking very bright-eyed for someone who was many centuries old and had just consumed several jugs of wine.

"All you need to do is figure out how to unlock it." Bianca reached behind her and pulled out a bright purple yoga mat, almost upsetting the massive bowl of popcorn on her lap. "Here, take this."

Julie reached for it hesitantly. "What's this for?"

"Sit on it so you don't get sand in your panties." Bianca gestured. "Sit."

Julie unrolled the mat and sat down.

"Cross-legged," Bianca added. "Then put your hands on your knees, palm up, and then touch your thumb and forefinger together."

"Okay," Julie mumbled, doing as she was told.

"Perfect." Bianca grinned. "Now close your eyes."

Julie closed her eyes.

"Now focus very, very deeply on your inner power," Bianca instructed. "Block everything out of your mind. And say 'ommmm' if you want."

"Ommm?" Julie attempted. She tried reaching deep as she had done with the dragon egg, but it felt empty and pointless without having the unborn dragon beside her.

"Let's try something else," Morgan suggested.

Julie opened her eyes. "I'm down for anything."

"Good." Morgan cleared her throat. "I want you to think about the person you care for more than anyone else in the world."

"Her hot elf boyfriend." Bianca snickered and took another fistful of popcorn from the bowl.

Julie flushed, but the first person she thought of was Rosa. "Okay?"

"Now imagine they're being charged by something dangerous," Morgan went on.

"A rhino," Bianca suggested.

"A rhino." Morgan nodded seriously. "Imagine what you'll do about it, and see if you can make it happen."

Julie closed her eyes, picturing it. Her mother would probably try to sell it some kind of natural elixir of life.

"Focus, Julie," Morgan urged.

Julie tried to imagine a hulking beast lumbering toward her mom, and adrenaline surged through her veins. She thought about the earthquake and imagined opening an abyss in front of the rhino to save her mother. The rhino tumbled into the abyss… Wait, weren't rhinos super endangered? She frowned.

"Why a rhino?" she asked, opening her eyes.

Something small and white landed on her nose. Julie yelped and jumped to her feet. It was a popcorn kernel, and it was rapidly followed by another, which hit her cheek.

"Hey, cut it out!" Julie yelled.

"Stop us, Julie! Use your powers!" Morgan shouted, hurling another piece of popcorn at her.

There was a crackle of thunder, and the moonlight faded. Julie looked up. Clouds were gathering in the night sky.

"It's working!" she exclaimed.

The next popcorn hit her in the eye, making her yelp.

"Woohoo! Good shot, bestie!" Bianca offered Morgan a high-five.

They kept pelting Julie with popcorn, and the clouds rumbled above her, then a burst of rain cascaded onto the lists. Julie laughed, delighted, holding up her hands as the thin drizzle splashed her face. It was bitterly cold, but it was something.

"It's working!" she cried.

"We need you to do more than summon rain. We know you can do that from your fight at OPMA Avalon North." Morgan's voice was serious. "You're not truly accessing your powers."

Julie's shoulders slumped. "What do I need to do to access them?"

"That's what we're going to find out." Bianca stood up. "I think you need to sing!"

"Sing?" Julie squawked.

Morgan nodded vigorously, shivering as the cold rain continued to pour down on them all. "Yes! It connects you with your, uh, your inner strength!"

Julie frowned. "You're making that up."

Bianca scrambled down from the grandstand. "Sing, Julie!" she commanded. "*SING!*" She burst into the *Anthem of the Eternity Throne*, which was old, boring, and filled with Old English words Julie didn't have the hang of. Julie knew the shape of it since it was sung at all PMA events, so she joined in with difficulty. Morgan's pure voice rose. Bianca belted out the words with the enthusiasm and the pitch of a barking dog.

Nothing happened except that the rain soaked deeper into Julie's clothes. "I don't understand," she spluttered, turning to Morgan. "Why isn't this working?"

"I don't know." Morgan frowned. "This usually works."

"Well, it's not working today," Julie blurted. "Do I even *have* powers when I'm alone? I need the dragon egg!"

"You have to be able to harness your magic, Julie. Otherwise, you're a danger to yourself and others." Bianca stepped back.

Julie's annoyance rose as the rain made its icy and wet way into her underwear. It was unpleasant but far less so than the knowledge that she had to get this right to protect the people she loved and go back to doing what she wanted to do. Her hands clenched.

"This is pointless!" she yelled. "All I can do is make it rain!" A scream of anger burst from her, and fire flashed over her body.

CHAPTER THIRTEEN

The roar of flame made Julie gasp in shock. Stumbling back, she raised her hands, staring as fire—genuine yellow fire—surged over her skin. The flames licked her arms, shoulders, and legs and flickered in front of her eyes.

Then, as suddenly as it had come, the fire was gone. Julie ran her hands over her bare arms, shaking. There was no damage. She'd felt only a tickle as the flames danced on her skin.

"What! *What?*" She turned to Bianca and Morgan, wide-eyed.

Bianca snickered. "Told you she was going to be the emotional type."

Morgan sighed and handed over a small pouch of gold. "I'll get you next time."

"Wait, you guys knew this would happen?" Julie squeaked.

"We had our suspicions that you could summon fire," Morgan told her, "if we got you riled up enough."

Julie wanted to be mad about being manipulated, but instead, she found herself staring at her hands, heart thudding. "How do I do it again?" She clenched her fists and let out a half-hearted yell, but nothing happened.

"Your power over the elements is linked to your emotions," Bianca explained.

Morgan nodded. "You can use fear to manipulate earth and anger to control fire. You need to master your emotions before you can control the elements at will."

"How very kung-fu guru of you," Julie muttered.

Morgan laughed. "It's a truth even older than kung fu, Julie."

"Eh, I don't know." Bianca spread her hands. "I think a fuck-around-and-find-out approach would work just as well."

Morgan sputtered with laughter. "Well, you're not wrong."

"I like Bianca's idea." Julie snorted.

Bianca chuckled. "Okay, let's throw you off a cliff and see if you can fly."

"Bianca!" Morgan chided.

The succubus dissolved into an infectious belly laugh, and Morgan and Julie couldn't help joining in.

"Well, okay, let's discuss this over breakfast *after* some beauty sleep." Morgan got to her feet. "I could certainly use some, and I need to check on Arthur."

"Why don't you just kiss him?" Bianca asked, following Morgan back toward the tower. "He'll either come back to life or turn into a frog."

Morgan elbowed Bianca in the ribs. "You know it's more complicated than that."

"Yeah, I know, bestie." Bianca draped an arm around Morgan's shoulders. "Want me to come with you?"

"I'd appreciate the company," Morgan admitted.

Julie headed to the tower alone, changed into her pajamas, and sank into the incredible softness of the mattress. She lay staring up at the underside of the canopy, painted with an elaborate scene of a many-towered castle of white stone rising from a green landscape.

She lifted her hands and looked at them. Fire, real flames, had just...appeared all over her.

Lillie would be so proud.

The thought of her late landlady/substitute grandma made tears prickle in Julie's eyes. Lillie would have loved Bianca and Morgan, and if she'd known the paranormal world existed, she would be telling Julie to live up to everything a Lunar Fae could be.

You're a storm, not a ray of sunshine. Lillie's words, yelled on the Manhattan Bridge during a thunderstorm the day she died, filled Julie's mind. *You're a woman. You shake the world and water the earth. You hear me? You can destroy things and grow them. Don't turn your thunder down for anyone. No one.*

Julie smiled as the first rays of dawn's light pierced the window. She'd promised Lillie she would live with her volume turned all the way up. That had been the reason she'd left recruitment and joined the military instead.

"I miss you, Lillie," she whispered, "but I'm doing my best." She chuckled. "And I've found a perfect pair of hellions to help me fulfill my promise."

She rolled over, buried her face in her pillow, and fell asleep slowly, tears still staining her cheeks.

Brunch was a leisurely affair in the great hall, with late-morning sunlight streaming through the stained-glass windows. It turned into rainbows where it danced on the walls. As usual, the magical banquet table had produced a magnificent spread. Julie contentedly plowed through a heaping plate of Eggs Benedict, the Hollandaise sauce being the perfect balance between creamy and tangy.

"Okay, bestie." Bianca popped a blueberry into her mouth. "What's the plan for today?"

"Well, after our discussion last night, Bee-Bee, I think a

combination of our two approaches will work best." Morgan grinned.

"So, we're going to try controlling my emotions and find out?" Julie guessed.

Bianca laughed. "Something like that."

"I still hold that you need to learn better control over your emotions," Morgan explained. "At the same time, maybe some screwing around is in order."

"It's always in order if you ask me." Bianca smirked.

"What are we doing?" Julie ate the last bite of her Eggs Benedict.

Bianca's grin was as wide as the horizon. "We're going to have a dragon hunt you."

An hour later, Bianca, Morgan, and Julie stood on a heather-dusted hilltop a couple of miles from the castle. Its towers rose into the sky. The rest of the landscape was a dizzying array of green hills and shimmering sea.

Julie spotted the massive winged shadow on the water before she saw the dragon, who was a patch of darkness hurtling toward them over the water. The dragon was flying at an unthinkable height, the shape of his wings standing out sharply against the sky. With a flick of wings, the dragon swooped toward them. He flew in a wide arc around the trio, leathery wings outstretched and his many-colored scales flashing in the sun.

Gracefully, the dragon stretched out his legs and touched down with a final thump of wings a few yards from Julie. His giant talons churned the earth, and twin spires of aromatic smoke rose from his nostrils.

"Hey, Alugon!" Julie grinned.

"Greetings, Julie of the Meadows." Alugon's voice was deeper in his dragon form, and a fiery glow rose and fell behind the blue, gold, and purple scales over his ribs as he spoke.

Morgan bowed formally. "Thank you for coming, Deep Lord. I appreciate your presence."

Alugon chuckled. "You may dispense with the formality, Keeper. It does not go down well in present company." He winked a giant amber eye at Julie.

Bianca snickered.

"Very well, then." Morgan laughed. "Are you ready to put this one through her paces?"

"Ready and willing," Alugon rumbled.

"When they said I'd be hunted by a dragon, I didn't think it would be you," Julie admitted. "You've always encouraged me to take my time with my powers."

"I had not realized that your efforts, combined with those of the unborn dragon, had had such a profound effect." Alugon inclined his massive head. "I believed your aura would be visible to those with keen eyes."

"Keen eyes?" Julie raised her eyebrows. "Like a Woodland Fae."

"Indeed, young one." Alugon nodded. "But I did not imagine that your powers would burst out of control. It is necessary for us to train you for your safety and that of others."

"Now that you've long-windedly said everything we've already explained to Julie, shall we get down to business?" Bianca pulled out her hair tie, allowing her golden curls to rampage down her back. She grinned as she unfolded her wings.

"Indeed." Morgan gave a wild laugh and opened her hands. Droplets of water gathered in each palm, then rose to form a spinning ball that levitated. "Your aim, Julie, is to reach Tintagel alive."

Julie glanced at the castle. "*Alive?*"

"Yep." Bianca grinned.

Alugon's chuckle was like a small earthquake.

"Oh, yes. This is for you." Bianca reached behind her back and pulled out something that looked like a paintball gun except for the blue runes inscribed along the barrel. "This is a magic-nulling rifle. If its ammo hits one of us, it'll knock out our magic for five minutes."

"Knock out your magic?" Julie looked at Morgan. "Will Arthur be okay?"

"Of course. The enchantments I've woven over him will hold on their own for a time, and I'm fairly sure I could break free of the ward if I wanted to." Morgan winked.

"Am I supposed to use magic?" Julie asked.

Bianca shook her head and pointed at the sky. "Full sun. You likely won't be able to summon any."

"Instead, I want you to focus on summoning specific emotions as you head for Tintagel," Morgan interjected. She pointed at a distant Pendragon flag snapping on a pole beside the road to the castle. "From here to the flag, try to summon anger. After that, summon fear. Just hold those feelings steady."

Julie raised an eyebrow. "Why do I need to be chased by a dragon while doing that?"

"That was my part of the plan. I felt you needed a challenge." Bianca tossed her horns.

Julie clutched the rifle against her shoulder. "Last question. Do I get a head start?"

"Thirty seconds, young thing!" Bianca threw open her wings and leaped into the sky. Alugon followed, and Morgan spread her gossamer wings and fluttered after them.

"Not fair. I can't believe I don't get wings," Julie grumbled, but she set off for the nearest copse of trees at a dead run.

It seemed like much less than thirty seconds had passed when a blast of water appeared out of nowhere and slammed into Julie's ribs with the power of a river. It knocked her off her feet, and she tumbled down the hill, clinging desperately to her rifle. Surprise and pain washed through her in equal amounts. She hadn't had time to focus on anger yet, but it came on its own, running hot in her veins.

"Hey!" She rolled to her knees and brought up the gun.

Hovering above Julie's head, Morgan fired another blast of water.

Julie rolled aside and bolted for the trees again. She fired as she ran, missing Morgan by inches, then threw herself under the cover of the trees, panting.

They wouldn't protect her for long, she knew, but she had enough time to take a few deep breaths and focus on the rage boiling in her chest. *Stay angry. Stay angry!* It was easier than she'd expected. She gripped her gun firmly, inhaled, and darted deeper into the trees.

She spotted the gap ahead and was ready for the water blast when it came. She sidestepped, raised her gun, and fired. Morgan let out a yelp as the spherical round slapped her arm. "Ow!"

"Gotcha!" Julie shouted back.

"Get her, Bee-Bee!" Morgan called.

Julie put her head down and ran faster, sticking to the dense cover of the trees. At the edge of the copse, she hesitated, glancing up and around. There was no sign of Bianca, and a river wound quietly through the dale in front of her. The water was low, and there was plenty of opportunity to take cover under overhangs and the little caves she spotted in the bank.

Julie took a quick breath and charged forward. Manic laughter caught her ear an instant before a bolt of red magic slashed across her wrists, burning her skin. She squealed, then whipped around and fired, missing the succubus as she swooped toward Julie, hands outstretched and magic burning in her palms.

After firing two more rounds, both of which missed as Bianca plunged toward her, Julie fell to the ground and rolled. More magic shot over her head, scorching the green grass. The damaged areas instantly bloomed with wildflowers. It was fascinating, but Julie didn't have time to stare. She bolted, hugging her rifle, in a wild zigzagging pattern. Magic slashed into the ground on either side of her, but she kept dodging, kept going, and made it to the riverbank unscathed.

The anger was red-hot in her veins. She thought she felt heat on her skin, too, but it was hard to tell without losing focus. She leaped over the edge of the riverbank, landed heavily on the dry sand, and darted under an overhang.

Deep breaths. She channeled her anger, forcing it to calm her and slow her wild breathing. Slipping into a crouch, Julie raised the rifle and waited for anything to appear beyond the crosshairs.

There!

Julie fired. Bianca let out a yelp as the round exploded on her wing, and the magic in her hands flickered out.

"You magnificent bitch!" the succubus cheered. "Go, go, go!"

"Screw you, Bianca!" Julie roared. Anger bubbled again in her chest.

Bianca burst out laughing. "That's my girl!"

Julie scrambled out from under the overhang and ran on, zigzagging and darting, waiting for Alugon. She glanced around. Had she passed the red flag? Was she supposed to be concentrating on fear? The anger was so thick in her veins that she wasn't sure she'd be able to make the switch.

She leaped over a fallen log and landed heavily on the sand, and a fireball crackled over her head, so hot and close that it singed her arm hairs. A yelp tore from her throat, and she threw herself to the ground as the fireball crunched into the log she'd just scrambled over. It exploded into burning splinters and ash.

"Shit. Shit!" Julie shrieked, scrambling to her hands and knees. She crawled frantically under the overhang, hugging her rifle. "Are you trying to *kill* me, Alugon?"

The dragon's rumbling laugh shook the earth. He swooped past, his vast shadow falling over Julie. Clearly, turning anger into fear was not going to be a problem.

Julie panted. Alugon was heading away from her. He'd take a

moment to turn and come back. She had to move *now*. Despite the fear that froze her limbs, making them feel useless, she staggered out from under the overhang and jogged along the riverbank, glancing around as she went.

The dragon had turned around. She saw fire flickering at the back of his throat and ran faster, dodging wildly. Would it help? She heard the roar of the fireball before it came at her and scrambled sideways, tripped in the water, and fell to her knees with a splash. The fireball slammed into the river just ahead of her in a cloud of steam and smoke but was extinguished almost at once.

Maybe that was the key. The river. Julie lurched to her feet and ran through the calf-deep water, lifting her knees high with every stride. The shadow covered her again as Alugon swooped. Sucking in a breath, Julie whipped around and took aim. She couldn't miss since he was the size of a house. However, as her finger tensed on the trigger, Alugon turned deftly aside, and the round missed him by a hair's breadth.

Julie's heart hammered in her throat. She had no difficulty maintaining her fear as she ran. Her exhaustion grew worse with every struggling step she took in the water. She watched as Alugon wheeled up ahead, all wide wings and spiked tail. She needed a break. She needed—

Cover. Julie spotted the mouth of a small cave in the riverbank just ahead, half-hidden beneath the roots of the weeping willow that grew on the bank. Straining every fiber, she ran for it, spray drenching her legs. A fireball roared past and missed her by inches as she flung herself into the mouth of the cave.

It was cool inside, and Julie knew a moment's relief as she skidded into it, legs outstretched to hit the back wall. They didn't. She kept sliding, and the ground dropped away under her. She yelped as she tumbled headlong down a steeply sloping tunnel of loose earth, tiny pebbles bouncing around her as she slid.

She came to a halt at the bottom of the tunnel, breathless and battered, her rifle gone. The air smelled damp and stale. It was very quiet, and when Julie raised her head, she could hardly see anything in the faint sunlight trickling down the tunnel. The weak light showed her enough of the cavern she'd fallen into that she could tell it was huge.

Fear fluttered in her gut. *Pretty sure this is more than Morgan would think useful.* Julie took deep breaths and glanced at the narrow tunnel. Its floor was loose dirt, and she thought she could crawl back out.

"It's okay," she told herself aloud.

She rose to her hands and knees, and something stirred in the darkness.

It was huge.

Julie shimmied backward toward the tunnel, holding her breath. Maybe it had just been her imagination. Then she heard something heavy and scaly scrape the dirt and the crunch of claws. Before she could reach the tunnel, the weak light showed her the outline of a reptilian head the size of her body. The thing's nostrils flared, and as Julie's eyes adjusted to the darkness with the rapidity of terror, she made out giant red eyes that narrowed at the sight of her.

It looked draconic until it snarled. Then it showed brownish teeth at odd angles and a blunt, brutish nose. A reptilian tongue flickered between the gaps in its teeth, and a huff of rotten breath rolled toward her.

Wyrm, her training supplied. *A flightless, fireless, legless cousin of the dragons. Brutish and perpetually hungry, with a taste for flesh and fresh milk. The wyrm is an adept hunter, and its bite, so laden with bacteria as to be poisonous (similar to its distant cousin, the Komodo dragon), is almost always fatal.*

"Nice wyrm," Julie quavered.

The beast lunged. Julie threw herself aside with a shriek and rolled across the cavern floor. The wyrm's massive jaws chomped the air mere feet from Julie's body. It whipped around, several yards of sinewy coils moving against each other like the slithering of a snake, and the end of its tail wove as though it had a life of its own. Julie leaped to her feet, her heart hammering wildly, and fished for the Bowie knife in her boot.

"Come on, you ugly asshole!" she gasped, but there was no fire in her yell. She was looking at the tunnel and feeling the clutch of fear and wondering how much force it would take for that tunnel to collapse.

The wyrm let out a low hiss, its body puffing out sideways like an adder's, and raised its heavy head. Its tongue flickered, testing the air. Julie swiped at it with her knife. The creature lunged, its moribund breath washing over her, and Julie rammed the Bowie knife into its nose with all her strength. It rebounded off the scales like she'd rammed it into a brick wall and flew out of her hand, and the side of the wyrm's blunt nose slammed into her hip and knocked her to the side. She landed on her shoulder, and her head hit the dirt.

Julie scrambled back, dirt and blood mixing in her mouth. The wyrm snapped its jaws inches from her, its fetid breath filling her lungs. *I'm going to die down here.* The cavern trembled beneath her, and the wyrm paused its attack and raised its head, nostrils flaring. The cavern shook again. Tiny cracks spread through the roof. Small stones rolled from the walls to land on the trembling floor.

Julie glanced at the tunnel. Dirt filtered down from its ceiling. It was going to fall in, and she didn't have a second to lose. She scrambled to her feet and made a run for it, screaming, but the wyrm got there first. The end of its tail coiled about her chest, and her feet left the ground. She would have screamed if she'd had any air left. Instead, she landed on her back without a sound, her lungs burning, her vision blurring. The entire cavern was shaking.

A huge rock fell from the roof. Julie threw up an arm to

protect her face, but it thudded into the ground over the mouth of the tunnel, and the light faded.

"No!" she shrieked.

It was too late. Chunks of soil collapsed onto the rock, followed by showers of fine dirt, and the sunlight was reduced to chinks. The wyrm was still hunting. Its head swung toward Julie, its eyes twin spots of red light in the near-darkness. The cavern bucked around them, and more dirt rolled down the walls, encasing her legs. She was trapped.

CHAPTER FOURTEEN

The wyrm opened its jaws, and Julie raised her Bowie knife in a shaking hand. "Come at me, bitch!" she wheezed.

A deafening roar echoed through the trembling cavern. There was a crunching rumble, and more dust and dirt filled the air. Then, blessedly, fresh air and sunlight poured into the cavern. So did Alugon in human form, his hands glowing with silver magic as he stepped through the hole he'd blasted in the side of the cavern. His amber eyes locked on the wyrm, and the creature whipped around to face him.

Julie's chest rose with what felt like the first deep breath she'd taken in hours, and the tremors decreased. She kicked her feet free of the dirt and got up. The handle of the Bowie knife slipped around in her sweaty palm.

The wyrm hissed. Its tail whipped from side to side, and it lunged at Alugon. He shifted, his human form blossoming into the mighty shape of the dragon, and opened his jaws. Fire boiled in the back of his throat.

Instantly, the wyrm shrank. It cowered to the ground, its body deflating. The whipping tail stilled, and the creature's head snapped this way and that, searching for a way out.

Alugon shut his mouth with a bone-crunching snap. He lowered his head, drew back his scaly lips from teeth the length of swords, and let out a rumbling snarl.

The wyrm shrieked, then slithered toward the back of the cavern in a panicked side-to-side motion, blunt head slamming into fallen rocks and slabs of dirt as it went. The creature's movements were almost too fast to see as it shot along the back wall of the cavern, tongue flickering.

Sweat pricked Julie's palms as she watched the wyrm's frantic movements. Could it get away? Were they trapped in here with a monster? The cave floor juddered under her feet.

There was no way out. The wyrm snaked up and down the length of the cavern wall, then spun and hissed again in desperation, puffing its body up.

"It needs to escape," Alugon rumbled. "It won't go into the daylight, and you've caved in the back of the cavern. You need to open a tunnel for it to get away!"

"*Me?*" Julie shrieked, and the earth rumbled around them. "I can't. I don't know how!"

"You caused this cave-in. You can repair it!" Alugon's huge head swung toward her.

The wyrm hissed. A wave of its foul breath rolled over Julie, and she spun to face it, raising the knife. "I don't know how not to be scared!" she cried. Tiny cracks spread through the cave floor at her feet.

"Don't stop being scared." Alugon snarled at the wyrm again. "*Use* your fear! Think of all the times you've had to control your sharp tongue and use your quick wits for good instead."

Julie opened her mouth to protest but hesitated. Alugon wasn't wrong. She thought about Lotan and the way he'd responded to her, and the pressure in her chest eased.

The wyrm's hiss intensified. Its red eyes locked on Julie, and it coiled to strike.

"Now, young one!" Alugon roared.

Julie inhaled and held out her hand toward the back of the cavern. Her fear crackled in her chest, a contained ball of pure power, and the rocks and earth around her stirred in response to that power. She could feel every stone, every grain of sand, and the touch of scales slithering on dirt.

Julie pushed her power out of her chest, and the back of the cavern burst open. Dirt and rocks scattered in all directions. The huge black hole in the wall was filled with swirling dust.

With a last defiant hiss, the wyrm disappeared in a flash of scales.

There was a rumble of laughter from beside Julie, rising in pitch as Alugon shifted back to human form. He turned to her, his robes tattered and dusty. "Come on, young one." He held out a hand patterned with blue, gold, and purple. "Let's get back into the fresh air."

Julie sheathed the knife and clutched Alugon's hand in her sweaty palm. "I think I'm going to puke."

"Please refrain from vomiting." Alugon towed her to the gap he'd blown in the side of the cavern.

They scrambled over the rubble and finally, blessedly, stepped into the bright daylight and crisp air. Julie bent over, hands on her knees, and sucked in long breaths, squinting against the dazzling reflection of sunlight on the river.

"Julie!" Morgan's yell was followed by footsteps on the sand. "What happened?"

Bianca was close behind her. "Merlin's glorious round ass, you're bleeding."

Julie straightened and squeezed out a smile for them, then touched the damp spot in her hair. Her fingers came away sticky with blood.

"Are you hurt?" Morgan's hazel eyes were wide as she jogged up to Julie.

"I'm okay." Julie wiped her hand on her pants. "Just a little banged up."

"Banged up?" Bianca's eyes narrowed at Alugon. "What happened down there?"

"I sort of ran into a wyrm." Julie grimaced. "And then caused the cave to collapse around me."

Alugon put a hand on her shoulder. "She's only telling half the story. She finished by regaining control of her fears and opening the cavern so the wyrm could escape."

Morgan gasped. "You were able to manipulate earth at will?"

"Well, not like Korin does." Julie rubbed the back of her neck. "But I did move some shit around so that the wyrm could get away and quit trying to eat me."

"Yes! You glorious boss bitch!" Bianca slapped her on the back with a force that almost sent her face-first into the sand.

Morgan nodded. "You learned a valuable lesson, Julie, and far more quickly than we expected, too. I'm impressed that you could control your power in that situation."

"So, does this mean I get to go back on duty?" Julie straightened.

Alugon folded his arms with a rustle of robes. "I feel that Julie demonstrated impressive control in a difficult situation."

"Good." Bianca beamed. "Welcome back to the force, Private."

They exchanged high-fives, and Morgan wrapped her arms around both their shoulders. "But first, dinner," she announced.

There was a general murmur of agreement, and they walked back to Tintagel in the golden light of afternoon.

***

"Shit," Raven muttered, leaning back in her chair. "What a load of assholes."

Korin grunted. "I can think of a few stronger words for them."

Julie hovered at the door to the common room, peering inside. Her unit was lounging on a collection of couches and armchairs, watching a grim scene play on the TV against the wall.

It looked like news footage: a small granite fortress had gone up in smoke, and sirens and naiads in a fire engine were trying to control the familiar blue flames. Above the carnage, a Dark Moon League flag snapped on the battlements.

"We don't need to hear them, Korin," Isaiah chided. He was stretched out on the couch in his golden wolf form, nose on the armrest. "We *need* our whole unit back together."

Korin let out a sigh, her shoulders deflating. "Yeah. I hope Meadows is okay. We really need her back. I..." She paused. "I feel a little lost without her."

Julie smirked.

Really? You're going to ruin this sweet moment? Hat grumbled. She'd swung by Taylor's office to grab him and a brief kiss on her way in.

Good to have you back, you insolent piece of headwear. Julie tugged his brim.

You know *I'm a magical artifact.* The *magical artifact, arguably,* Hat snorted.

Julie ignored him. She stepped forward, spreading her arms. "Feel lost no longer, Korin! The prodigal daughter has returned."

Korin's face flushed to the shade of beet juice, and Raven flew up from her armchair. *"Julieeeeee!"* She dashed across the room and flung her arms around Julie's torso.

Julie couldn't help a burst of startled laughter. The six Weres scampered up to her, whining and barking, their wet noses shoving into her hands. Even the faeries flew a little arc around her head, then brought forth something that looked like a flower crown but turned out to be decorated with tiny rodent skulls. They placed it on her head before she could stop them.

"You're back!" Raven gave her an extra squeeze.

"Yep," Julie wheezed. "Could you, uh, not use the vamp-strength?"

"Oh. Yeah. Sure." Raven stepped back.

Jae materialized at Julie's elbow. "I'm glad you're here." She smiled and ran a hand through her long black braids.

"Seeing your face again is...tolerable," Korin growled.

Julie smiled. "It's good to be back. Looks like shit's going down." She nodded at the TV.

"Yep. The Dark Moons have escalated in response to Prince Lotan's address." Korin's expression darkened. "That's an OPMA branch near the Eyrie. Three good soldiers were killed, plus a civilian."

"Assholes." Julie frowned. "When are we going to get those suckers?"

"They've sent Griffin One." Raven rolled her eyes. "We're supposed to have *training* before we go back into the field."

"Training? What for?" Julie raised her eyebrows.

Chester jumped back onto the couch and stretched out to his full length with a yawn. "Something about the new systems and new weapons; that kind of thing. Sounds like it's going to be fun. We start tomorrow."

"Cool." Julie flopped into her usual chair. "Sounds like I got home just in the nick of time."

"Not a moment too soon, Julie." Jae fished out a smile. "We've missed your cool head."

Korin gave her a pointed look, and Julie had to hide her snort of amusement. She hadn't felt cool-headed in the cave yesterday.

That reminds me. She sighed, enjoying her familiar chair. *I'd better go to the room and do my meditation thingies before it gets busy like Morgan suggested.*

Probably, Hat agreed.

Julie got to her feet. "I'm going to unpack, guys. See you at dinner."

"We're going down early." Korin picked up the remote and flipped to a different channel. "Six o'clock start for training tomorrow."

"Looking forward to it." Julie grinned and headed to the door.

"Hey, Julie?" Jae called.

Julie turned, her hand on the doorknob, and the elf's brown eyes deepened as she smiled.

"Are you sure you're fully healed from your injuries?" Jae asked.

Julie felt a cold dagger plunge into her gut. *I hate lying to Jae.*

You need a cover story. You can't tell them you lost control of your Lunar Fae powers and needed training, Hat told her. *The thought that you were injured and the barracks damaged in an explosion involving the new thaumatech is a much easier pill to swallow.*

Yeah, yeah. Julie sighed.

"Julie?" Jae's brow creased.

Julie forced her grin back into place. "Recovered and raring to go!"

She cringed as she scuttled off to the barracks to meditate in secret.

The elevator in the military wing was much less glitchy than the one in the main PMA building. Julie was half-nostalgic for the moments when the elevator would unexpectedly spit her out into Switzerland or on a clifftop where scientists were studying rocs. This one opened obediently on a sublevel of the military wing, and they all shuffled out onto a metal walkway overlooking a space so huge that she couldn't help gasping in surprise.

Hat chuckled. *Bigger on the inside, remember?*

The space was the size of a city block. Two city blocks, Julie guessed. It was hard to tell since the edges of the room were lost in the misty darkness. Pinpricks of light in the high ceiling cast a dim glow over the scene. Julie could make out sharply cut hedges, dark and rustling, forming a massive labyrinth that covered the floor. She tried to trace a path through the maze with her eyes, but it was a crazy mess of dead ends and twists and turns.

"Whoa," Julie murmured. "I've never been down here."

Isaiah chuckled. "This is going to be fun. We were here for a training exercise once."

"Hey." Teddy looked daggers at him. "We all promised not to talk about that."

The other Weres snickered in unison.

Marching in columns with Julie and Korin side by side at the head of the line, they strode up to a huge metal platform overlooking the labyrinth. Griffin Six was already there, the unit waiting in neat ranks, as well as Droppelheimer and Sergeant Derek Adamos.

"This is going to be fun," Julie muttered to Korin.

Korin stifled a groan. Derek was a minotaur. Over eight feet tall, Droppelheimer looked like a toothpick beside him. His bull's head rose from a physique that rippled with muscle and ended in shaggy legs with cloven hooves. He held a club the size of a small tree in one hand, swinging it idly as though it weighed nothing.

Griffin Seven came to a halt in front of the two sergeants and saluted sharply.

"At ease, soldiers," Droppelheimer growled.

Julie clasped her hands behind her back and stood comfortably with her feet apart. In unison, the rest of her unit did the same, and a familiar thrill coursed down her spine.

"Your training today will be focused on introducing two of our newest upgrades to your tech and weaponry," Droppelheimer told them. "You've already visited the armory."

Both units nodded enthusiastically, and grins flashed in the gloom. Stepping into the armory had been like visiting a futuristic new world. The racks of weapons had been moved back, and they had walked into a large space lined with a long row of platforms, bordered by a white counter that offered a glimpse of tightly packed weapons racks beyond.

The moment she'd stepped onto her platform, biometrics had scanned her eyes and hands and identified her as Private First

Class Julie Meadows. With a clank of machinery and a hum of magic, her assigned armor and weapons had appeared on the counter, and a team of brownies had slapped them on her. It had taken thirty seconds to arm her entire unit.

"The weapons you are holding might look similar to the trank guns you're used to," Droppelheimer went on, "but there have been significant upgrades. Qtana and the rest of the IT department have worked out a way to stabilize Sandman dust to the point where it can be built into bullets instead of just stun grenades. Your mission is to fire these bullets directly into the faces of your targets."

Julie winced.

"The dust is contained inside a soft casing that will explode on contact," Droppelheimer added. "It causes no permanent damage, so don't hold back. Your opponents will be unharmed."

Julie glanced at her rifle, gripping it tightly. This was going to be useful. Her pistols could fire electric stun ammo, but the rounds caused damage, and the pistols were far less accurate over long distances.

"There's more." A grin flashed over Droppelheimer's face, which he quickly smothered. "Please engage your telechips."

The other members of Julie's unit touched their helmets, activating the new microchips inside. Hat was one step ahead. He hummed for an instant, and Julie blinked as the labyrinth appeared in sharp relief, the darkness banished. She could even see the walls of the huge room in the distance.

"Telechips are the cutting edge of thaumatech. They present a heads-up display—a HUD—directly into your mind, a combination of technology and Satori magic, I'm told." Droppelheimer's voice bubbled. "Qtana will continue your briefing. Over to you, Qtana."

Julie glanced around for the blonde troll, but she spoke in Julie's mind.

Good morning, Griffin Units Six and Seven. Qtana's voice

carried its usual enthusiasm. *I'm so excited to show you the cool new innovations we have developed for you!*

"Keep it professional, Qtana," Droppelheimer cautioned.

Yes, sir. Qtana cleared her throat. *Okay, teams. Sergeant Adamos will run today's exercise. It's going to be a game of capture the flag. Each unit will be given a base. Griffin Six, this is your base.*

A bright yellow arrow throbbed in Julie's vision on her left. She turned sharply and raised a hand to her face. The arrow turned into a yellow circle that pulsed over a location at the extreme left of the labyrinth.

It's like a video game! she exclaimed to Hat.

Griffin Seven, this is your base, Qtana went on.

Julie didn't jump when the white arrow appeared. She turned to her right, looking for the white circle, which was halfway down the right edge of the labyrinth.

Qtana chuckled. *Having fun yet?*

"Professionalism, Qtana," Droppelheimer reminded her.

Yes, sir. Qtana cleared her throat. *The flag is here in the center of the labyrinth.*

A blue arrow pointed at the middle of the maze, and an image of the PMA flag appeared on the lower left of Julie's vision. It revolved gently.

Your objective is to capture the flag and take it to your home base, Qtana explained. *The first unit to bring the flag to their base will be the winner. The point is not the competition, however. The point here is to get used to the new thaumatech in advance of the raids on Dark Moon cells that Captain Kaplan and Major Hartshorn have been planning.*

"Now tell them the best part!" Droppelheimer's hands curled into fists, his eyes gleaming.

Uh, yes, sir, Qtana mumbled. *To guide you through your mission and to test this tech, which I hope to issue on the next mission, you will follow Ariadne's thread.*

"Ariadne's thread?" Julie asked aloud.

Since the original Ariadne's thread, which guided Theseus through the labyrinth, was instrumental in building this piece of thaumatech, we've called it that. Qtana sounded sheepish. *No offense, Derek.*

"None taken," Derek boomed cheerfully. "Theseus was an asshole, but the thread is brilliant."

On your HUD, you'll see— Qtana went on.

"It's a guidance system that works inside your mind!" Droppelheimer burst out, waving his hands above his head. "It lays out the path you have to take next, just like Ariadne's thread. This is going to revolutionize missions in so many ways and almost completely remove the possibility of miscommunications and navigational errors!"

The units stared at him in silence.

"Put it on, Qtana!" Droppelheimer shouted.

Yes, sir. Qtana stifled a chuckle.

A silver line appeared in Julie's vision, running down the center of the night vision goggles that doubled as a heads-up display. It curved gently down the stairs to her left.

"Just follow the silver line." Droppelheimer was practically jumping up and down by this point. "Just go where it sends you, and you'll head straight to your destination!"

So, a GPS, but telepathically transmitted, Julie sent to Hat, bemused. *We were overdue for upgrades.*

Hat snorted. *That's what happens when you lock one of the most powerful magical artifacts in the world in a Warehouse for so many years.*

Droppelheimer took a deep breath and tugged his service cap, straightening it. Everyone was staring at him.

"Well, what are you looking at?" he snapped. "You have your orders. Over to you, Adamos." The orc strode away, straightening his tie as he walked.

Derek grinned, his droopy ears perking up. "To your bases!" he thundered. "I will give the go command when you're in position."

The air was filled with the deafening clatter of boots on the metal staircases leading down to the labyrinth. Julie and Korin led their unit at a jog around the outside of the labyrinth, following Ariadne's thread. They ended up at an entrance to the labyrinth, an arch of greenery, and stepped through it into a round grassy space enclosed by hedges. A gap on the far side of the space led to the rest of the labyrinth.

"Okay." Julie turned to the unit. "What's our plan?"

"Get to the flag first and avoid confrontation?" Jae suggested.

Korin nodded. "Good. If we move fast enough, they'll never catch us." She turned to the Weres. "This fancy new HUD can tell us where to go, but your noses can tell us where Griffin Six is."

"Affirmative." Isaiah slung his rifle onto his back and slipped into wolf form. The rest of the Weres followed.

"Faeries, can you fly over the hedges?" Julie asked.

"Isn't that cheating?" Raven raised an eyebrow.

Julie shrugged. "It's not cheating to use natural advantages."

One of the faeries fluttered up to the top of the nearest hedge and reached out. There was an electric crackle, and she snatched her hand back with a yelp. "Nope. There's a force field over the hedges."

"It figures," Korin growled.

"Worth a try, though." Julie looked around. "Jae, can your magic affect the hedges? As in, could you make them open a path to the flag?"

Jae shook her head. "I've tried. They're warded."

"Okay, then we have to do this the old-fashioned way," Korin concluded. "Follow Ariadne's thread."

"The Weres can go ahead," Julie suggested. "They can smell out Griffin Six, and they move the fastest of all of us. They can get the flag and head for the base, and we'll cover them from behind."

"Good idea." Korin nodded at the team. "All clear?"

There was a chorus of affirmatives, and a moment later, Derek's voice crackled in their minds.

All teams are in position. At the count of five, you may begin, he ordered.

The Weres moved to the entrance of the labyrinth and crouched, ready to sprint. Julie cocked her rifle.

Five. Four. Three. Two. The minotaur let out a rippling guffaw that dissolved into a roar. *One. GO!*

CHAPTER FIFTEEN

The Weres sprinted forward, muted barks escaping them as they ran in a tight pack. Korin and Julie followed, then Raven and Jae, circled by buzzing faeries.

Ariadne's thread twisted sharply to the left, then to the right. The Weres flowed around the tight turns effortlessly, their claws digging into the dirt. Julie's ankles protested and her combat boots strained as she threw herself around the turns. Korin had an even harder time. The dwarf's short, stout legs pistoned frantically as she strove to keep up with the Weres.

For the first few minutes, Julie focused on trying to keep the Weres in sight. Soon, though, she began to wonder what Ariadne's thread was up to. The path it took twisted and turned in wild zig-zags up and down the edge of the labyrinth. Korin kept glancing at Julie, then looking forward again, perhaps training her eyes on her silver thread.

Even the Weres' enthusiastic barks were quieter. Sweat trickled down the small of Julie's back by the time the Weres slowed to a confused trot, glancing left and right and sniffing the air. In the lead, Isaiah's and Chester's tails hung between their hind legs, and Isaiah's neat pointed ears flicked forward and back.

"This doesn't seem right." Chester stopped, and the rest of the unit stumbled to a halt behind him. "Look. We're heading directly away from the flag, and we have been for a while."

"He's not wrong." Julie squinted at the mental HUD. "The flag's behind us, and we're heading away from it."

"It *is* a labyrinth," Isaiah pointed out.

Chester huffed. "Yes, but surely we should be making *some* progress toward the flag? It feels like we're being led away from it."

"Maybe we should retrace our steps," Raven suggested. "Get back to the entrance, then split up and see who gets to the center first. We'll have a better chance of finding it then."

Julie bit her lip. "Qtana seemed very sure of her tech."

"Yeah, but we're also 'testing' it." Korin enclosed the word in air quotes. "Maybe *we're* the ones being tested. Maybe Derek wants to see us not just blindly following the new thaumatech instead of using our brains."

Julie gazed at the silver thread that stretched down the center of her vision, heading away from the flag.

"Should we vote on it?" Raven suggested.

Korin snorted. "This is a military unit, not a democracy." She turned to Julie. "What do you think?"

Julie blinked, suddenly aware that the entire unit was staring at her, even Korin. The Weres wagged their tails.

"I..." Julie paused. "I first met Qtana when her 'baby,' the IRSA 4000, accidentally drafted me into the PMA."

Korin raised her eyebrows. "Well, that inspires confidence."

"It turns out that Qbiit had been sabotaging her work on the IRSA and on other projects." Julie squared her shoulders. "Once he was out of the way—"

"You mean after his head exploded during his murder and malfeasance trial?" Raven corrected helpfully.

"Well, yeah." Julie cleared her throat. "*Anyway*, once he was out of the way, Qtana could really shine. Since then, she's done great things for the PMA. She's now the brave, intelligent troll she always had the potential to be." Julie raised her chin. "I believe in her, and I believe in Ariadne's thread. We need to keep following it, even when it doesn't make sense."

Korin held her gaze for a few moments, then nodded. "Then that's what we do. Come on. Move out!"

The Weres whirled and bolted forward, their happy yips bouncing off the labyrinth's walls. Once again, the rest of the unit followed at their best pace.

Believe in Qtana, do you? Hat sniped. *The troll who called me senile?*

Not everything's about you, Hat, Julie grumbled.

No, only most things. Hat sniffed.

The thread's path through the maze changed so gradually that it was several minutes before Julie realized that they were being led along a series of switchbacks that inched toward the center of the labyrinth. The Weres' barks grew louder and higher-pitched.

"The flag must be gone by now," Korin panted. "Griffin Six must have taken it. We wasted time by stopping."

"No!" Teddy called from the pack. "There's no one else. Just us...and Derek!"

The words had scarcely left his mouth before the labyrinth opened ahead of them. They piled into a circular open space at its center that was bathed in an ethereal light and wreathed in mist. There was a hillock in the middle of the grassy circle, and on top of the hillock was the PMA flag, hanging limp in the motionless air.

Derek stood beside the flag, and as Griffin Seven bounded into the clearing, he threw open his arms and let out an earth-shaking laugh.

"You've made it!" he boomed. "Well done. Griffin Six doubted Ariadne's thread. They wasted several minutes trying to find the trail on their own. They've only gotten back on track now."

Julie and Korin exchanged grins, and the dwarf nudged her

with a shoulder. It was the equivalent of a giant bear hug coming from Korin, and warmth bloomed in the center of Julie's chest.

Chester trotted up to the flag and transformed, then stretched out his huge hands and tugged the pole out of the ground. The rest of the unit cheered.

Julie punched the air. "Yeah, Ariadne!"

"Come on!" Chester changed back into wolf form and clutched the flagpole in his jaws. "Let's go!"

Ariadne's thread disappeared for a moment. When it returned, it led back the way they'd come. Chester let out a muffled howl and bounded along it.

"Defensive position, ladies!" Korin ordered.

The Weres moved off at a purposeful trot, and Raven and Jae ran after them, with the faeries flitting overhead. Korin and Julie followed to the edge of the labyrinth, then stopped, glancing back, guns at the ready. There was no sign of pursuers.

"I don't think they'll catch up with us," Julie muttered.

Korin shook her head. "Me neither."

In position! Raven called.

Julie and Korin broke into a run again and passed Raven and Jae, who waited with raised guns at the next corner, providing cover. They leapfrogged toward the base like this, Chester leading the way with the flag, his packmates surrounding him, with the rearguard covering the back of the pack.

The motions had become automatic during training. Go, stop, cover. Go, stop, cover. They were halfway back to their base when Julie stopped again, raised her rifle, and swept it left to right. A yeti appeared in the crosshairs.

"Shit!" Julie sputtered, her finger jumping on the trigger.

Graupel, the yeti, threw himself aside, and the ammo punched into the dirt in a puff of golden sand. Julie swung the barrel after him, but Korin was quicker. Her shot landed squarely on his nose, and Graupel's head snapped back. He blinked, raised his rifle sluggishly, and fell to his knees. The big dark eyes unfocused, and he fell forward on his face, furry ass in the air, and began to snore.

"Where are the rest of them?" Korin gasped.

Contact! Contact! a faerie screamed in Julie's mind.

They bolted down the path and rushed around a corner. The rest of the unit was in a tightly packed cluster up ahead. Chester still clutched the flagpole in his jaws. The rest of the pack was bunched around him, and a volley of Sandman bullets rose to meet the naiad towering over the group. The bullets popped harmlessly through her as if they'd been fired into a waterfall.

"Merlin's asshole," Korin cursed. "It's Minerva."

The most powerful naiad in Special Forces reared over Griffin Seven. Taller than a building, she had transformed her willowy form entirely into water. *That's how she caught us,* Julie thought dimly. *She went through the earth in the form of moisture.*

Regrettable, yet true, Hat confirmed.

Minerva let out a triumphant roar and reached for the flag with a hand the size of one of the wolves. They snapped at her, but their jaws met only water. Chester paced backward, growling.

"Chester, run!" Julie shouted, tossing her rifle into its sheath on her back.

She charged as Minerva lunged for the flag. Chester lunged back, and instead of grabbing the flag, Minerva's fingers closed around Julie. Julie had just enough time to take a deep breath before water enclosed her.

The water instantly soaked her to the skin. Julie squirmed and struck out for the surface, but she was trapped in Minerva's grip, and panic surged through her body. Bubbles streamed over her face, precious oxygen escaping her lungs, and her body screamed for her to take a breath and flail her way to safety. To—

She felt the trembling of her muscles pass into the earth.

Julie. Julie! Hat yelled. *You can't do this now. Not now!*

Julie closed her eyes and forced her limbs to grow still. Even as her burning lungs begged for air, she allowed herself to float untethered. Morgan's words, the ones she'd told her to use for meditation, drifted slowly through her mind. *Still as the moon. Serene as a calm night.*

The tremor stopped. Julie opened her eyes. *Jae!* she yelled.

Julie? Jae gasped.

Grow a black wattle. The biggest one you can! Julie shouted.

What? Jae spluttered. *Wait...oh! I understand! Because the black wattle—*

Julie finished her sentence. *Is one of the thirstiest trees in the world.*

Minerva's fingers opened. Spray and air filled Julie's world, and she gulped in a huge breath before she realized she was falling. She flailed and screamed and squeezed her eyes shut as the ground rushed up to meet her—

"Gotcha!" a faerie cried.

Julie's eyes opened. She was suspended a foot off the ground. Tiny hands clutched her clothes, and her ears were filled with buzzing.

"Thanks," she wheezed.

The faeries let her go, and she landed heavily on her hands and knees. She rolled to her feet as the eerie screech of whitewater tore the air and shadows fell over the labyrinth. Jae had both hands pressed to the dry dirt, her face twisted in concentration, and from her fingers, a tree grew at superspeed. Branches unfolded from the rising trunk, leaves burst out on the twigs, and more branches appeared at an incredible rate. As the tree grew, Minerva, screaming, shrank.

In moments, the naiad was no taller than a human. With a last defiant shriek, the water that formed Minerva bubbled, gained color, and turned to flesh. She fell to her knees, a sodden woman in a PMA uniform, coughing and gasping as she pawed at her throat.

Jae sighed and fainted.

"I've got her!" Korin grabbed Jae and flung her over her shoulders in a fireman's carry. "Go, Chester, go! Get back to base!"

Raven, the faeries, and three of the Weres guarded the back of the path, firing stun bullets into the rest of Minerva's unit. Chester, Isaiah, and Teddy bolted, the flag streaming out behind Chester as they headed for the base.

"Cover me, Julie!" Korin rasped.

Leaving the rest of the unit to hold off Griffin Six, Julie ran after Korin, rifle in both hands. "Is she okay?" she yelled.

"Breathing," Korin panted.

There was no time for talking after that, only for running. Raven and the rest caught up a few minutes into their mad dash for the base, and then it was a flat-out race to reach their base before Griffin Six woke up from their Sandman sleep. Julie thought she could hear footsteps behind her when the path curved sharply to the left, then they tumbled into their base, Chester leading the way with the flagpole still clutched in his jaws.

Derek stepped out of the hedge as the last faerie flitted through the entrance. The minotaur carried a curly ram's horn in one hand, and with a grin, he lifted it to his lips and blew it a long, solemn note. It was still ringing when Graupel stumbled to the entrance of their base, panting.

"Too late, Graupel!" Derek boomed. "Griffin Seven won the game!"

Julie whooped, and the rest of the unit broke into breathless cheering. The minotaur dissolved into thunderous laughter that resounded over the misty labyrinth.

Julie stepped out of the armory door, having returned her equipment as quickly and easily as she'd retrieved it. Raven, Korin, and a pale-faced Jae were right behind her.

"This new armory is awesome." Julie straightened Hat, in service cap form, on her head.

"Not as awesome as Ariadne's thread," Raven gushed. "That worked *very* well."

"I'll be sure to tell Qtana. I'm meeting her and Taylor and a few friends tonight." Julie grinned. "The Weres are coming too. Do you girls want to join?"

"Are the faeries coming?" Korin asked.

Julie offered an arm to Jae, who leaned on it gratefully. "They couldn't make it. They've got a rave, I think," Julie answered.

"I don't even want to know what a faerie rave is like." Raven raised her hands, palms out.

Jae chuckled weakly. "I'd love to, but my bed is calling me."

"What were you thinking, by the way?" Korin demanded. "I've never seen you use that much magic in one go. It was a training exercise!"

Jae shrugged. "Seemed like I could push my limits since it wasn't real combat."

Korin threw up her hands.

"Was Minerva okay?" Julie asked.

Jae grinned. "Oh, yes. Dehydrated, I'm sure. I thought she was going to drown you, so if she's sore and parched tonight, she earned it."

"Did you hear Derek chewing her out about that?" Raven grimaced. "I felt bad for her. Anyone can get carried away in a training exercise, and to be fair, Julie was fine."

"Power can be hard to control," Julie murmured. She cleared her throat. "I mean, I guess it can. Anyway. Raven, Korin, you coming?"

"Sorry, Juju. I've got a word sprint with my fanfic group tonight, so rain check?" Raven smiled apologetically.

Korin stifled a yawn. "Yeah, I'll hang with Jae if it's all the same to you. I'm exhausted."

"That's cool. I'll see you girls tonight, then." Julie waved as they reached the end of the hall. "I'll come in quietly to avoid waking you."

The others headed down the corridor that led to the barracks, and Julie took the elevator to the main lobby. She'd barely hit the button when her phone buzzed in her pocket. It was Rosa.

Julie answered. "Hey, Rosa."

"*Julia!* Rosa, is it?" Rosa asked.

Julie grimaced. "Sorry. It was kind of an intense day. Slip of the tongue."

Rosa chuckled. "It's okay, honey. I understand."

"You do?" Julie raised her eyebrows.

"Of course I do." Rosa sighed. "You're much too fancy now with your highfalutin' corporate job to go around calling me 'Mom' anymore."

Julie groaned. "Seriously? That's not—"

"No, no, I understand. My sweet baby, with her travel allowance and her conferences and things, is on her way up in the world," Rosa teased. "I guess I shouldn't call you my sweet baby anymore, either. Would you like to go by Miss Meadows?"

"*Mooo-ooooom,*" Julie moaned.

Rosa laughed. "That's more like it, honey. Now, how are you? How are your bowel movements doing?"

"Seriously? You're going to ask about my bowel movements?" Julie rubbed the bridge of her nose.

"Of course I am, baby. Your regularity is a very important part of your overall health," Rosa lectured. "I've been doing research—"

"Googling, you mean," Julie pointed out.

Rosa ignored her. "And I've discovered an incredible new remedy I think you'll absolutely love."

"I'm sure I will," Julie muttered. "I can't wait to hear about it."

"I knew you would!" Rosa crowed. "Ernesto. *Ernesto!* You were wrong, dear. Julie *does* want to hear about the turmeric!"

Julie heard her stepfather rumbling in the background and

seized upon the opportunity to change the subject. "So, how is Ernesto? Do you guys have any plans later this month?"

"Oh, he's good, honey. We don't, actually. Why?" Rosa asked.

"I thought I'd come over. We could get burgers. Maybe stop by Dad's grave." Julie's voice softened. "If you want to."

"That would be lovely, honey." Rosa paused. "I miss you."

Julie felt an unexpected prickle behind her eyelids. "I miss you, too." The elevator door binged, and she blinked rapidly, then straightened up. "Hey, Mom, I'll call you later, okay? I'm having dinner with Taylor and some friends."

"Tell Taylor I say hello and want to know when he's planning to pop the question." Rosa cackled.

"*Mom!*"

"I'm kidding, honey. You have a good time." Rosa took a deep breath. "Julia?"

"Yeah, Mom?" Julie stepped out of the elevator.

"I'm proud of you, baby. You know that, don't you? I'm so proud of you." Rosa choked up. "You've come so far, and you've done so well."

"Aw, Momma. Don't cry." Julie swallowed hard.

Rosa laughed softly. "I love you, honey. Bye."

"Bye, Mom." Julie waited for Rosa to hang up before she tucked her phone back into her pocket.

She strode into the cafeteria, which was crammed with hungry soldiers in navy uniforms, plowing through a magnificent buffet of roast lamb, vegetables, and heaping portions of rice and potatoes, and gravy. Before she could head to the buffet table, she spotted a figure in green near the back, waving to her. It was Taylor. He flashed a grin and pointed at the two laden plates in front of him.

The tightness in her chest dissolved. She waved back with a huge grin and pushed her way through the crowded room to join him at one end of the long table on the far side of the cafeteria. The Weres were already there, shoving each other and having a boisterous shouting match about who had been the most physically impressive during today's training. Qtana, Ellie, and Olena were in deep discussion about how thaumatech was affecting PMA operations, and Malcolm sat beside them, looking befuddled but interested.

"Hey, beautiful," Taylor whispered to her.

Julie pecked him on the cheek before sliding into the spot beside him. "Hey." She squeezed his knee under the table. "Where's Cassidy today, Mal?"

"She's gone shopping in Avalon Town." Malcolm waved a hand. "I love my wife, but I'm quite happy to skip shopping with her, thanks."

Julie laughed. "Yeah, I feel you."

"Teddy, you do *know* you're eventually going to rupture your stomach if you eat at that speed, right?" Olena asked with horror.

Teddy looked up with bulging cheeks. "Is that your medical opinion, Doc?"

"It's my common sense opinion." Olena laughed.

"I'm a werewolf." Teddy scoffed. "I'm designed to eat fast."

"In your wolf form, maybe, but you look human to me tonight." Olena raised an eyebrow.

A spirited discussion arose, and Ellie leaned over the table, keeping her voice low. "Hey, Julie! How are things going with, uh, the glowing?"

Julie's cheeks burned. "Things are okay, but I'd appreciate you keeping that to yourself."

Ellie winked. "I *am* a secret agent, you know. I can keep a secret."

Taylor chuckled. "You only recruit the best, Julie."

"Mmm, but you're running the department now." Julie beamed at him. "How are the new systems doing?"

"Amazing. They've almost doubled productivity." Taylor's eyes shone. "We don't have to go to Admin to get those stupid forms for traveling anymore! We just fill them out online. How cool is that?"

"Waiting in the admin department *sucked*," Julie moaned. "I do *not* miss it."

"It's a good thing." Qtana frowned. "With the Dark Moon League on the move the way they are, we need to streamline everything we can."

"Do you know anything about the raids they're planning?" Isaiah leaned closer.

The others fell silent.

Qtana shook her head solemnly, blonde ponytail whipping. "Nothing confirmed yet, but I know the defeat in Piñon Pines hardly slowed them down."

"I've heard rumors from other agents that they're planning something big. Something to do with beefing up their numbers." Ellie shuddered. "Might just be a rumor, but it worries me."

"I can't believe they're still so strong after Prince Lotan's statement." Olena laid down her fork and stared at her half-empty plate. "I really thought things would get better after he… after he said those things, but…" She took a shaky breath. "The damage has been done."

"Lotan did make *some* difference," Qtana pointed out. "With his support, we've been able to limit the Dark Moons' use of para social media to spread propaganda. It's a big step."

"Yes, I-I know, but I still can't go into Avalon Town." Tears shimmered in Olena's eyes. "The last time I walked into the grocery store in Avalon where I used to shop, the cashier wouldn't serve me. He called me a—" She stopped.

"Called you what?" Julie asked gently.

"It's unrepeatable." Olena wiped at her eyes. "I had to leave. Now I only shop in human stores here in the city. I haven't even been back to my apartment in Avalon Town. Kaplan let me have a room in the barracks."

Julie's heart stung. "Olena, I'm so sorry."

"You don't deserve this speciesism." Ellie put a hand on Olena's shoulder. "Just because paras who look like you have done horrible things doesn't mean that you should be tarred with the same brush. It's shameful, and I'm sorry you have to deal with this."

"I hate it. I hate the things the Dark Moons have done." Olena shook her head. "I've treated the victims of their riots. I've looked into the eyes of soldiers, good paras standing up for what's right, dying from burn wounds inflicted by Sylthana fire." She held out her hand, and a tiny blue flame danced in her palm before she clenched her fingers shut. "It shames me to know that I'm healing them with energy that comes from the same source."

"Stop that." Julie's voice was more forceful than she'd meant it to be. "You're using that power for what it was designed to do. They're the ones who've twisted it."

"Yeah, and if anyone in the barracks ever gives you trouble, you come to me." Chester slapped a clenched fist into his opposite palm. "You've saved our asses too many times for us to let anything happen to you."

The Weres murmured agreement, and Olena smiled through her tears. "Thanks, guys. There's been some harassment." She flushed. "You know, pushing and shoving when I'm walking through the building. High school stuff."

"Well, then you won't walk on your own anymore." Chester let out a low growl. "If we're not around, our friends will be."

"Thanks, Chester." Olena wiped her eyes. "It's just hard. Part of me can't help but feel that my people deserve the rejection. Look at what elves like me are doing. I've seen so much pain. I can't believe so many people want to dethrone a queen who brought peace and prosperity to Avalon and the rest of the paranormal world."

"Lotan's address helped, but the Dark Moons have simply changed their narrative." Qtana sighed. "I've been helping scrub their communications from the dark web, but anytime I shut one site down, a hundred more pop up out of nowhere. The chatter on these sites is about putting a commoner on the throne and ending the monarchies and nobility forever. They've rejected Lotan, while supporters of the Sylthana Throne have turned away from the Dark Moon League."

Julie took a deep breath. "Lotan will do what he can to keep helping. I'm sure of it."

Ellie raised an eyebrow. "Why so sure?"

"Because, well, Taylor and I were the ones who talked Lotan into giving that address that renounced the Dark Moons." Julie paused. "I saw genuine regret in him. I think he's going to be a better prince for going through this."

"Wait, hold up." Malcolm held up his hands. "You two confronted *Lotan*, Prince of the Sylthana Elves? *How?*"

"He needed an ass-kicking." Julie grinned at Taylor. "And I do like to kick royal ass."

Taylor laughed and put an arm around her shoulders. "I agree with Julie. Lotan was not that different from the way I used to be, apathetic and controlled by his parents. He's determined to change now."

"He might not have control over the die-hard Dark Moons, but at least now we know who really is against the Eternity Throne," Julie added. "That way, they can be arrested."

"Or killed," Olena growled.

Julie stared at her.

The Sylthana Elf sighed. "I'm sorry. I know how harsh that sounds, but this is tearing my people apart."

Qtana rubbed her chin. "You know, there might be something we can do about that. Lotan's working to change the narrative about the Sylthana Throne, but ordinary paras really need to hear from paras like them."

Malcolm sat up straighter. "Are you thinking of a media campaign, Qtana?"

The troll nodded. "Yes. Remember how successful the recruitment drive was, the one where we interviewed Ellie and Blake? It didn't just bring in new recruits. It also helped change the narrative about the PMA as a whole because we were hearing from real recruits, not just the brass."

"I like the idea. Ordinary trolls and elves could dispel the false narrative the Dark Moons are spreading." Malcolm turned to Olena. "A message from Sylthana Elves who want this divide to end."

Olena's eyes widened. "You want me to help?"

"If you agree." Malcolm spread his hands.

Olena nodded vigorously. "I will do anything I can to put an end to this."

"I'll brainstorm in the morning and send you both an email." Qtana bit her lip. "Maybe it's time people heard my story, too, so we can put an end to all that 'justice for Qbiit' bullshit."

"Amen to that," Noah growled.

Chester sat back in his chair with a sigh, clasping both hands over his muscular abdomen. "I'm so full I could puke, but I need more roast lamb. Anyone else?"

"Chester, you're going to damage your GI tract," Olena chided.

Julie leaned to the side, resting her head on Taylor's shoulder. He absently traced the outline of her jaw with his fingertips.

"Look at Malcolm and Qtana," she murmured. "They're changing the world."

Taylor kissed her forehead. "It all started with you, babe."

CHAPTER SIXTEEN

The Griffin units sat at sharp attention in the conference room. Julie and Korin were in the front row with the rest of their unit right behind them as Shulme strode into the room. The clopping of the white centaur's hooves brought an instant hush to the conference room.

He stopped in the back corner, nodding to the gathered soldiers, and Droppelheimer and Bianca followed him. Bianca winked at Julie as she stepped up to the lectern.

"Griffins, you were all impressive in training yesterday." Bianca grinned. "Well done. I look forward to seeing how the upgrades to your tech and weaponry are going to improve your performance in the field, and I don't have long to wait. We had hoped to do another day's training before sending you on your next mission, but urgent intelligence has reached us, and you are all being deployed on an emergency mission today."

Julie sat up straighter, exchanging glances with Korin. *This sounds serious.*

It is, Hat agreed grimly.

"Our agents have located a large Dark Moon cell operating out of an abandoned castle, once known as Lockerfell, on the outskirts of the Deadwoods." Bianca nodded at the hologram behind her, and Julie recognized the tangle of dead, twisted branches. These were the same woods where the Haunted Hill was located and she and Taylor had saved the dragon egg from the clutches of a necromancer named Kevin. "The cell is not only large but also appears well-organized. These are trained combatants, not ordinary paras caught up in rioting. Worse, they have a plan, and it's a dangerous one."

Shulme's eyes narrowed, and Droppelheimer crossed his powerful arms.

Bianca went on. "Lockerfell was a guard tower for the Locker before its security was upgraded fifty years ago." Behind her, the hologram changed into a towering Victorian Gothic building. "This is where the Dark Moons and other criminals captured by the PMA and Palace Guard, including you, are kept before their transfer to the prison realm."

Droppelheimer stepped forward. "The Dark Moon cell plans to break their arrested members out of the Locker. There are one hundred twenty-one Dark Moons currently imprisoned there, not to mention hundreds of other dangerous inmates."

Julie's gut clenched. She heard a low growl rumble from Chester, who sat behind her.

"Your mission is to assault Lockerfell and arrest every member of the cell," Bianca went on. "You will take the new magic-powered transports through the portal and into the Deadwoods, then launch a surprise aerial assault on Lockerfell. Units will attack from all directions on both levels of Lockerfell. We're going to slip a noose around the neck of this cell and hang them." Bianca's eyes narrowed. "I don't want a single one of them to escape. I want them in the Locker by nightfall."

Shulme stepped forward, holding out a big, calm hand. "Lethal force is the last resort, soldiers. We want all the Dark Moons to face justice, which means bringing them in alive."

"Sir!" A Sylthana Elf from Griffin Two jumped to her feet, her blue eyes ablaze. "With respect, sir, the only justice these Dark Moons deserve is a bullet."

"Yeah!" Another Sylthana Elf, this one from Griffin Five, got up and folded his arms. "I'm with my prince. Those traitors should be put down like mad dogs."

There was a rumble of agreement from other Griffins. Julie saw Korin nodding out of the corner of her eye.

Shulme's voice sliced through the hubbub. "You may be with your prince, Private, but you swore allegiance to the PMA. Do you wish to desert, or will you follow orders?"

The elves were both silent.

"Sit down and listen to the rest of the briefing." Shulme didn't raise his voice. He didn't have to; the elves sat immediately. The centaur gazed at them icily for a few moments, then softened. "A life without magic awaits these traitors and criminals in the prison realm. Don't let your emotions get the better of you. You are not executioners. You are soldiers for peace and justice. Don't forget it."

"You will be using your new rifles with Sandman bullets," Bianca chipped in. "Once your targets are tranked, you'll cuff them with your magic-nulling restraints. Agents will be on standby to transport the arrested to the prison realm portal. They've proven too dangerous to serve time in the Locker."

"Qtana has uploaded the mission's specifics to your telechips." Droppelheimer nodded at them. "Once activated, Ariadne's thread will guide you to your targets. Any questions?"

There were none, and Shulme gave the order. "Move out!"

***

Minutes later, thanks to the efficiency of the new armory, Julie and the rest of her unit were jogging out of the military wing and into the large paved parking area at the back of the building.

"Have you seen the new transports yet?" Julie panted to Korin.

The dwarf shook her head. "We were supposed to train on them tomorrow, but now—"

The unit stumbled to a surprised halt. Julie's jaw dropped.

The transports, at first glance, looked like ordinary sand-colored light armored vehicles, broad and spacious to accommodate an entire Griffin unit apiece. However, they didn't have windshields. They had...were those *eyes?* There were two, dark and round, on the front of each vehicle where the windshield should be, with pinpricks of blue light darting within them. There were no wheels, either. Instead, the vehicles hovered two feet off the ground, blue light glowing beneath them. The same light oozed from the cracks in their doors and from the bodywork.

There were seven, and they hovered in a row above the parking lot, their engines emitting a deep hum as the Griffin units assembled. Shulme was a glowing white beacon in the middle of the navy-uniformed group.

Overwatch to Griffin Seven. Do you copy? he asked in Julie's mind.

Copy, Julie confirmed.

All units, board your transports! Shulme ordered.

Julie stepped forward with the rest of the units, and the transport in front of her wriggled from back to front like an overexcited dog. Its engine's hum rose to a high-pitched whine.

"What the—" Julie scrambled back.

The vehicle floated nearer to her, all of its doors swinging open at once, and the hum intensified.

"Seems like it's happy to see us," Raven commented.

"I think I liked the SUVs better," Korin grumbled.

Julie stepped forward and reached out, and the vehicle pressed its hood against her palm. There was a glowing blue numeral 7 etched on the hood. She stifled a giggle. "It's okay, guys. It's just friendly. Come on. Let's go!"

They scrambled into the vehicle. That was not made easy by

the occasional wriggling, but at last, they were all inside. Julie and Korin sat in the front seats, peering through the side windows. It was disorienting not to have a windshield, just a small glass slit above the vehicle's eyes or whatever they were.

"How do you drive this thing?" Korin asked aloud.

The last door slammed shut, and the vehicle's engine roared. It wheeled around of its own accord and surged after the other six vehicles, which were heading for the enormous portal in the back of the parking lot.

"Seems like it drives itself," Julie squeaked, clutching the edge of her seat.

"We need seat belts!" Raven wailed.

The vehicle bumped into the one in front of it with a bone-rattling thud.

"Merlin's asshole!" Korin cursed.

"*Korin!*" Raven exclaimed.

The other vehicle bumped back. Theirs let out a low growl and bumped harder, then pushed forward, jostling to get to the front of the pack. The other vehicles pushed and shoved each other, engines grumbling.

"Seven, could you calm down?" Raven squeaked.

"Seven?" Korin glared back at her.

"He wanted a name," Raven protested.

"Can you please *try* to focus on the fact that you are a professional soldier?" Korin barked.

"I think I need this spell for Genevieve," Julie commented. "Imagine what she'd be like with a mind of her own."

Chester grinned. "Sounds like fun to me."

The portal was just ahead of them, and Seven butted to the front of the line as they reached it. Julie clenched her eyes shut and rode out the portal dizziness. The morning light was gone. So was the ground. When she looked out of the window, she was staring down at a tangle of dead branches and thick silver cobwebs. The Deadwoods were a hundred feet below them.

"Shit the bed." Julie gasped. "We're *flying*."

Griffin Seven, do you copy? Shulme asked.

Copy, Overwatch, Korin responded.

Lockerfell is four clicks ahead. Ariadne's thread will be activated now, he told them.

A moment later, the silver thread appeared in Julie's vision, floating just beyond Seven's hood. There was a half-moon in the sky, and by its light, Julie could make out Lockerfell on the edge of a cliff, its bare, rocky flanks jutting from the chaos of the Deadwoods. Beyond the cliff, Julie saw an open expanse with the Gothic shape of the Locker in the middle of it.

Now that they were through the portal, the vehicles fell into neat pairs. Griffin One led the way. Seven obediently stayed in the back beside Six.

Griffin Seven, your target is the east wing, lower level. As Shulme spoke, a white dot overlaid the thread, highlighting a row of windows at the bottom of the Lockerfell. *Griffin Six will take the upper level.*

Copy that, sir. Julie pulled out her rifle.

You will engage your target by HALO jump from your vehicle, Shulme added.

Ahead, Griffin One's vehicle pointed its nose straight up and shot into the sky. Julie had just enough time to grab her seat as the rest of the vehicles followed, but magic glued her safely in place as Seven climbed into the star-dusted night. They leveled out again after a few minutes and began to circle. When Julie looked down, Lockerfell was a speck far below her.

In position, Overwatch, Griffin One's unit leader reported.

Griffins, engage! Shulme shouted.

Trapdoors opened in Seven's floor. Julie grabbed the straps of her parachute, which the armory had automatically strapped on, and exchanged grins with Korin. "Ready?" she yelled against the howl of the wind through the trapdoors.

"Go!" Korin shouted.

Julie stepped to the edge of the trapdoor and then through it.

Surrounded by her unit, she free-fell through the night, arms and legs raised to keep from spinning. The wind whipped her hair and cradled her body as she plunged toward the white target hovering over the toy castle that was Lockerfell. An altimeter counted off the feet in the bottom left corner of her HUD.

She glanced at the rest of her group, and her eyes met Chester's. The werewolf's pale blond hair streamed in the wind, and he gave her a toothy grin and a thumbs-up. Julie laughed and returned it. Adrenaline, thrill, and *life* burned in her veins, and she had to control her urge to let out a whoop of excitement.

The blue glow of the vehicles was far above them, and she began to make out the target's details: tall, arched windows, many still with glass in them, the ruins of a tower broken off halfway up, leaving a jagged edge of ruined stone. The white target on her HUD hovered over the lower east wing's windows.

The altimeter had reached four thousand feet.

Ready! Korin sent.

Julie rested a hand on the ripcord of her parachute.

Three thousand seven hundred. Three thousand five hundred. Three thousand two hundred. Three thousand.

Now! Korin bellowed.

Julie pulled her chute and heard the silken thump of it unraveling. She gripped the handles, bracing herself against the inevitable jerk of the harness around her body. Black chutes bloomed in the night as the rest of the unit did the same, and they floated toward the white target on Julie's HUD, quickly and silently.

Contact! Contact! Griffin One exclaimed. Blue fire exploded from the broken tower, and Julie spotted a trio of Sylthana Elves near a massive cannon that spat Sylthana fire. A Griffin One's parachute caught fire, and Julie heard the distant scream as a soldier fell from the sky.

Julie! Two o'clock! Hat yelled.

Julie's head snapped back. They were drifting toward the battlements, and she saw movement on the battlements just before a massive ball of white-hot electricity, spitting and crackling, headed right for her. Its stench filled her nostrils. Julie pulled on one of the handles and swung hard to one side, and the ball missed her by feet.

It exploded into the woods, yellow fire flaring in the trees. Another boom shook the air, but Julie didn't have time to determine where it was coming from. The window was rushing up to meet her, stars and chutes reflecting in the glass, and she only had enough time to bring her boots up.

Glass shattered when her heels slammed into it. She swung through the window, with broken glass accompanying her, and cut her chute loose in one movement. When her feet hit the ground, Julie's rifle was in her hands so that when the first troll ducked out from behind a pillar with his gun raised, her round hit his face before he could pull the trigger.

They were in a huge hall lined with pillars. It had been the great hall but was now littered with rubble, and moonlight poured in through a huge gap in the roof. Julie felt it course through her veins, and energy crackled into her muscles. Bursts of rifle fire exploded around her as her unit moved forward as one, taking cover behind the pillars. A swarm of disorganized Dark Moons struggled to find cover in the rubble. Upturned tables and chairs lay everywhere, with plates of food strewn over the floor. They'd interrupted dinner.

Julie stepped over a snoring elf, reached her pillar, and took cover beside it, panting as she checked the magazine in her rifle. Still plenty of ammo left. She darted away from the pillar and fired as a troll rose from behind a slab of concrete. Her shot hit his arm, and he spun, roaring, before her next round struck him in the face. The troll staggered back and fell into a chair, his gun rolling from his limp hands.

Raising her rifle, Julie spun, scanning for more targets.

Nothing stirred except her unit. Dark Moons lay scattered over the floor, snoring.

Griffin Seven, lower east wing is clear. Korin calmly reported. *Restraining targets.*

Copy that, Griffin Seven. Good job, Shulme added.

"Aw, boring." Chester slung his rifle onto his back and pulled out a fistful of magic-nulling zip-ties. "I was hoping for more action."

Julie laughed. "There's always tomorrow."

She crouched and rolled the elf at her feet onto his face, then held his wrists steady while Chester zip-tied them. They left him contentedly slumbering in the recovery position and headed across the hall, working their way through the snoring Dark Moons quickly. The Sandman dust wouldn't last long.

"You looked tired," Julie commented, tipping the troll in the chair forward so Chester could get to his wrists. "Everything okay?"

"Oh, yeah. I slept outside Olena's door. Growled at a few creeps." Chester grinned sheepishly. "Teddy will take tonight's shift."

Julie laughed. "Olena's honor guard, huh?"

"Thought she could use the reassurance." Chester shrugged. "Until we get these assholes under control."

"Sooner rather than later, I hope." Julie straightened. "Hey, do you think we should—"

Griffin Seven! Griffin Seven! The panicked cry came from Minerva. *Do you copy?* Her voice rasped through Julie's mind.

Copy, Griffin Six, Korin answered.

Footsteps thundered beyond the ruined banqueting hall, and gunfire ripped through the air.

Reinforcements! Minerva screamed. *They're coming right at you!*

Shit! Korin cursed. *Griffin Seven, on alert!*

Julie reached for her rifle, but before her fingers could close on the grip, the wrecked wooden door at the end of the hall burst open, and Dark Moons poured through it in a bristling mass of guns. Julie yanked her rifle around on its sling, but it was too late. The elf at the head of the group had taken aim. She saw the flash of the muzzle, felt the thump of impact, and hit the ground on her side, her helmeted head smacking into the rubble with enough force that darkness covered her eyes.

She shook her head hard, blinking, and patted over her body, looking for blood and the hole. As her vision cleared, she realized the impact hadn't come from a bullet. It had come from Chester. He was on the ground beside her, and gunfire punched into the slab of concrete they were lying behind. He'd tackled her to the floor.

"What in Merlin's name, Chess?" Julie snarled as she dragged her rifle out from behind her back and rose to a kneeling position. "I can take care of—"

"I know, I know." Chester chuckled, but the sound was a pale ghost of its usual self. "You can take care of yourself."

He fell back against the floor, his face twisted in pain, and blood surged from his chest. A black pool spread through the dust below him.

CHAPTER SEVENTEEN

"Chess. Chester!" Julie threw her rifle aside and grabbed his shoulders.

Chester's eyes fluttered open, unfocused and hazy. He lay on his back, one hand clasped to his chest, blood oozing between his fingers. Julie grabbed his wrist and pried his hand away. A fresh gush of blood ran over his armor. It was bright red and pulsing, and smoke rose from the wound. She heard distant sizzling from the depths of the massive hole in his chest.

Silver. Hat's voice slammed in her head like a coffin lid.

"No. *No!* You're going to be okay, Chess." Julie's fingers tore open the tiny first-aid pack on her belt, and she fumbled out gauze and pressed it against the wound. "Put pressure on it. Come on." She grabbed his hand and clasped it over the wound, but his fingers were cold and limp.

"It's okay," Chester wheezed. Flecks of blood came out with them, and they fizzled in the corners of his mouth. "It's okay, Julie."

"You're going to be fine. You've got to be fine." Julie's voice and hands wouldn't stop shaking. She packed more gauze into the wound. "We just need to stop the bleeding."

She was only vaguely aware of the rest of the unit striving to get to them. Of the gunfire that had turned into a strangely soft popping noise in her ears. Of the bursts of dust from the concrete slab as bullets slammed into it. Far more real was the warm, sticky blood on her hands, smelling smoky and burned, and Chester's soft, ragged gasps, each weaker and shallower than the last.

"Julie," he croaked.

"Shhh. Save your strength. You're going to be fine." Julie's throat felt like a noose was tightening around it.

"Julie." Chester moaned with pain and effort. He reached up and gripped her arm, his hand slick with blood on her armor. "Please."

She forced herself to look into his eyes. They were glassy, but they locked on hers.

"You saved me," she whispered. The tears escaped down her cheeks. "Why would you do something so dumb?"

Chester smiled again, the one that had flashed opposite her as they rumbled to their next mission. The smile that had preceded a hundred stupid jokes. The smile that held all his chill and his ferocity and his strength, and suddenly all she could think of was his hulking lupine figure guarding Olena's door all night and his hairy form against her knees as he held back the Dark Moons in the Avalon riots. His body slamming into hers, taking her bullet.

"You saved us by recruiting us." Chester struggled for a wheezing breath that sucked appallingly through the wound in his chest. The smile didn't slip, and his eyes brightened for an instant. "I'm returning the favor, is all."

"Chess," Julie whimpered.

His eyes did not close, but she saw him go. The light left them. His smile faded, and the big hand grew limp on her arm. Everything that was Chester left the bloody shell that lay on the floor beside her.

"CHESTER!" Julie screamed. She knew he was gone, but she grabbed his shoulders and shook him anyway. *"CHESTER!"*

Jae was suddenly beside her, bandages spilling out of her pack like guts while blood ran from a wound in her temple.

"Where was he hit?" she asked, then froze as her eyes found Chester's face. Very delicately, with a hand gloved in purple nitrile, Jae pressed two fingertips to Chester's carotid artery.

Julie searched the elf's face, desperate. Maybe... Jae looked up, and her eyes told Julie what she already knew.

Chester was dead.

"No." Julie sagged and rested her forehead on the once-powerful shoulder of the corpse of her friend. "No, no, no."

She heard wild barks behind her. The other Weres were still fighting, protecting their brother. How was she going to tell them Chester was dead? How was she going to tell his parents? Panic sucked at her like a whirlpool, and she wobbled on the edge of it, dragged toward an abyss of fear that made nausea climb into her throat and dizziness grip her brain.

The castle shuddered, the great ruin moaning with the force of Julie's fear. Dust fell from the walls and ceiling. The earth juddered beneath Julie as she knelt beside what was left of Chester.

No. Julie raised her head, and the shuddering stopped. She looked at Chester's motionless face, and something cold surged through her body. She glanced around and instantly found what she was looking for: the Sylthana Elf who'd shot and killed Chester. He was in the back corner of the hall, his rifle gone, trying to fend off Isaiah and Austin with wild swings of a saber as they snarled and lunged at him in wolf form.

The shudder that ran through Julie's body ended her trembling. She leaned down and pressed her lips to Chester's dusty forehead, then brushed his eyes closed with her fingertips. When she rose, she glanced down at the rifle lying beside his body and kicked it aside.

"Julie?" Jae gasped.

Julie ignored her. She ignored everything except the feeling coursing through her body, bleeding from the center of her chest, which hurt as sharply as though the bullet had pierced her after all, and the face of the Sylthana Elf as he tried to keep Isaiah and Austin at bay. The battle raged around her, but Julie didn't care.

She strode toward the elf. The instant she stepped into the moonlight, fire blazed to life in her hands, forming balls. The flames were gentle on her skin, but she felt their heat. She knew they'd burn.

"Isaiah! Austin!" someone snapped. It took Julie a second to realize the voice was hers. It was deep and harsh, and it startled both wolves, even in their battle rage. They looked at her, hackles raised and blood and foam dripping from their jaws. The elf stared at her and froze.

"Step back," Julie ground out, walking faster, the flames rising higher on her arms. "He's mine."

Julie? Hat gasped.

Neither wolf asked questions. They read what had happened in her eyes and backed away, snarling, their bodies trembling with fury and pain.

The elf didn't move. He just stared as she strode toward him, cold rage drenching her.

Julie! Hat cried.

Julie stopped two feet short of the elf and raised her clenched fists. "You killed him," she hissed. "You killed my friend, you bastard."

"P-please," the elf whimpered.

Flames roared between Julie's fingers. She could imagine him burning. She could see him suffering as Chester suffered.

Julie, please, no! Hat begged. *This isn't who you are.*

The elf threw down his saber and stepped back, raising his empty hands. "Don't kill me," he pleaded.

The flames grew, licking hungrily toward the elf's flesh. "Why shouldn't I?" Julie snarled.

You're not a murderer. Julie, remember who you are! Hat cried.

I don't know who I am! Julie raged. *I've never known! Human, fae, powers, no powers—* She took a step nearer to the elf, and he cowered into the corner, crying out. *Maybe I* am *a murderer.*

No, you're not. Remember what Alugon always says. Who you really are is something only you can decide, and you're deciding it now. If you do this, you're crossing a line you can't come back from.

The elf cowered. Julie wanted to see him burn. She wanted to hear him scream.

"Do it, Julie!" Austin snarled.

Julie raised her hands. The elf shrieked and she closed her eyes, desperate for clarity. The image that filled her mind was Lillie Griswall, laughing in Genevieve's passenger seat, and the flames shrank in her hands.

Julie opened her eyes. The elf stared at her, pale and trembling. She took the last stride toward him so they were nose to nose and pinned him against the wall.

"You're the murderer," she hissed.

The flames in her hands went out, but when she raised her right hand, her palm was red-hot and blazing. She grabbed his throat with her cool right hand and held him still as she pressed her burning palm to his cheek. The smell of sizzling skin and hair filled the air, and the elf's high-pitched screams echoed above the noise of battle.

When Julie lowered her hand, the elf's face bore a scarlet handprint. She leaned close, spitting the words in his face. "Now you'll never forget what you've done."

She stepped back. The elf collapsed to the floor, sobbing.

"Trank him," she snapped.

Isaiah and Austin transformed and fired, and the two Sandman bullets slammed into the elf's burned face. Julie strode back into the battle.

All seven Griffin units waited in the hallway outside the conference room, but not a word was spoken. A deathly silence hung over the soldiers. There was no shoving, no joshing, no wisecracks or retellings of epic feats. The smell of blood and smoke draped them like a pall.

Julie sat with her back to the wall, so tired that her bones felt like water. Her knees were drawn up to her chest, her forearms propped on her knees. She noticed that her limp hands were still flecked with Chester's blood.

The six Weres—the *five* Weres—sat in a huddled heap in human form. None spoke. Isaiah stared into the middle distance, his eyes blank.

A door creaked. "You may enter." The voice was Droppelheimer's.

The Griffins shuffled forward. Julie dragged herself to her feet and trailed after them as they headed into the conference room. Droppelheimer held the door. Before she could step inside, he held out a hand. "Private Meadows, a word?"

Julie didn't care. She stopped and nodded.

Droppelheimer closed the door, and then his eyes searched her face. "I saw what happened via HUD footage." The orc paused, his voice deeper than usual. "I need to know if you're fit for duty."

Julie stared at her bloody hands.

"I know what you've been through." Droppelheimer rubbed a scar on his forearm that was almost obscured by black tattoos. "But I need people that I can trust."

Julie raised her head. *So my leak-in-the-PMA theory isn't wrong.*

Hat said nothing.

"Justice needs to be served, sir." Julie clenched her fists. "Whether I'm grieving or not. You can count on me and my unit."

Droppelheimer's stern features relaxed into a smile. "Make

sure you keep focusing on that, Meadows." He paused. "I saw what you did to the elf, too."

Julie looked away. "He deserved it, sir."

"I saw that you didn't kill him, even though you could have." Droppelheimer's voice stayed gentle. "I'm not sure most of us would have had your restraint in that situation." He laid an oddly delicate hand on her shoulder. "Chester knew what he was doing."

"Yes, sir." Julie swallowed.

Droppelheimer nodded at her and headed into the room. Julie followed. Her unit wasn't sitting in their usual places. Instead, they'd tucked themselves into a back corner. She sagged into a chair between Jae and Isaiah and sat staring at the floor as the briefing began.

"Griffin units, your performance was exemplary." Droppelheimer gripped the lectern tightly. "I see the holes in your ranks today. More than one of you has lost a brother or sister, and that is an irreconcilable loss, one I feel with you."

There was a soft whimper from Julie's right. Isaiah clasped a hand over his mouth and nose, tears coursing down his cheeks. She grasped his free hand. Jae was pale and silent beside her.

"Rest assured that we will not stop until all those despicable murderers have been captured and justice has been served." Droppelheimer's voice trembled with emotion. "The sacrifices of these brave paras will not be in vain. The Dark Moon League will be stopped, whatever it takes. They will pay for what they have done, and the peace that our brothers and sisters believed in will be returned to the paranormal world."

The briefing went on. Droppelheimer gave statistics and doled out praise for a job well done.

Dark Moons all restrained, huge disaster averted, whatever. It was hard to listen. Julie's brain felt like it had been stuffed with straw. She couldn't stop staring at the fat white number on the hologram beside the words PMA Losses, *4.* How could four young, healthy, vibrant paras who'd headed out today to save the world be gone?

The briefing ended. The units began to shuffle out of the room. Julie dragged herself to her feet, let go of Isaiah's hand, and stumbled toward the stage, pushing past the other Griffins as Droppelheimer turned to go.

"Sir," she choked out.

The orc turned to her. "What can I do for you, Private Meadows?"

Julie was vaguely aware of the rest of the unit behind her. "Sir, request permission to go to Montana and tell Chester's pack what happened in person." She swallowed hard. "Please, sir." Her voice only broke a little.

Droppelheimer nodded. "Your unit has been granted several days' leave and a travel allowance. You will return his body to the pack for burial with full honors."

Julie's eyes blurred with tears. Korin had to step forward and say, "Thank you, sir," because Julie had neither words nor the strength to say them.

The hot, dry wind blowing across the prairie cooled the tears on Julie's cheeks. She didn't try to wipe them off. In full dress uniform, she stood at solemn attention with the rest of her unit, lined up beside the grave that contained all that remained of her friend and comrade.

Droppelheimer had offered to hold a full military funeral at the PMA, but Isaiah had asked that Chester be buried the way wolves traditionally honored their battle dead. Julie had been at a PMA memorial, and this was very different. There was no music or guns, just the wolf pack on the windy prairie and the grave marked by a simple wooden cross jutting from the flat landscape.

"Traditionally, we bury our dead where they fall," Isaiah had told her on the flight. "Death is not something we segregate from life. It is not an end but a beginning, a leap into the joyous beyond. Mourning is for those left behind."

He'd said the words like he was reciting them, and Ezekiel Woods was doing the same right now. The alpha of the pack and the mayor of the nearby town where they lived was struggling with the same words. He stood over the fresh grave, his neatly cut black hair whipping in the wind, an all-black suit tracing the outline of his powerful frame.

"Mourning is for those left behind," he finished. The alpha stopped and took a long breath, then squeezed out a few more words. "Chester stood against a tide of evil that has begun to feel overwhelming. We've seen the suffering those terrorists have caused. We feel that suffering now."

He lowered his head, rubbed his eyes, and went on. "But because there are paras like Chester in the world, paras as strong and loyal and...and compassionate as he was..." Ezekiel took a shuddering breath. "His memory gives us hope."

If there was more to Ezekiel's speech, he couldn't finish it. Instead, he stepped back, and Cironius Achilleos raised his head. The centaur's long brown hair and tail streamed in the wind.

"Lisa, do you want to come forward?" he asked softly.

A petite blonde wolf at the front of the pack transformed into a plump middle-aged woman with streaks of gray in her hair. She looked so ordinary. So normal. A normal woman whose son had been torn from her. Julie's hands trembled uncontrollably on the PMA flag in her grip. Somehow she walked up to Chester's mom and held out the flag.

"I'm sorry," she croaked. "I'm so sorry."

Lisa accepted the flag, then her soft white hands wrapped around Julie's, and they weren't shaking. "You're Julie, aren't you? The one who recruited him."

Julie swallowed hard. "Yes. I'm so sorry. If I hadn't—"

"Julie, darling." Lisa squeezed her hands. "If you hadn't

recruited Chester, he would not have lived. He was born to do what you helped him to do. Serving was the best thing that ever happened to him." Her lip trembled. "Thank you for giving my baby boy the best life he could ever have had."

Lisa took the flag and left, and Julie made her way back to the row of soldiers, then found the strength to sob quietly instead of falling to the ground in tears.

Ezekiel had transformed into a huge black wolf with streaks of gray in his ruff and muzzle. He raised his head, and a soft, low howl rumbled from deep within his chest. It rose slowly into the blue sky.

One by one, the wolf pack added their voices. Young and old, deep and high, male and female, their howls rose together, a song of hope and mourning as old as the prairie. Julie closed her eyes and lost herself in the song of the wolves.

CHAPTER EIGHTEEN

They held the wake in the town hall, which wasn't very big and felt even cozier with the entire wolf pack, the unit, and other local paras crammed inside. As soon as Julie and the rest of the unit squeezed through the doors, she felt a sudden surge of hunger.

The table at the back of the hall was laden with food. Everyone in town had brought something: sausage casseroles, chicken pot pies, enormous vats of macaroni and cheese, creamy mounds of potato salad, dinner rolls still hot from the oven, and trays of pies and cakes and cookies and a big bowl of green Jell-O with fruit. Julie felt like she'd stumbled into a potluck at the church where she'd grown up.

"You look pale, dearie." A comfortably-proportioned elf stood at one end of the buffet table, doling out plates. "Eat something." She shoved a plate into Julie's hands.

Julie had not been able to do more than nibble anything since Chester had died last week, but she piled her plate high with food. Everything was wholesome and home-cooked. Her unit huddled around a table in a corner, but before they could dig in, Lisa strode up to them.

"No, no, no." She gently took Isaiah's arm. "Come on, honey. You were Chester's family, too. Come and sit up here with us."

Julie followed the rest of the unit to a long table in front. Ezekiel and Cironius were also sitting there, the centaur's equine part lying down so he could fit at the table. Two elderly werewolves smiled and nodded at the unit as they sat down.

"You're all looking well, Isaiah," the elderly female creaked.

Isaiah managed a faint smile. "Thank you, Nana Beaumont."

"I have such nice pictures of Chester from his time serving with you all," Nana Beaumont quavered. "He was very handsome by then."

"Chester was always handsome, Mama." Lisa's smile blurred with tears.

"You have to believe that, don't you?" Nana chuckled. "You're his mother."

"Aw, Mama, don't say that! He was a beautiful little boy." Lisa wiped her tears.

Nana cackled. "Honey, when he was thirteen, he was all armpits and Adam's apple, and you know it." She fumbled in her purse. "Here, let me show you."

Julie didn't think she could face a picture of Chester. She couldn't even look at his photo on the memorial wall on the main floor of the military wing. But when Nana held out the picture, everyone burst out laughing. The little guy in the photo was a long way from the slab of muscle Julie had known. He was wearing only a blue Speedo, and his ribs stood out like hoops, knees and elbows enormous and out of place.

Korin guffawed. "Look at tiny Chessy!"

"I'd forgotten about that." Isaiah chuckled. "He was *such* a weed. He only turned into something when he took up wrestling in high school."

"He was a good wrestler, too." Nana grinned toothlessly. "Kicked your butt plenty of times, 'Saiah."

"Yeah, yeah. Either way, he was pretty impressive by the time he was sixteen." Isaiah snorted, then turned to Teddy. "Hey, Ted, do you remember that time that the jocks from the football team were picking on you, and they turned around, and Chess was standing right behind them?"

Teddy scoffed. "I had them right where I wanted them."

"Yeah, especially when they all scattered at the sight of Chester." Noah snorted.

The Weres laughed, and it was hard not to join in. Cironius shook his head, smiling. "I can't believe you all were a bunch of good-for-nothing scoundrels chasing my horses around during foaling season a year ago."

"Oh, Cirry, would you give it a rest with those horses of yours?" Lisa laughed, the tears drying on her cheeks. "Chester and this lot got up to *far* worse things than chasing your horses."

Cironius raised an eyebrow. "You don't consider living wild in the woods and terrorizing innocent horses to be the worst of their crimes?"

"Certainly not." Lisa grinned. "Austin, do you remember Lizzy Ellis' sixteenth birthday?"

Austin's cheeks turned scarlet, and the other Weres burst out laughing.

"Wait, this sounds good." Julie leaned forward. "What happened?"

"Lizzy was a beautiful girl." Lisa smirked at the deepening blush on Austin's cheeks. "A Sylthana Elf with long hair. Down to her heels, I think."

"Even when braided." Austin let out a tiny sigh.

Julie joined the chorus of chuckles.

"Austin here had a crush on Lizzy." Lisa patted his hand. "The only trouble was that he was painfully shy, and Lizzy was one of the popular girls. She didn't even know Austin existed. Besides, she was with one of those jocks who terrorized Teddy, and he was no good for her. So, Chester came up with a plan."

"Chester and his plans." Noah groaned.

"Lizzy's sixteenth birthday was that summer. I knew Chess was up to something, but I didn't know what," Lisa went on. "I kept asking, and he kept telling me not to worry about it." She leaned forward and said the next words in a stage whisper. "Spoiler alert. I should have worried about it."

Blake snickered. Austin's blush deepened.

"On the big day, Lizzy's parents had hired a local band to play at her party, but Chester had other ideas. Austin's something of a guitar player." Lisa nodded at him.

Julie turned to Austin, grinning. "You *are?*"

"Shut up," Austin mumbled.

"Chester's brilliant plan was to replace the band's lead guitarist with Austin here." Lisa grinned. "The night before the party, Chess and the rest made their move. He slipped a bit of copper into the guitarist's drink at the bar that night, although *what* you were doing in the bar, I don't want to know." Lisa frowned.

"No, you don't," Isaiah admitted.

"Most werewolves are sensitive to copper since it behaves a little like silver. The result was that the guitarist spent the next twenty-four hours on the john, poor guy." Lisa shook her head. "Of course, when that started, Chester was ready with Austin to be the emergency stand-in. The band had all had enough to drink that it worked. Austin got his chance."

"Chess was just trying to help," Austin added. "What happened next wasn't his fault."

"What *did* happen?" Julie asked, intrigued.

Austin grimaced.

"This poor sad soul—" Blake slapped Austin on the shoulder, "got up on stage, took one look at the crowd, saw Lizzy staring at him, and couldn't play a single note. Not one. Bummed out her entire birthday party. She was *pissed.* She left angry notes in his locker for a year."

Julie snorted. "That's what happens when you act weird when trying to get a girl's attention, dude."

"I know, I know!" Austin moaned.

"Well, technically, Chester's plan worked," Isaiah pointed out. "She *did* know who you were after that, Austin."

"Yes, and she hated me!" Austin wailed.

Laughter rippled around the table, and Lisa shook her head.

"Okay, but you got him back for it," Teddy piped up. "Do you remember that time with the full moon coming-of-age ritual when you stole the Moonlight Chalice and hid it under Ezekiel's robes?"

"That was *you*?" Ezekiel rounded on Austin. "I thought I was losing my mind!"

Once more, the town hall filled with laughter, and this time, it was easy to join in.

Julie settled into her seat and looked back at Great Falls as the jet took off. The city grew smaller and smaller and finally dwindled into a glittering speck on the vast prairie, then was swallowed by clouds as the jet kept climbing.

Jae put a hand on her shoulder. "Looks like you slept better last night."

Julie glanced at her. "I-I did, actually." She paused. "I think I slept through the night." She smiled. "It must have been all that good food at the wake."

Jae shrugged. "Good food and good feelings."

"I don't know." Julie pressed a hand to the hollow spot in her chest, which still had a dull, bone-deep ache. "I don't know if I'll ever be able to feel *good* about Chester. I don't know how we'll go on without him, but after this time with the wolf pack, I feel like we *must*."

"How so?" Jae asked.

Julie gazed back again, though Montana was now hidden by clouds. "Because of what we saw back there, Jae," she murmured. "Ordinary paras living ordinary lives, supporting each other. Paras who've lost so much and still found the courage to be good to one another.

"Look at Lisa. She lost her son, and you know she loved him, but she was so kind to us. She..." Julie swallowed. "She healed so much guilt in me with just a few words."

"They all stood together," Jae agreed. "And they found so much to celebrate. I don't know how that wake ended with so much laughter."

Julie wiped her eyes. "Paras like that deserve to be protected. They should be able to live together without having to worry about being bombed by Dark Moons or losing their kids in a senseless war." She looked at Jae, her jaw clenched. "We need to make that possible again."

Jae nodded. "Chester knew that. He believed in it, and he died for it."

"We all risk our lives for that." Julie clenched her fists. "But it's worth it."

"I'm with you." Jae's voice was soft.

"So are all of us," Korin called from the aisle seat. The Copper Dwarf's eyes burned with passion. "To the death, just like Chester."

Julie grinned. "Those Dark Moons better watch out. We're coming for them."

I know that voice. Hat groaned. *You have a plan, don't you?*

Julie settled back in her seat, smiling. *Oh, you bet I do.*

Julie knocked on Bianca's office door. "It's me."

"Hey, girlfriend!" Bianca chirped from inside. "Come on in!"

Julie pushed the door open and couldn't help gazing around

the office in awe. The chaos she'd seen here last time was replaced by sleek efficiency. The Gleipnir wires were practically invisible along the walls, and Bianca's desk, which had always been a mass of paperwork, was clean. She sat behind a shiny silver laptop, eating gummy bears with her feet on the desk.

"Want one?" Bianca offered the bag.

"No, thanks." Julie approached the desk.

Bianca waved a hand. "Sit down." She closed the laptop and planted her boots on the floor instead. "What's up? Any trouble with your powers?"

"Oh, no. I haven't had *that* trouble since the fight at Lockerfell." Julie winced at the memory.

"That was impressive, I must say, but I understand if you don't want to go over all that right now." Bianca twirled a blonde curl around one finger. "So, what can I do for you?"

"I have an idea." Julie grinned. "I thought I'd run it by you so I can officially go rogue if you say no and I do it anyway."

Bianca chuckled throatily. "I like it already."

"I want to set a trap for the Dark Moon League." Julie took a deep breath. "And whoever is helping them inside the PMA."

Bianca raised an eyebrow. "How did you know that that was a concern?"

Julie snorted. "If I said it was because of my Lunar Fae juju, would you believe me?"

"Categorically no, but that's an awesome answer, so I'll let it go." Bianca folded her arms. "What do you have in mind?"

Julie smiled. "I want to use Malcolm Nox as bait."

"Stop right there." Bianca held up a hand, a grin tugging the corners of her lips. "I'm not shooting you down, but we're going to need to talk to Kaplan if we're going to dangle the Nox heir in front of the most dangerous terrorist group in the world."

"I thought you'd cut down on the red tape." Julie planted her hands on her hips.

Bianca laughed. "Yes, but not *that* much, girlfriend. Let me give him a call." She picked up her phone and tapped the screen, then put it on speaker and set it on the desk.

Kaplan answered on the third ring. "*What?*" he snarled.

Bianca cut to the chase. "Julie's in my office, and she has a brilliant idea to capture our mole. We need approval from the top if we're going to make it happen."

There was a beat of silence.

"You don't know my idea yet," Julie mouthed.

The succubus grinned and waved a hand.

"Meadows has good ideas," Kaplan muttered.

"Why, *thank* you, sir!" Julie cooed.

"Didn't know you were listening, Meadows," Kaplan growled.

Bianca snickered.

"Knowing you two are in one room without adult supervision makes me nervous. Get your asses to my office. I've got twenty minutes." Kaplan hung up.

Bianca leaped to her feet. "Let's go!" She opened a side door of her office. "Malcolm! Come on. We've got a plan, and it involves you."

Bianca, Malcolm, and Julie hurried out of the elevator onto the fourth floor of the main building, and a painful wave of nostalgia washed over Julie. The communal office, with its ringing phones and the bowed heads of recruiters, was still familiar despite the lines of Gleipnir steel and the shiny new laptops.

Automatically, she glanced at the office she and Taylor had shared for so long. Its door was open, and she could see the dreadful portrait of the scantily clad mermaid, but Taylor wasn't at his old desk. Instead, two dwarves were bent over their laptops.

Julie let out a breath.

"You okay?" Bianca asked, striding toward Kaplan's office on the other side of the floor.

"Yeah." Julie laughed. "Lots of memories here, that's all." She ran a hand over her navy uniform, missing the green.

You've outgrown that role, Hat told her softly. *You'd hate it if you had to go back.*

I know, but it was special. Julie sighed.

"Are you guys going to tell me what this is about?" Malcolm asked, raising a slender eyebrow.

Julie grinned. "Soon."

Bianca's old office door opened when they were halfway across the floor, and Taylor hurried out, frowning at a clipboard in his hands. He looked up as they approached, and a smile blossomed on his face.

"Julie! Malcolm!" He stepped forward, then hesitated. "Major Hartshorn."

"You can smile at your girlfriend, Taylor. I won't eat you." Bianca chuckled.

"Where are you going?" Taylor asked.

Julie grinned. "Your favorite place. Kaplan's office."

"I have to talk to him about these numbers." Taylor waved his clipboard. "Mind if I tag along?"

"You might as well." Bianca gestured at him to follow.

The four of them piled into Kaplan's office, which was less changed than the rest of the floor. There was still a portrait of Kaplan, mounted on a rearing horse and looking imposing, on the back wall, and big windows overlooking the campus. Kaplan was sitting behind his desk, fingers steepled and amber eyes burning as they entered.

"You're late," he snarled.

Bianca and Malcolm sat. Julie hovered near Bianca's chair, and Taylor set his clipboard on the desk. "Captain, I have—"

Kaplan pushed the clipboard aside. "I know, the stats. Deal with them, Woodskin. You know what you're doing."

Taylor lifted his chin, shoulders squaring. "Yes, sir."

"Now, what's all this about?" Kaplan demanded.

Bianca nodded at Julie. "Tell him your plan."

Julie straightened and met Kaplan's eyes. "Sir, I know how we can capture whoever in the PMA is feeding intelligence to the Dark Moon League."

Kaplan's face showed no surprise. "Are you going to tell me, or are you just going to stand there basking in your cleverness?"

Julie folded her arms. "Sir, we've already established that whoever is behind these attacks is out to get the heirs and councilors from the seven Royal Families. I think we should lay a trap for them." She raised an eyebrow. "I think we should give them what they want as bait."

Everyone stared at Malcolm.

"*Me?*" The vampire laughed. "I've already been kidnapped twice in a year, so why not?"

"That's my point, Mal. Whoever they are, they want *you*." Julie grinned. "I think you can help us catch this son-of-a-bitch."

"Or daughter," Bianca chipped in.

Kaplan pinched the bridge of his nose and took a calming breath, then glared at Julie. "How do you propose to do that without getting the prince of vampires killed?"

"You could send him on a bunch of 'secret' assignments across Avalon, sir." Julie spread her hands. "Only they won't be secret. We'll let one spot on his itinerary slip to each department in the PMA. That will narrow it down, depending on where our traitor shows up."

"And when he shows up, I get kidnapped?" Malcolm asked, quirking an eyebrow.

"You'll have the faeries from my unit with you for backup. They're easy to conceal and pretty deadly," Julie explained. "What's more, a trusted team will monitor each location on the set time and day. Whoever arrives, we'll whisk you out of danger, but we *won't* arrest them."

"We won't?" Kaplan raised his eyebrows.

"No." Julie grinned. "We'll tail them and track them back to whoever's instigating the League's efforts to spark a war over the Eternity Throne."

Kaplan sat back in his chair, rubbing his chin with a vast hand.

"Sir, you can't actually be considering this," Taylor spluttered.

Kaplan's eyes narrowed. "I don't take well to being told what I can and can't do, Woodskin." He turned to Julie. "I don't think it will work, Meadows. If a full team swoops in and rescues Malcolm, our target will be suspicious."

"Hopefully, Malcolm and the faeries would be able to get out of trouble *without* needing a full team, sir. Either way, if we follow the target, they'll have to take us to their boss at some point." Julie paused. "Even identifying them without tailing them would be useful."

Kaplan folded his arms. "What about the leaks to each department? How do you propose we keep those secrets from slipping *between* departments?"

"They might," Julie admitted, "but we can appoint paras we trust in each department—paras who are low in the ranks and trusted by their colleagues—to monitor chatter as it passes through the department. They'll be able to keep tabs on whatever rumors are spread."

"I..." Kaplan stopped and frowned. "I like it."

"You do, sir?" Taylor spluttered.

Julie shot him a glare.

"You have my permission to go ahead, provided Major Hartshorn personally leads the op." Kaplan nodded to the succubus.

Bianca punched the air. "*Yesssss!* A chance to get out of my office." She turned to the vampire. "Now all we have to do is persuade Malcolm, and by Malcolm, I mean Cassidy."

"I agree that Cassidy might take some persuading," Malcolm

acknowledged, "but I want to be part of this." He turned to Julie and Bianca, grinning. "I'm in."

Kaplan rose to his feet. "Then it's settled. I have a meeting with Commander Lapp." He shuddered. "Dismissed."

"You can talk in my office if you want," Taylor offered.

"That's fine. Thanks." Bianca chuckled. "I look forward to seeing what you've done with the place."

"Are you sure, Mal?" Julie asked as they left Kaplan's office. "We'll do our best to keep you safe, but there are always risks."

"I am, but I want this person to be brought to justice." Malcolm flashed a fanged grin. "And let's be honest; I miss the action."

"Me too." Bianca smirked. "I can't wait."

Taylor held the door, and they filed into his new office. The chaos Bianca had left it in was gone. Julie was startled by how precise and tidy everything was. There was a nice new emerald-green carpet, and the desk was spotless, with pens and notepads lined up with geometric precision next to the gleaming laptop.

There was a coffee table in the corner, surrounded by comfortable seating, and Bianca threw herself into one of the chairs. "You think you can persuade your wife, Malcolm?"

"Cass is intimidating, but she won't infringe on my independence. We'll talk it out." Malcolm sat opposite her. "She might want to be involved, though."

"I'm cool with that if you are, Bianca." Julie took her seat, pulled Hat off, tossed him onto the coffee table, and ran a hand through her sweaty hair. "I've been with Cassidy in a fight. She's a little crazy, but she's fearless. I'd fight beside her any day."

"What about me?" Taylor asked, perching on the edge of an armchair.

"You?" Bianca raised her eyebrows.

Taylor spread his hands. "Yeah, me. What can I do?"

"Nothing. You're the head of recruitment, not a soldier. This is going to be a dangerous op," Bianca told him.

Taylor sat back, staring at Julie. "We've fought side by side, Julie."

"Yes, but that was before I was a professional soldier." Julie kept her voice gentle. "You've always had my back, T, but this is just like any other mission. I've got this."

Taylor seemed about to speak, then closed his mouth and sagged into his chair.

"There's a price for being in a leadership role." Bianca's smile was kind. "That price is a nice, comfy desk and saying farewell to anything remotely adrenaline-inducing."

"But *you're* going on the op!" Taylor protested.

"I know, right? The trick is to keep getting promoted until you get to the level where you can pretty much do whatever you want." Bianca winked.

"You could take it up with Kaplan if you wanted." Julie folded her arms, irritated.

Taylor squirmed. "I don't care about going on the op. I just—" He stopped.

Don't say it, Julie snarled inwardly. *Don't you say it.*

He's going to say it, Hat predicted.

"I don't want you to get hurt," he muttered, dropping his eyes.

Yep, he said it, Hat commented.

"I'm not having this discussion with you. I'm a soldier. You need to learn to be okay with that." Julie got up.

Taylor's head snapped up. He turned to Malcolm, his fists clenched on his knees. "So, Cassidy will be okay with you being dangled like a juicy worm in front of the traitors who want you dead, Malcolm?"

Hat gasped, and Bianca's jaw dropped. Malcolm, always pale, lost what little color he had had in his face. His skin was almost translucent.

"Okay, that's it." Julie grabbed Taylor's arm and yanked him out of his chair. "We need to talk. *Now.*"

She was trembling with anger as she dragged Taylor to the

other side of his office. Reaching the corner, she whirled to face him, still holding his arm. "What is your problem?"

"I'm just…oh!" Taylor gasped and snatched his arm back. Smoke rose from the sleeve of his uniform, and he rubbed his arm, staring at her.

"Sorry." Julie gritted her teeth and took a deep breath, forcing her burning palms to cool.

"It's okay. I know it wasn't on purpose." Taylor interlaced his fingers. "Julie, I'm just scared for you."

"Scared for me, huh?" Julie folded her arms. "Are you as scared for Malcolm?"

Taylor just bit his lip.

"I didn't think so. You've got to let go of this, Taylor. I've been a soldier for seven months now. I'm going to be a soldier for a long time, and there are always going to be risks," Julie spat.

"I know." Taylor looked at her, and tears glittered in his eyes. "I-I tried to ignore them, Julie, but after Chester—" He looked away.

Julie felt a pang of guilt. She'd almost forgotten that Chester had been Taylor's friend too.

"I get that. I do." Julie clenched her fists. "But it doesn't change anything. You can't interfere with my job, Taylor!" She furiously gestured at the other side of the room. "You undermined me in front of my commanding officer. Do you know how disrespectful that is? You can't keep doing this!"

Taylor turned away, running his hands through his hair. "I don't know how not to care about you."

"You're not caring for me when you do this. You're being an ass!" Julie retorted. "You're telling me you don't value my choices or acknowledge my strength, and if you're going to be in a relationship with me, I need you to do that."

"I do value your choices. You're the strongest person I know, Julie," Taylor choked out, keeping his back to her.

"Then act like you believe that!" Julie snapped.

"I'm trying, okay?" Taylor spun to face her, his face ashen. "I'm also trying to look out for the woman I love!"

The word broke over Julie's head like a blinding light. Her words stuck in her throat, and she stared at him in silence. Taylor froze, tears in his eyes. She'd never seen him look so hopelessly afraid.

"I..." Julie took a long breath. All the things she wanted to say evaporated from her head. What came out of her mouth was, "I love you, too."

Taylor looked away, taking deep, shaky breaths.

"I do." Julie stepped forward and laid a hand on his arm. "I really do, T, but you can't cage me."

Taylor just gazed at her, eyes wide.

Julie's voice was steady, her palms cool. "I'm not going to turn my thunder down for you or anyone. I get more powerful every time I visit the egg, and I don't know where that's going to take me. I can't live my life making decisions based on your fears."

She paused. "So you need to think long and hard about how we can come to an agreement."

CHAPTER NINETEEN

Julie's words slammed into Taylor's chest like punches. They were cold, and her eyes were hard as they drilled into his.

I love you, too. Her words echoed in his mind, but they seemed less real than what she had just said.

"Come to an...agreement?" Taylor echoed in a croak.

Julie nodded. "And we'll have to talk this through later. After we've plugged this leak." She frowned, storm clouds gathering in her eyes, and looked at Bianca. "I'll meet you in the ops room, Bianca."

Then she was gone, stalking out of the room. Taylor's sleeve cooled where her hand had rested. He let his hands fall to his sides, empty. When she slammed the door, it rattled his bones.

Malcolm's awkward chuckle broke the silence. "I think you need to choose the hill you want to die on carefully, Taylor."

Bianca burst out laughing. "Julie isn't a *hill.*" Her blue eyes sparkled. "She's a mountain range. Get used to it, or get used to the idea of being without her."

Taylor's cheeks flushed.

"Well, speaking of dying, I need to go talk to Cassidy."

Malcolm got up and headed for the door, pausing to pat Taylor on the shoulder. "Good luck."

Bianca left on Malcolm's heels, and Taylor reeled over to the coffee table and flopped into an armchair. He covered his face with his hands. It felt like there was a cannonball in his chest.

"Looks like it's just you and me, huh?"

Taylor jumped. He'd forgotten that Hat was still lying on the coffee table where Julie had flung him.

"She doesn't often forget me, but maybe it's not a bad thing this time." Hat jumped onto Taylor's lap, his peak curling into what might have been a smile.

Taylor leaned back, rubbing his face with both hands. "I'm so afraid for her, Hat." He had to take a deep breath to choke back his emotion. "I saw Chester the day he was killed. That morning, lying in front of Olena's door. He said hello and chatted with me like guarding her was nothing for him, but I know how much it meant to her. Chess was a good guy, a *great* guy, and he's gone just like that." He paused. "I just don't want that to happen to Julie."

"You're not wrong. It might happen." Hat's crown sagged. "But this is who she is."

"Maybe..." Taylor swallowed. "Maybe I can't deal with it. I don't want to hold her back, but I don't know how to cope with the thought that I could lose her as suddenly as we lost Chester."

"Think about your options, Taylor," Hat murmured. "Julie's not wrong to be angry, and she's trying to hold back. She's trying to give you a chance to work through this, but she's right. You've been given enough time. You can't burden her with your fears."

Taylor stared at the carpet. "I don't know how not to." Nausea gripped him.

"Then maybe you should learn." Hat's voice was firm. "Don't you think she's worth growing for?"

Taylor groaned, pressing his fingertips into his temples, miserable. "More than anyone I've ever known, Hat. I don't mean to overstep her boundaries. I just want to protect her, and I feel like I'm failing."

Hat chuckled. "You'll be surprised to find that she feels the same way. This war puts *you* in danger, too, you know. Julie has a lot of reasons for doing what she does, and you're one of them."

Taylor hesitated. "I've never seen it that way."

"I know you kids think my views are somewhat archaic," Hat went on, "but women—most of them—are better equipped for dealing with tricky emotions. Less so now that men are encouraged to express how they're feeling, but there's a lot of catching up to do in that regard for males of most species. Simply put, you're being a guy about this, Taylor."

Taylor took a deep breath, straightened, and stared at Hat. "How do you know all this stuff?"

"Oh, I've been around," Hat told him airily.

How does a hat get dates? Taylor pushed the thought aside, certain he didn't want to know. "Well, what can I do to make it right?"

Hat's peak curved up. "You can keep trying to fix things she doesn't want fixed, or you can be a good boyfriend and ask what you can do to support her while her life is changing."

Taylor nodded, turning the thought over in his mind. "Thanks, Hat." He managed a faint laugh. "I've never loved anyone like this, you know? I feel so clueless."

"You'll learn." Hat chuckled. "Start by trying to grasp that you can be happy together your whole lives and *still* be two separate people with separate needs and goals."

Taylor thought for a moment. "I don't want it to be different. I don't want her to be less *her*. That's who I'm in love with."

"Then hold onto that," Hat encouraged him. "Also, take me to the military wing, please. *You* might be missing out on this, but I'm not."

"Out of sympathy, are you?" Taylor raised his eyebrows.

"Just do it," Hat grumbled.

Taylor tucked Hat under his arm and headed out of the room.

"I'm so sorry about that," Julie groaned as she and Bianca left the elevator and strode through the lobby. "My boyfriend is a total idiot."

Bianca shrugged. "Eh, not a *total* idiot. He's just being a dude."

"I don't know about that," Julie admitted. She raked a hand through her hair. "Ah, shit. I left Hat in his office."

"We'll send some boot to go get him. First, we need some girl talk." Bianca draped a sisterly arm around Julie's shoulders and squeezed her, then let go as they stepped out onto the campus. "Tell me what's on your mind."

Julie chewed her lip before answering. "I wasn't lying. I do love Taylor. There's a lot about him to love. I just don't understand why we keep having these problems."

"Hey, girl, problems are normal." Bianca smiled. "Take it from a succubus. Everyone has problems, and as problems go, Taylor's not throwing up any red flags." She shrugged. "Pink ones, maybe, but nothing you can't solve with clear communication."

"I don't know." Julie huffed. "I just want us to get along and agree on everything."

Bianca emitted a merry peal that rang across the campus. "Girl, that would be boring as all hell."

Julie stared at her.

"Sure, you need to agree on the important things," Bianca went on, "but nothing ruins people's relationships like giving up their individuality for the sake of an easy ride." She raised an eyebrow. "You want a lover who makes you feel like you've got your foot on the gas of that Mustang of yours, or do you want to be stuck doing the speed limit in a Prius all your life?"

Julie rubbed the back of her neck. "You have a point."

"Of course I have a point. I'm amazing." Bianca tossed curls over her shoulder. "Thing is, it's not going to be the last time Taylor messes up. You're going to mess up, too. Neither of you will ever be perfect."

"Let me guess." Julie raised her eyebrows. "It doesn't matter if we're 'perfect for each other?'"

"No. That's sentimental bullshit, even when it comes to love." Bianca grinned. "Thing is, arguments can be the best part of a healthy relationship. They push us to grow and see a different perspective. To become better people, as long as you remember what really matters: that you love the person, even though you're equal and different. That you agree on the most important things."

Julie nodded and took a deep breath. The tightness in her chest lifted. "Thanks, Bianca."

"Anytime." Bianca slapped her on the back and grinned. "So, are we going to catch ourselves a traitor?"

Julie laughed. "Let's do this!"

The giant owl clicked her beak, sneering down at Malcolm from her towering height. Evening light fell through the tall, thin windows of her home. Malcolm tried to resist the urge to stare around at it. The building was vaulted, cathedral-like in its gray stone and Gothic curves, and there were perches built into every crevice. In the spire above him, the shadows were filled with the rustling of wings.

"Your documents mean little to us, mammal," the owl hooted.

"Yes, you said," Malcolm muttered. She had said that at least four times, and it struck him as irrelevant, considering that a hapless goblin servant had brought them to the inner chamber.

The owl's eyes narrowed. "The Parliament is not impressed with your insolence."

The Parliament can go screw itself. Malcolm kept that to himself. He bowed deeply, glancing into the shadows again.

Relax, Mal. Julie's voice came through his telechip. *We've got you. The faeries are just outside, plus the one in your bag.*

"The Eternity Throne sends its regards." Malcolm forced a smile for the owl's benefit. "Thank you for your time."

As he spoke, he ran a hand over the leather satchel on his hip and straightened. The faerie inside buzzed in annoyance, and he felt the reassuring bump of the glass vial in there with them—Cassidy's blood. It clinked against a bottle of silver antidote.

Besides, it appears that nothing's going to happen, Bianca grouched.

Somehow, that's not reassuring, Malcolm grumbled.

The owl blinked. "Leave us. You bore us, mammal."

"How is that an insult?" Malcolm muttered to himself.

The owl didn't hear him. She had already turned away. Throwing open her enormous wings, she sprang into the air and flew soundlessly up to the rustling spire.

Malcolm headed for the tall door at the other end of the building as quickly as his feet could carry him.

Why so nervous tonight? Julie asked. She sighed. *It's been two weeks, we've been dragged all over Avalon, and nothing's happened to you.*

Yeah. Bianca snorted. *I can't believe Kaplan sent the rest of the unit back to the OPMA. I think he only agreed to let Julie, Cassidy, the faeries, and me babysit you because he knows you tend to be rash.*

Thanks, Malcolm grumbled.

To be fair, it is starting to look like no one's going to take the bait, Julie pointed out.

Don't sound so disappointed. Malcolm paused as he reached the door and nervously peered outside. The building was surrounded by a forest of aged pine trees interspersed with ancient, motionless dryads. The branches groaned in the wind. *Something just feels different about tonight,* he admitted.

We're only a few hundred yards away, Bianca assured him, *and we can see you standing in the doorway. Come on out and get in your carriage. I have dinner plans.*

Oh? With who? Julie asked.

Bianca snickered. *Don't you want to find out!*

Malcolm took a deep breath. The wind moaned in the trees as he stared across the clearing. His carriage waited on the drive, the pair of black horses stirring restlessly in the shafts. Perkins was at the reins, and he had his hands full, trying to get them to stand quietly.

The sight of old Perkins was the reassurance Malcolm needed. He stepped forward, feet crunching on pine needles, and started the trek across the clearing. It felt like the carriage was getting farther away, like a nightmare. The hairs rose on the back of his neck, and Malcolm stopped and whipped around, his nails lengthening into claws.

There's nothing there, Malcolm, Julie told him.

There *was* nothing except the spooky old building and the hooting of owls. Malcolm took a deep breath and brushed off his suit, feeling stupid. He turned toward the carriage.

The wind changed. It blew suddenly from behind Malcolm, ruffling his hair, a chill breath on his neck.

The horses lunged. The carriage jerked forward, and Perkins let out a cry while hauling back on the reins. Panicking, both horses reared and snorted, and white sweat burst out on their shoulders and necks.

What's going on? Julie yelled.

I don't like it. Go, go, go! Bianca screamed.

Malcolm spun to face the woods, his fangs and claws lengthening, but he barely had time to brace himself before the woods exploded in a wild mass of fur and feathers. He caught a glimpse of a fox with teeth bared, crows plunging from the sky toward him, and a lumbering bear bursting from the bushes with a deafening roar.

Faeries flitted around him, but there was no time to fire a single shot before a huge stag plunged out of the mass of animals, antlers first.

———

Julie clutched her pistols as Seven plunged through the trees. Branches ripped the camouflage tarp off the vehicle, squealing across its body, but it didn't slow down.

"What just happened?" Bianca yelled. Red magic swirled in her hands.

"Where is he?" Cassidy shrieked. The vampire clutched the edge of her seat, eyes wild and face ashen.

"I have no idea," Julie stated. "Where were the faeries?"

"I don't know! I just saw those animals pop out of the woods, then they and Malcolm disappeared!" Bianca shouted.

Seven spun to a halt in the clearing. It was empty except for the wreckage of the carriage. The horses were gone, and Perkins stood beside the ruined carriage, horrified.

"That way. They went that way!" he cried as Julie kicked the door open and jumped out. He pointed into the woods. "The horses ran after them. They were—" He swallowed. "Different."

"I can feel them," Hat agreed. "They're under an enchantment."

"So Bambi didn't kidnap Malcolm on his own," Julie growled.

"No. Someone's behind this." Bianca slammed Seven's door. "Julie, come on!"

"We have to find him!" Cassidy snapped.

Julie scrambled into the vehicle, and before she could close the door, Seven raced into the woods, careening off trees with bone-jarring thumps and crashing madly through the undergrowth.

"I feel lost without Ariadne's thread," Julie admitted.

"You don't need that silly bit of thaumatech. You have me," Hat announced. "I'm guiding the vehicle."

"And I know where my husband is," Cassidy hissed. Her eyes glowed red, and she flexed her long white claws. "Hat, I'll guide you."

Seven wove between the trees, humming with speed and magic. Julie caught glimpses of the animals' passage: the white flesh of a tree exposed in a snapped branch and hoofprints in mud, but she couldn't see them.

A rock rushed up to meet them, and Hat yelped. Seven's nose rose, but the rock slammed into his undercarriage, and the vehicle bucked madly. Julie squealed, bounced off her seat, and threw out her hands to keep from smacking her face into the dash.

"Slow him down, Hat!" Bianca snapped.

"No!" Cassidy snarled. "They're getting away from us."

"What's that?" Julie pointed through the slit window on the front of Seven. There was a huddled brown lump on the ground a few hundred feet ahead.

Cassidy inhaled sharply.

"Stop!" Hat ordered.

Seven hummed to a halt near the lump, and Julie leaned out the window. It was a wild boar, newly dead, its carcass bloodied. Hoofprints patterned its hide, red and angry, and there was a pool of blood around its mouth. Its ribs were misshapen and squashed.

"They trampled it to death," Julie murmured.

"Who cares? It's not Malcolm. Go!" Cassidy snapped.

Seven surged forward, and Julie turned to Bianca. "I have an idea."

"Any idea is a good one right now. Do it!" Bianca barked.

Julie leaned out of the window, hoping she wouldn't get her head smacked off by a tree. She filled her lungs with air and yelled with all her might, "Hey, come merry dol! Green Man, hear us!"

"Wish I'd thought of that," Bianca muttered.

Seven surged onward, and Julie looked up at the silent dryads, searching for the giant flying leaf Green Men rode upon. She saw nothing but branches and sky. They skimmed past the carcass of a crushed hare, and Julie's palms began to sting.

"Where *are* they?" Cassidy cried.

"Why isn't he responding?" Julie demanded.

"Don't look at *me!*" Hat spluttered. "I'm busy controlling this thing!"

"Hey, come merry dol!" Julie tried again. "Green Man, hear… *shit!*"

Seven swerved to avoid one tree, but another appeared out of nowhere, and the vehicle's nose slammed into it with a sickening crunch. He spun helplessly, throwing Julie against the door. Cassidy's shriek pierced the air as Seven careened across a clearing sideways. His hum turned into a screech. Julie saw the woods rushing up to meet them and braced herself into her seat, throwing her arms over her head. She gritted her teeth and waited for impact. Instead, Seven jerked to a halt.

When Julie looked up, the vehicle was mere inches from the nearest tree.

"What happened?" Bianca demanded. "These things are supposed to be sentient enough to avoid collisions!"

"That wasn't a simple collision. That tree *moved*," Hat whispered.

There was a long, creaking moan from the woods. Julie picked up her pistol from the floor where it had fallen in the chaos and cocked it. She felt a crackle of magic through the metal.

"Great," Bianca snapped. "Just what we need. This is why I go to the beach instead of the woods."

The dryads at the edges of the clearing had come to life. Their branches rose, leaves rustling as shudders ran through them. The earth cracked, then exploded as roots burst from it, then plunged back into the ground, dragging the dryads nearer to where Seven stood.

"This forest is an army on its own." Bianca cocked her rifle.

Cassidy opened the door. "I'm going after Malcolm."

"You're staying in this vehicle, Cassidy," Bianca ordered. "Without you, we have no way of tracking him."

Julie kicked her door open and stepped out into the clearing. The dryads were coming closer. She could see their twisted, gnarled faces deep in the trunks of the trees, and they were furious.

"Green Man!" she shouted. "You might not care about us, but what about your animals and trees? They've been enchanted, and they're being murdered! You're supposed to care for these woods!" The sting in her palms turned into a burn. "You're supposed to be taking care of them, and if you want to save them, you must come to us *now*!"

"Silence, worm!"

The voice roared through the trees, bending their boughs and making the grass hiss against Julie's legs. She stumbled back, throwing up a hand to shield her face as wind thundered through the woods. A black shape blotted out the sunlight for a moment. Then a giant leaf swooped down to the clearing, borne on the wind, and a slender humanoid stepped off it and strode toward Julie.

This Green Man was nothing like the yellow-booted, jovial Ember Floraison from Fernwood Deep. His face was flesh, but it was gray and shrunken flesh with deep wrinkles in the cheeks and brow. The eyes were flint-gray, and instead of green leaves, his beard was composed of jutting brown pine needles that stuck out in every direction. Animal skins were wrapped around his body, some still reeking.

"Leave my forest." The Green Man's words rattled like the wind in dry twigs.

Bianca stepped out of the vehicle and slammed the door. She strode over to the Green Man. Her wings were half-unfolded, and she cradled her automatic rifle in her arms.

"Respectfully, sir, we're not going to do that. Something's happening in your woods. Someone's enchanted your animals and probably your dryads, and they've taken Malcolm Nox, the prince of vampires." Bianca raised her head, tilting back her horns. "We're not going anywhere until we find him, and we'll need your help."

"Help?" The Green Man ground his yellow teeth behind the pine-needle beard. "You will get no help, stranger. Leave my forest! You have no place here."

"We'll leave as soon as we retrieve our friend," Julie offered.

Bianca snorted. "You are the caretaker of this forest, Green Man. You're bound to help us locate Malcolm Nox and free the animals from their enchantment. Are you going to?"

The Green Man's eyes narrowed.

"Oh, and if you don't help us, you should know one thing." Bianca grinned. "Bacchus is only a phone call away."

Julie raised her eyebrows. *That is a story I'll need to hear after all this.*

Focus! Hat chided.

The Green Man threw back his head with disconcerting suddenness. Julie gasped and raised her pistol, and an eerie shriek emanated from the Green Man's wide-open mouth. It was the sound of a gale in a dead tree and of a dying deer, and goosebumps rose on Julie's skin in response.

"Get on the ground!" Bianca had her rifle aimed. "Get on the ground and put your hands behind your head!"

The Green Man let out a screeching cackle and leaped onto his leaf.

"This is your last warning!" Bianca flipped off the safety.

The Green Man glanced at her, his dry-grass hair windblown around his face. "*I* am the enchanter of this wood," he hissed. "And all that lives within it shall do as *I* say."

Julie saw the root ripping through the dirt toward Bianca's ankles just in time. "Bianca, look out!" she yelled and whipped around, firing her pistol into the dirt. A root stopped inches from Bianca's legs, and there was a creaking moan of pain from the nearest dryad.

They were closing in. The Green Man was gone and dryads surged toward them, roots and branches reaching for Julie's face. She fired into the trunk of the nearest tree. Splinters flew, and Julie stared through the bullet hole, but the dryad only shrieked in pain and came faster. It drew back a branch and struck. Julie leaped back a split second too slow, and the tip of the branch lashed her cheek.

Julie raised a hand to her cheek and felt hot blood on her fingertips. A surge of rage crackled through her, and she holstered the gun.

"Fine," she spat as the dryad's branches pulled back for another blow. "Have it your way."

Flame roared in her hands. The dryad's mouth opened in a moan of terror, but it was too late. Julie raised her blazing hands, and fire touched the dryad's leaves. They stayed green, but the flames scorched a black scar on the branch.

The dryad shrieked and stumbled back, and Julie looked for Bianca. The succubus was high in the air, her leathery wings beating, firing blasts of red magic into the trees. Julie spotted a vine crawling up one of the dryads, about to lunge toward Bianca. She raised both hands and concentrated, and a tongue of flame launched from her palms and slashed the vine. It shriveled to ashes.

"You go, girl!" Bianca cheered, then sent another blast of magic into the nearest dryad's face. It stumbled back, shrieking, and its branches tangled with its neighbor's. Both trees fell to the ground.

Cassidy was suddenly beside her, hissing and slashing at the trees. "We have to get to Malcolm!"

"Which way is he?" Julie yelled back. She grabbed the nearest dryad by the branch, her hands sizzling with fire. The dryad pulled back with a scream, waving its burning branch, the flames roaring as they were fanned by the movement.

Cassidy pointed.

"Leave Seven. He can't move through these trees!" Hat shouted. "Just go!"

"I'm covering you!" Bianca called from above.

A bolt of red magic punched a hole in the ring of dryads ahead, and Julie and Cassidy raced through it. The vampire's eyes blazed scarlet, but there was none of the madness in her face that Julie had seen there during the Quickening.

Cassidy's mouth was set in a grim line, and her blazing red eyes looked dead ahead. Whenever a branch or a root crossed her path, she threw it aside with a slash of her claws or a snap of fangs, not slowing down.

She's even scarier like this, Julie observed.

Three o'clock! Hat screamed.

CHAPTER TWENTY

Julie threw up her right arm and sent a blast of flame into a charging dryad. The tree fell back in a plume of smoke, screeching.

"Look out!" Bianca shouted. "There's a creek just through these bushes!"

"Come on!" Julie called to Cassidy. "They might not follow us through the water!"

They plunged into the bushes, and Cassidy let out a high-pitched shriek and disappeared from beside Julie. Julie skidded to a halt. Leaves flew into the air, and Cassidy was on the ground, roots wrapped around her ankles, being dragged back into the wall of angry trees pursuing them.

"Cassidy!" Julie yelled.

Bianca fired red magic at the roots and missed. Julie rushed forward, sheets of flame stretching up her forearms as rage blazed in her chest.

"Let her go!" Julie bellowed.

More roots surged from the ground, wrapping around Cassidy's arms and her torso. The dryads' branches stretched toward Cassidy, their leaves shaking violently. A bolt of red magic fell from the sky, cutting through three of the roots, but there were five more to take their place. A root burst out of the earth and twined around Cassidy's neck, and the vampire's eyes widened with terror.

"*NO!*" Julie clenched her fists, and flames roared up her arms to her shoulders. Heat surged through her body, and she spread her arms. "Stop. *Stop!*"

The trees didn't listen. Cassidy's face was turning blue.

Julie brought her hands together, skin meeting skin with a soft *slap.* Then a whirling torrent of flame burst from her joined hands and sped into the trees. It raced from dryad to dryad where their branches touched, and the air was filled with their screams and moans as flame danced along their branches, thick white smoke billowing into the air.

The roots shriveled and collapsed around Cassidy. Julie ran to her, the fire dissipating in her hands as horror replaced the rage in her chest. Limbs dropped from the trees as coals and ash.

Cassidy was sitting up, clutching the red marks around her throat.

"Come on!" Julie grabbed Cassidy's arm.

"Go, go!" Bianca shouted.

Dragging the vampire with her, Julie bolted through the bushes, her free hand clutching her pistol. The bushes gave way to the wide, slow-moving creek, and Julie plunged into it, finding it only knee-deep. Cassidy regained her strength as they waded across it. When they reached the opposite bank, she was leading the way, and she fell to her hands and knees as soon as her feet hit dry land.

Julie stood over her, looking back into the woods. The dryads had rushed down to the creek. Some had fallen in, moaning, with black smoke rising from their charred trunks. Others soaked their scorched bark in the water. The smoke had already lessened.

"What did I do?" Julie stared down at her hands. "They were being enchanted!"

Bianca landed beside her, folding her wings. "You saved Cassidy's life, that's what. Probably Malcolm's, too." She grabbed Cassidy's arm. "Get up, Cass. We still need to find him."

"What is *that*?" Cassidy shrieked.

Julie turned and forgot the burning dryads.

The ground was not only clear ahead of them but blasted. There was no grass, no wildflowers, no ferns. Bare dirt ran up the hill, on top of which stood an enormous building stepped like a Mesoamerican pyramid. However, this wasn't carved from stone. It was made of whole trees, their branches tangled with each other, their butchered trunks stacked like corpses in a pyre. They were gray and dead.

Julie shuddered. "Creepy."

"Not just creepy." Bianca sucked in a breath. "Those aren't trees, Julie. They're—"

Julie gasped. "Dryads." She could see their faces in the trunks, twisted in death grimaces.

"He's in there," Cassidy rasped. She rose to her feet. "Malcolm's in there." Her voice trembled.

Julie clenched her fists. "Then we're going to get him out."

There was no cover. They strode onto the bare dirt, which smelled scorched and bitter. Bianca had her rifle in her hands again. Julie had her pistol in one hand and flames in the other. Cassidy's fangs were extended. As they approached, sound seeped through the walls: yelps and screeches, barks and squeals. Animal sounds.

"They're still in there with him!" Cassidy lunged forward.

Bianca grabbed her arm, stopping her. "Stay with us. We'll do this together."

They moved quickly, feet almost silent on the dirt, toward the black gap in the bottom of the temple formed by an arch of twisted trees. The trunks that formed the foundation of the temple were huge—redwoods—but these were supple and green. Barely more than saplings. Julie couldn't look at their faces.

"He did this," Bianca whispered as they stepped into the darkness. "The Green Man built this thing."

"He's controlling the animals, too," Julie realized.

Bianca nodded. "This is all his doing."

Cassidy stared at the twisted figures of the saplings. "He was supposed to protect these dryads, and look what he did to them."

They were in a dark hallway bordered by more dead dryads. The golden flicker of Julie's flames lit the way, and as they advanced, the animal noises got louder.

They heard a scream, masculine and painfully human.

"Malcolm!" Cassidy yelled.

"Wait!" Julie exclaimed, but it was too late. The vampire charged toward the sound.

Julie and Bianca followed at a dead run, and the hallway spat them out into a huge open pyramidal space. The walls were jumbled roots and branches. The floor was dirt, churned up by the hooves and paws of the horde of animals gathered in the center of the room, in which stood a great stump, eight or nine feet in diameter, like an altar.

"*Malcolm!*" Cassidy cried.

"*Cassidy!*" Malcolm screamed.

He was spread-eagled on his back on the stump. Blood ran from a cut in his cheek, and his arms and legs were tied down with vines that tugged and writhed as they threw more coils around his limbs. The vampire's black suit was torn, and he looked panicked as he thrashed against the vines that held him down.

A ring of animals lunged and snarled at him, a badger's teeth snapping inches from his heels. There was a tiny gunshot, and a puff of sparkling gold fairy dust exploded in the badger's face. It fell on its side, instantly sedated.

The faeries hovered in the air, surrounding Malcolm, firing

their rifles into the animals. Piles of sedated animals lay all over the temple, but hundreds more poured through the gaps in the tree-trunk walls. One faerie lay weakly on the edge of the stump, her left wing crumpled like paper, still firing into the fray.

Julie set her pistol to stun and fired. A ball of crackling electricity thudded into a charging doe, and her slender legs buckled. She fell and slid across the dirt. Julie fired again, but more animals poured through the trees.

"We have no choice," Cassidy snarled. "We must kill them all."

"We can't!" Julie cried. "There are too many!"

"You know Green Men. Talk to him!" Bianca snapped. "Cassidy, we'll hold them off!"

The succubus and vampire charged as one, punching and kicking. When Bianca locked horns with a fierce stag, Julie forced herself to turn away. She clenched her fists, and fire exploded over her hands.

"Green Man!" she shouted at the top of her voice. "I'll cut to the chase. I'm going to burn this entire forest down if you don't call these animals off!"

Wild windblown laughter rushed through the temple.

"Don't think I'm serious?" Julie strode to the nearest of the giant trunks. "Let's start right here!"

She held up a blazing hand, and a roar of wind almost knocked her over. It fanned the flames on her hands, and they flared over the trunk. Black scorch marks formed on the wood, and the wind stopped. The Green Man melted out of the dark passage, his gray eyes locked on hers like a hunting wolf's.

"You cannot stop this," he hissed.

"Really? Watch me, bitch." Julie held out a burning hand to the trunk.

"Fool!" the Green Man roared. "You would burn the temple down around us?"

"I can control fire. I'm pretty sure I can get my friends out alive." Julie's eyes narrowed. "Now call off those animals, or your little temple will be ashes."

The Green Man sneered. "My beasts will kill you. They will fight you though they burn."

Julie shuddered at the mental image, the flames flickering in her hands. She squeezed her fists tight, willing them to keep burning.

"There is nothing you can do, child." The Green Man grinned, his teeth crooked behind the pine needle beard. "I will wash this temple with the vampire's blood. I have spent centuries building the magic here. All it requires to work is a sacrifice."

"Work?" Julie stalled, her mind racing. "What do you mean?"

"This temple will return the world to the old ways." The Green Man's cackle was a storm wind in the woods. "A time when the wilderness was king and the lesser groups knew their place. When fae and elves huddled in fear of the dark, for the dark contained my beasts and *me*."

His laugh echoed around the temple, coming at Julie from all directions. "Your petty thrones and foolish kingdoms, your pomp and frippery, your meaningless nobles and orderly agencies will fall. There will be sacred chaos once more, where the world is pure, driven by survival alone and governed by the bloodthirsty and the strong."

Julie's eyes widened. "You," she snarled. "You're the one who's been stirring up the Dark Moons. You're the reason they never seem to run out of resources."

The Green Man sneered. "Those fools were useful for a time. They will soon learn to be subjugated as *we* have been subjugated." He stepped back, his gray eyes sliding to the altar. "I was surprised when the vampire spawn came into my woods, but he was a gift. I wanted the Sylthana prince after that pompous fool rejected the assistance he was offered, but this is better."

He let out a harsh, wheezing cackle. "When Julius Nox finds out how his heir died, he will scourge Avalon. He will be part of plunging the world into the darkness it once enjoyed. The world will be pure once more. The world will be ruled by—"

"Okay, okay, we get it," Julie groaned, rolling her eyes.

The Green Man stared at her.

"Like, your monologue was pretty cool. I liked the wording. But I'm done with it now. Basically, you're not going to call off the animals?" Julie raised her eyebrows.

The Green Man sneered. "No. You will die, and your blood—"

"Whatever, man. Suit yourself." Julie shrugged, and flames roared up her arms, engulfing her torso and dancing over her eyes. "One major bonfire, coming right up."

"*No!*" the Green Man screeched. He threw back his head and let out that wild, mournful cry again, and the walls of the temple began to tremble.

No! Hat gasped.

What? Julie held her burning hands to the nearest trunk.

They're here! Hat cried. *The Dark Moon League!*

The Dark Moons came from all directions. They poured through the hall, squeezed through the gaps between the trees, and abseiled in through the hole in the pyramid's roof. Trolls, elves, dwarves—all had their faces painted black, with the white sliver of the crescent moon on one cheek.

An elf dove from halfway up the wall and yanked a knife from its sheath, his eyes fixed on Malcolm.

"No!" Julie yelled. She whipped around, jabbing a fist in his direction, expecting a gout of flame to leap from her arm. Instead, a ball of fire launched from her fist, white plasma shimmering with heat in its center. The fireball punched into the elf's chest, threw him across the temple, and scorched a hole in the wall.

"Shit!" Julie yelled.

"Woohoo! you go, Julie!" Bianca cheered. She had a bear in a chokehold, and it was slowly losing consciousness. "New moves for the win, girl!"

"Thanks!" Julie grinned back.

"There are too many!" Cassidy cried. She was kneeling over Malcolm, slashing at the vines that clutched at his arms and legs, but they kept coming.

There was a familiar creaking moan from the hallway. Julie sent another fireball thundering into the chest of a charging troll and looked up as a stream of furious dryads, dripping wet and scorched with fire, poured into the temple.

Julie shot a fireball into the leader of the dryads. It ripped off two of its major branches, steam sizzling from the ruined trunk, but the dryad didn't slow down, and its sodden flesh didn't catch fire.

"Merlin's asshole," Julie cursed.

Bianca screamed. The bear lay senseless at her feet, but she was faced with a pike-wielding elf, and blood dripped from a gash in her left wing. She brought her good wing around in a thunderous blow that sent the elf flying, but a pack of enraged foxes swarmed around her legs, snapping and snarling. She jumped, kicking at them with her boots as she fired magic into the Dark Moons at the same time. Her right wing flapped desperately but couldn't lift her out of their reach.

"There are too many!" Julie screamed. She kicked a dwarf in the guts and spun to launch another fireball at a charging dryad.

"We need reinforcements," Hat cried.

"Reinforcements, or fewer enemies." Julie's eyes narrowed, and with a fireball in each hand, she scanned the temple for a gray figure. "How do I get rid of the enchantment on the animals?"

"If you can distract the Green Man—" Hat began.

Julie slammed a blazing fist into the blackened hole where a dryad's branches used to be. The inside of the trunk caught fire, and the dryad stumbled back, screaming, black smoke rolling thickly from among its branches. She ducked a vicious swipe from a troll's saber, feeling a line of fire open on her cheek, and launched a fireball into his face.

"Find him, Hat!" she snapped.

"Help!" Cassidy's voice was a hoarse shriek of terror. "We need help!"

Julie's head snapped around. Malcolm was free, his wrists bruised and clothes torn, and he and Cassidy stood back-to-back on the altar, animals clawing and snapping at their legs. Above them, a cloud of irate birds flew in a tight-packed circle, their deafening chatter rising above the noise of battle. Julie glimpsed flashing beaks and tiny claws. They rose, their circle forming a vortex. They were preparing to dive at the stricken vampires.

She felt the fist coming at her and grabbed it just in time, using the dwarf's momentum to spin him around and fling him into a charging knot of Dark Moons. Fending off the dryads with one arm, Julie searched for a way to get to the vampires.

"Bianca!" Cassidy sobbed.

Bianca, hopelessly beleaguered, didn't hear. Her ruined wing scattered blood everywhere as she strove to gain air over the sea of animals and Dark Moons overwhelming her.

"*Malcolm!*" Cassidy screamed.

A massive stag slammed his antlers into Malcolm. The vampire was tossed into the air, blood soaking his tailored suit from the shallow cuts the antlers slashed in his skin. He snarled and clawed at the stag's face, but he was too late. The birds were about to dive.

"*There!*" Hat bellowed. "Julie, there he goes!"

Julie whirled. She saw the whipping dryad branches first, then the giant leaf soaring into the air. The Green Man crouched upon it like he was surfing.

She didn't think, just punched a fist in his direction, aiming a little ahead of him, and a ball of burning plasma hurtled across the temple. For an instant, Julie thought it would hit him in the chest. Instead, it seared through the leaf, and flames sprang to life on his legs. His scream shook the temple. Leaf and Green Man plummeted to the ground in a cloud of smoke.

"Julie, look out!" Bianca shouted.

Julie spun as the stag, his antlers bloody, hurtled toward her. She screamed and fell to her knees, throwing her hands up over her head. Her heart stuttered in her chest. Instead of lowering his antlers, the stag let out a snort of effort, drew up his knees, and jumped, sailing over her head.

Julie slowly raised her head.

Something close to silence had fallen over the temple. There were no growls, no yelps, no shrieks, just the thunder of hooves and paws and wings as the forest animals fled, their eyes liquid and frightened. The enchantment was lifted. They poured toward the hall that led to the door. A scattered cloud of birds flew frantically toward the hole in the roof. Small creatures squeezed through the gaps in the walls and disappeared into the woods.

"Yes! *Yes!*" Bianca bellowed, punching the air.

Hisssss! The thin whine of an arrow came out of nowhere. It landed with a sickening meaty slap, and a wooden shaft jutted from Bianca's shoulder, ending in gray fletching.

There was a moment of utter silence. An elf stood among the chaos of half-trampled Dark Moons, bow raised, bowstring still quivering.

Bianca stared at the arrow, and her face twisted. She clenched a fist around the shaft, ripped it out, and threw it. It thudded into the elf's throat, and he fell to the ground with a gargling scream.

"Come at me, bitches!" Bianca roared, red magic glowing in both hands.

The Dark Moons roared in response, and a wave of them rushed at the succubus, closely followed by the dryads. Julie broke into a sprint, jumping over the fallen, and reached Bianca as the first Dark Moon slashed at her with a sword. She blocked the blow with an armored forearm and kicked the troll in the nuts, then rammed her knee into his nose as he doubled over.

"*There are still so many!*" she shouted.

"Get to Cassidy!" Bianca snapped back.

Julie slammed both hands into the trunk of the nearest dryad. Flames roared over its bark, and it stumbled back on its roots, shrieking. When it collapsed into the ranks of its fellows, flames spread through them in a yellow sheet.

Through the heat haze, Julie saw Malcolm, white-faced and motionless on the stump altar. Cassidy stood over him, her black hair wild around her head, blood pouring from her slashed hands.

Julie sent another fireball into the Dark Moons in front of her. As they fell back, shrieking and beating at their burning clothes, Julie sprinted toward the altar. She punched her attackers aside with fiery fists and reached Cassidy, who was locked in a tooth-and-nail brawl with a wereleopard, just as a troll swung his club toward her face.

Julie planted a foot on the edge of the altar and jumped over the fighting vampire and her opponent. She launched a fireball when the club was just inches away. It exploded in a shower of splinters, searing the troll's hands, and when he fell back with a scream, Julie landed on his shoulders. She slapped her burning hands against his face, and he shrieked and fell to his knees, raising his hands to his scorched cheeks.

Julie tumbled off, rolled to her feet, and scrambled onto the altar. Malcolm still lay there, groaning softly. Cassidy kicked the wereleopard away and swung to face Julie, panting and bleeding.

"Is he okay?" the vampire asked.

Julie touched Malcolm's neck. "Strong pulse. He's out cold, but he's fine. The bleeding isn't bad."

"He hit his head when he fell off the stag." Cassidy shook her hair out of her face.

The Dark Moons were regrouping. A ring of them marched toward the altar, pikes at the ready.

"We can't win," Cassidy murmured.

Julie flexed her fingers. Flames roared up her forearms and licked around her elbows.

"Not alone," she agreed. "But I can buy us some time."

She rose to her feet, stood on the altar, and raised her arms in front of her. *Fire*, she begged her powers. *Not fireballs.* When she felt heat crackle through her arms, she released it in a spitting gout of flame. A roar of fury ripped from her throat, and Julie spun in a circle, fire spraying from her hands. In seconds, Cassidy, Malcolm, and Julie were surrounded by a ring of fire, smoke, and screams.

"It won't hold them back for long," Julie gasped. "I think we should—"

Claws slammed into Julie's shoulders, causing a pain as sudden and frigid as having a bucket of ice water thrown over her head. The flames disappeared from her hands, and cold spread through her body as her feet left the altar. She heard wings thud as hot blood coursed down her skin. She was being lifted off the ground by vicious talons that gripped her shoulders, and when she managed to squint upward, she spotted a skin made of cracked, worn stone.

Gargoyle! Hat screamed. *They can't burn!*

Julie wanted to curse, but her head was spinning. She summoned a brief spark of fire to her hands and snatched at the gargoyle's limbs, but her fingers scrabbled harmlessly over unyielding stone. Someone was yelling her name from far below, and her head was swimming.

The bolt of red magic was blinding. Julie raised her hands to her face as the gargoyle's scream echoed through the temple. The talons disappeared.

Then she fell.

Taylor kicked Kaplan's office door open and rushed inside.

Kaplan looked up, bushy eyebrows knotting and big hands bunching into fists on his desk. In one of the cushy leather armchairs facing the desk, Julius Nox raised a questioning eyebrow.

"Woodskin!" Kaplan thundered, his teeth lengthening. "I am engaged in an important meeting. Get out!"

"Sir, this is urgent!" Taylor's heart thudded as he crossed the office.

Kaplan's burning amber eyes narrowed. "You listen to me—"

Taylor strode over to the desk and slammed both hands on the smooth surface. "No, Captain! *You* listen to *me!*"

Kaplan's eyes widened.

"Contact from Hat." Taylor trembled. "They need us. *NOW!*"

Kaplan's brows rose, and he and Julius exchanged glances. The captain leaped out of his chair, grabbed an earpiece, and thrust it into position. A second later, the telechip's comm blared in Taylor's mind.

Emergency mobilization! All resources to the portal now! Kaplan's voice was cool and sharp.

"I'm coming, Jack." Julius got up.

Kaplan nodded curtly, and the captain and the vampire king strode toward the door. Taylor was left in the office, hands shaking, drenched in a cold sweat.

Julius swept through the door first. Kaplan paused and looked back, his brows butting heads like angry, wooly bulls.

"Well, what are you waiting for?" he snapped. "Aren't you coming?"

Taylor grinned. "I'm coming."

CHAPTER TWENTY-ONE

"Julie! *Julie!*"

The desperate cry came from above Julie's head. Her body ached. She was lying on something hard and cold. Dirt. Dirt in her mouth, too. And in her bra.

Crap.

"Julie, wake up!"

Julie's eyes opened, although the left one would only open a slit. She spat out dirt and groaned.

"Get up!" It was Bianca who was yelling. "We need you!"

"Mmm." Julie closed her eyes. "Coffee first."

An electric shock zapped Julie's head. She let out a yell and scrambled to her feet, fists raised to her face.

"Hat!" she spluttered.

"Sorry, not sorry," Hat gasped. "We're in trouble!"

Julie's blurred vision cleared, and the smells and sounds of the battle flooded back. Flames covered her hands, but it was all she could do to stop the earth from trembling underfoot.

"What happened?" she asked.

"Bianca caught you," Cassidy snapped.

Julie, Bianca, Malcolm, and Cassidy were pressed against the back wall of the temple shoulder-to-shoulder, pale and bleeding. Bianca's face was twisted into a snarl. Malcolm's mouth was stained red, so Julie guessed he'd drunk Cassidy's vial of blood to regain his strength, and Cassidy was missing a clump of her thick dark hair. The faeries buzzed overhead, looking helpless.

"We're out of faerie dust," one of them growled.

Bianca stared at them. "Don't you make it?"

"We can't just shit it out, you know," the faerie snapped.

"Well—" another began.

"Here they come!" Cassidy exclaimed.

The temple was swarmed by Dark Moons and dryads. There were so many that Julie struggled to make out individual attackers. They were a single mass of seething violence, bristling with branches and limbs and weapons, and they were advancing. There was no rush in their charge. They simply walked forward, chuckling and yowling, the dryads' branches rustling in anticipation like porcupine quills.

"They think they've won," Malcolm whispered.

"They can't win," Hat cried.

Julie's flames flared. "We'll go down fighting."

"You don't understand," Hat groaned. "You can't go down at all. The Green Man wanted to fracture the world by sacrificing Malcolm. Do you have any idea what will happen if all of you die here?"

Julie's eyes widened.

"*It would be catastrophic!*" Hat screamed.

Julie stared at Bianca, and the succubus' elegant lips pulled back, baring her teeth. She tossed her horns.

"Then I guess we can't go down," she snarled. Balls of red magic crackled in her hands. "Come on!" she roared.

"Yeah, come and get us, assholes!" Julie raised her blazing hands.

They struck together. Fire and magic surged into the enemy, filling the temple with red and yellow light. A rank of them fell, screaming, but there were always more. No matter how much fire Julie poured into them and how many smoking bodies fell, more Dark Moons pushed through the flames.

The club came out of nowhere and slammed into Julie's ribs, sending her flying so suddenly that she didn't have the breath to scream. She landed on her back and skidded into the mad mass of the Dark Moons, and before she could move, they were on her. Armored hands gripped her arms, pinning her down. She screamed, but a fist slammed into her lips, and blood filled her mouth.

A female Sylthana Elf straddled her, silver hair shorn. Her blue eyes shimmered as she raised a knife over Julie's throat. The temple floor trembled.

No, no, no! Hat screamed. NO!

Julie forced down the fear. She couldn't die afraid. She'd bring the entire temple down on their heads.

"FOR THE ETERNITY THRONE!"

The roar shook the temple to its roots. It was followed by the thunder of trees shattering, then blinding sunlight poured into the temple from above. The Sylthana Elf froze and looked up, and an arrow slapped into her chest, glowing blue. She fell back with a scream, and that was when Julie saw him.

He was surrounded by a mass of soldiers in navy uniforms that was pouring through the hallway, swarming down the walls, and swooping through the vast hole that had been ripped in the roof, but Julie's eyes found him at once. Taylor. His gilded Aether armor flashed in the sunlight, and he leaned low over Sleipnir's mane as the eight-legged stallion galloped into the fray on thin air.

The sight sent heat and power surging into Julie's arms. She let out a roar, and the Dark Moons on her arms screamed and leaped back, their metal gauntlets melting. She rose to her feet and blasted a smoking hole in the enemy ranks.

Sleipnir cantered to the ground, and his hooves thudded on

dirt. He halted beside Julie. Taylor grinned down at her, Robin Hood's bow in his hands and his hair windblown by the wild ride.

"Just when I thought I'd get to rescue a damsel in distress," he teased.

Julie rolled her eyes. "Can I have a lift, please?"

"As long as I can have a bodyguard." Taylor winked. "I hear you shoot fire. Think it could be helpful."

"Deal." Julie laughed. She quenched the flames on her right hand and reached up. Taylor gripped her arm, and she swung up onto Sleipnir's broad back behind him. The stallion reared, pawing the air with four front feet, as a gang of brave Dark Moons edged toward him, pikes outstretched. Around them, Griffin units launched into the battle. The air was thick with screams and roars of triumph.

Taylor strung three arrows on his bow and fired them in unison, clearing a path to the pikemen. Sleipnir charged. Julie sank her weight down into his back and stretched out her arms on either side of her, sending gouts of flame into the Dark Moons. Taylor's arrows cleared the way ahead, Sleipnir's hooves crushed attackers underfoot, and Julie's fire roared all around them. She didn't think her heart had ever beaten this quickly.

Breathless, Sleipnir pulled up on the other side of the temple and wheeled on his hind legs to face the battle. Everywhere Julie looked, the PMA banner flew high; the orderly ranks of navy uniforms were winning. Her unit had formed up around Bianca and the vampires. She saw green shoots bursting from the ground, turning into vines and wrapping around the dryads, restraining them—pure Shajara magic countering the dark enchantment.

NO! Hat screamed in Julie's ear. *Look! Two o'clock! KAPLAN!*

Sleipnir was already plunging forward when Julie turned her head. Kaplan, in tiger form, stood over a fallen troll, his giant paws planted on the troll's shoulders, snarling into its face as

Droppelheimer slapped restraints onto her wrists. Behind them loomed the Green Man. Sparks and smoke flew from his ruined hair. He stumbled forward on bare, blackened feet, teeth bared behind the pine-needle beard in a grimace of rage, and he carried a sharp, jagged length of charred wood in one hand.

The world slowed. The Green Man raised his makeshift spear over Kaplan's unprotected back. Julie gathered power in both hands and shouted Kaplan's name. As the tiger looked up, she sent a blazing fireball winging through the air.

The Green Man barely had time to look up before it hit him in the chest. For an instant, fire flared behind his eyes. Then he exploded into a shower of sparks and ash.

Well. Hat cleared his throat. *That was graphic.*

Sleipnir skidded to a halt beside Kaplan. The tiger gaped up at Julie.

"You're welcome." Julie smirked.

"Fight's not over yet, Meadows," Kaplan growled.

The tiger launched at the nearest elf, all teeth and claws. Droppelheimer gave her a dazzling smile and brandished a broadsword at her. "He means thank you!" The orc let out a terrifying battle cry and followed Kaplan into the fight.

Taylor grinned at her over his shoulder. "Shall we, my love?"

"Together," Julie agreed. "For the Eternity Throne!"

"For the Throne!" Taylor echoed, and they charged into battle.

It was over.

A black pall of smoke hung over the battlefield. From where she sat in the back of a PMA ambulance, Julie had to squint through the smoke and dust to see the crews of red-clad agents and healers in purple jumpsuits hurrying across the temple. The stump had been destroyed, and the surviving Dark Moons had been restrained and were being marched in orderly rows to the waiting prison vans.

"Justice will be served, you know." The silver-haired dwarf tending to the cuts on Julie's shoulders gave her a faint smile. "They'll live out their days in a world without magic."

"Pfft. I could handle that." The other dwarf medic sported a black beard and a cheeky smile. He handed his partner a roll of bandage. "It's a world without sexy asses that I couldn't stand."

The silver-haired dwarf rolled his eyes. Julie tried to summon a laugh, but nervousness prevented it. She could see Taylor standing halfway across the temple, bright in his armor, helping a group of green-leafed Fernwood dryads to start the long process of taking down the dryad bodies that formed the temple walls.

They'll be given to their people and buried in the knowledge that their murderer is dead, Hat told her gently. *It's the best outcome we could have hoped for in this situation.*

That's not what's bothering me. Julie frowned. *Look at the Dark Moons.*

They watched in silence for a few moments as a line of shackled Dark Moons moved quietly past on the way to a prison van. The agents surrounding them clutched their guns tightly, but none of the paras offered any resistance.

They look meek to me, Hat offered.

That's just it. They're meek, but they're not defeated. Julie narrowed her eyes.

All the Dark Moons walked with straight backs, staring straight ahead. No, not walked. Marched in perfect time, their knees lifting high like they were on parade. A chill crept down Julie's spine.

I see what you mean, Hat murmured. *They seem...*

Undefeated, Julie finished.

Another line of Dark Moons was led past a few feet away, and Julie shrugged off the dwarf's hands. She pushed off the ambulance and landed lightly on the charred earth.

"Hey!" the dwarf protested. "Come back here! We're not done with you!"

"Thanks for the help," Julie called over her shoulder. Wincing as her bandaged ribs complained, she strode across the dirt.

The agent leading the group of Dark Moons gave her an appraising glance. "What—"

"Don't even." Julie held up a hand. "I'm not in the mood."

Before he could say anything, Julie pushed past him and walked up to a tall Sylthana Elf in the middle of the group. She remembered him yelling commands in the battle. He stared at her imperiously as she approached.

"What's up with you?" she demanded, planting her hands on her hips.

The elf arched elegant eyebrows. "I don't follow."

"None of you are protesting your arrest or imprisonment. I would be if I was being sent to the prison realm." Julie frowned. "So, what gives?"

The Sylthana Elf grinned at her, the expression sudden and brilliant in his soot-streaked face.

"You don't understand, do you?" he purred. "This imprisonment won't last long."

"Uh, as far as I know, you're getting life," Julie retorted.

"Under the current regime." The elf raised his chin. "But a time will come when the Eternity Throne falls, and we will be released and return as heroes to our people."

"Good luck with that," Julie snapped.

The elf didn't respond. He merely smiled and turned away, and the line of prisoners marched on to meet their fate.

Taylor opened his office door so quickly that Julie wondered if he'd been standing there waiting for her to knock. His lips curved in a sheepish smile.

"Hey," he managed.

Julie folded her arms, trying to return his smile. "Hey."

Taylor stared at her for a few moments. He smelled like summer rain, and it made it very difficult for her to remember why she was here.

"Uh, can I come in?" Julie prompted.

Taylor cleared his throat, stepped back, and pulled the door wide. "Sure. Uh, sure. Yeah. Come in. Coffee?"

"That'd be great." Julie headed over to the couches and gingerly sat down, wincing.

Taylor fumbled with the coffee machine. "How's the, uh…" He gestured at his chest.

"The ribs?" Julie absently tugged the bandage. "They're okay. Just cracked. Olena says she might be able to heal them, depending if I have any reactions to the cuts and bruises she fixed by magic yesterday."

"It's a relief that she can use magic on you now." Taylor brought over two mugs of coffee and set Julie's down in front of her. Black and bitter, just how she liked it. "How are Bianca and the others?"

"They're fine, thanks to Olena. Bianca's wing has a scar. She's stoked about it." Julie laughed. "She says that what doesn't kill you makes you hotter."

"She'd know." Taylor chuckled and slowly sat down opposite her.

"Have you heard any more news about the Dark Moon League?" Julie asked.

Taylor nodded. "It's official. The League's been disbanded. Oh, there'll always be a few nutcases sharing photos of their flag on the Internet, but it's effectively gone. There won't be any more trouble from them."

Julie's shoulders relaxed. "Good. That's so good."

Silence fell over them like a damp towel. Taylor stared into his coffee. Julie took a gulp of hers, but it was too hot. She tried not to splutter overtly. To his credit, Taylor ignored her.

It was several moments before he spoke. "You were amazing yesterday."

Julie couldn't stifle her smile. "Not too bad yourself, T. Someone's been practicing in secret."

"I like to keep fit." Taylor shrugged one shoulder. "But I can't blast fireballs from my bare hands."

"That was epic. Not gonna lie." Julie leaned back on the sofa, laughing. "It came as a surprise even to me."

"If this is what your powers are like when the concealment spell still isn't gone, then I'm excited for you for whatever comes next." Taylor's smile crinkled the corners of his eyes this time.

"Excited or scared?" Julie folded her arms.

Taylor dropped his gaze. "Both."

The silence returned.

Julie broke it this time. "I'm sorry, Taylor. I know I've been unfair and overly harsh, and you didn't deserve it."

"I'm sorry, too. I've been stifling you, and I know it." Taylor sighed. "We're both in the wrong."

"I know how close I came to getting killed yesterday, and I know you saved me, but there might come a day when no one saves me." Julie bit her lip. "I've accepted that, Taylor. If you can't, things are going to be difficult for us both. I need you to decide—"

Taylor raised a hand. "Please."

Julie leaned forward, listening.

"The thought of losing you terrifies me more than anything." Taylor swallowed. "But the sight of you in battle awes me. You're amazing, Julie. You're doing incredible things. I know that doesn't make fighting any less dangerous for you, but it's what you are meant to do right now." He looked up at her, his chocolate-brown eyes soft enough to get lost in. "I'll never not be scared for you, but I give you my word that I'll never stand in your way again."

Julie's breath caught. "You know you could lose me violently, T. If you're not up for that, I get it. There are no hard feelings."

"I am up for it." Taylor's fists clenched. "I know it's a risk, but you're worth it. I hope you don't think I was trying to be your rescuer yesterday. I—"

"Let's be real." Julie laughed. "I needed rescuing at that moment, and you were there for me. I'll never be mad about that. You weren't standing in my way. You were standing *with* me. That's what I need from you."

Relief blossomed on Taylor's face. "I'll always be there for you. *Always*. I promise."

"And I'll always support you because you're pretty incredible yourself, you know." Julie chuckled. "Julius told me about you bursting into the office and yelling at Kaplan."

Taylor's cheeks grayed with embarrassment. "It was a dire situation."

"It was sexy." Julie smirked.

Taylor giggled uncomfortably.

Julie got to her feet, then held out her arms, tears stinging her eyes. Taylor ducked around the coffee table and wrapped her in his embrace. She buried her face in his shoulder, breathing his unbelievable scent and feeling the steady thump of his heart against her chest.

"I love you," she blurted.

Taylor's arms tightened around her. "I love you, too."

Julie's chest felt filled with warm honey, and she held him closer. "My petrichor prince," she murmured.

He drew back, his eyes darting from her eyes to her lips and back. She tipped her head back, and her heart began to thunder. He leaned closer, and his lips found hers, and—

Sorry to interrupt, Hat broke in, *but there's something you both should know.*

Julie stepped back with a groan. "Not now, Hat!"

"How are you even talking to us?" Taylor glanced at Julie's bare head.

Hat scoffed. *You think I can't communicate with you from the barracks? I summoned you from the middle of a battle in Avalon, which is literally a world away.*

Julie sighed. "Okay, what do we need to know?"

Kaplan wants to see you in his office. Hat paused. *I wouldn't keep him waiting.*

Taylor shook his head, but he was smiling. He held out an arm. "Shall we, my lady?"

Julie held up a finger. "Don't push it."

"Okay, okay." Taylor laughed and offered his hand instead.

Julie took it. Fingers interlaced, they walked out of the office side by side.

AUTHOR NOTES RENÉE JAGGÉR

WRITTEN MARCH 20, 2023

Thank you for reading through to the back of book six!

As in my last author notes three weeks ago, life is still quiet. Well, not as quiet. I'm getting ready to leave for the UK. The weather gods gave it their all and dumped ten inches of snow on us poor souls here in the desert, but since then, we've had occasional rain and some nice days. I actually went out without a jacket the other day! Woot!

Tonight, I proved to my satisfaction that I can only cook for armies. I had a taste for beef Stroganoff, so I made some. A huge pan full, plus egg noodles (I didn't make those, but they were good ones). Yum! However, I will be eating it for days. Thank goodness I've made friends here that I can ~~dump some on~~ give some to, and they will appreciate it. I can only eat something for two meals. Then I'm done.

Are y'all weird like that? I mean, Jo would help, but I don't think she needs people food.

Starting to pack and trying to find the stuff I bought to take over for friends, like Trader Joe's Everything but the Elote Seasoning and ghost peppers. There are also llama stickers, but I know where those are.

Exciting news! My friend Isabel Campbell, one of the people I visit in Scotland, just had two series accepted by LMBPN! I can't say much more now, but I'm very excited for her. More news in my next author notes, along with the blurb for the first series. We authors have to support each other, especially those who like scones and haggis.

Hope you found Book one of _Piercing the Veil_ when it came out a week or so ago, if it sounded interesting in the blurb I included in my last author notes. I really hope you enjoyed it if you bought it. Let me know what you think. Book two comes out on April 14, so you won't have long to wait for the next one.

The next book in this series is in. Julie's world keeps getting more complicated, and it will continue to do so. Many shenanigans to come. We have a ways to go yet!

Until we speak again, I hope your skies are sunny and your days are filled with happiness and good books!

Renée

BOOKS FROM RENÉE

Para-Military Recruiter
(with Michael Anderle)
Drafted (Book 1)
Recruiter (Book 2)
Accepted (Book 3)
Lead (Book 4)
Recruited (Book 5)
Soldier (Book 6)
Tactical (Book 7)

Piercing the Veil
Dangerous Opportunities (Book 1)
Dangerous Responsibilities (Book 2)

Reincarnation of the Morrigan
Birth of a Goddess (Book One)
The Way of Wisdom (Book Two)
Angelic Death (Book Three)
A Cold War (Book Four)
A Battle Tune (Book Five)

Broken Ice (Book Six)
A Torn Veil (Book Seven)
Sins of the Past (Book Eight)
The Wild Hunt Comes (*Book Nine*)

The WereWitch Series
Bad Attitude (Book One)
A Bit Aggressive (Book Two)
Too Much Magic (Book Three)
Were War (Book Four)
Were Rages (Book Five)
God Ender (Book Six)
God Trials (Book Seven)
The Troll Solution (Book Eight)
Winner Takes All (Book Nine)

Callie Hart Series
Thin Ice (Book One)
Cold Blood (Book Two)
Feelings Run Deep (Book Three)

BOOKS BY MICHAEL ANDERLE

Sign up for the LMBPN email list to be notified of new releases and special deals!

https://lmbpn.com/email/

For a complete list of books by Michael Anderle, please visit:

www.lmbpn.com/ma-books/

CONNECT WITH THE AUTHORS

Connect with Renée

Facebook: https://www.facebook.com/reneejaggerauthor

Website: https://reneejagger.com/

Connect with Michael Anderle

Website: http://lmbpn.com

Email List: https://michael.beehiiv.com/

https://www.facebook.com/LMBPNPublishing

https://twitter.com/MichaelAnderle

https://www.instagram.com/lmbpn_publishing/

https://www.bookbub.com/authors/michael-anderle